"YOU'RE A BEAUTIFUL WOMAN, GINNY.

After you get over the hurt, you'll find someone else to love."

"Don't talk to me like a Dutch uncle," she said, her voice ready to break. "You're not my relative. We're not friends; we're not even acquaintances. You're just walking through my life, and I wish you'd keep going."

Tony smiled, as though he could see something that was hidden from her view. His smile transformed his face, lighting it up the way moonlight brings texture to a darkened landscape. "Good luck in your new job, Ginny."

Dear Reader,

When two people fall in love, the world is suddenly new and exciting, and it's that same excitement we bring to you in Silhouette Intimate Moments. These are stories with scope, with grandeur. These characters lead the lives we all dream of, and everything they do reflects the wonder of being in love.

Longer and more sensuous than most romances, Silhouette Intimate Moments novels take you away from everyday life and let you share the magic of love. Adventure, glamour, drama, even suspense—these are the passwords that let you into a world where love has a power beyond the ordinary, where the best authors in the field today create stories of love and commitment that will stay with you always.

In coming months look for novels by your favorite authors: Maura Seger, Parris Afton Bonds, Elizabeth Lowell and Erin St. Claire, to name just a few. And whenever you buy books, look for all the Silhouette Intimate Moments, love stories *for* today's women *by* today's women.

Leslie J. Wainger
Senior Editor
Silhouette Books

IMRL-7/85

Stardust And Sand

Amanda York

Silhouette Intimate Moments
Published by Silhouette Books New York
America's Publisher of Contemporary Romance

SILHOUETTE BOOKS
300 E. 42nd St., New York, N.Y. 10017

Copyright © 1985 by Amanda York

Distributed by Pocket Books

ISBN: 0-373-07107-8

First Silhouette Books printing August, 1985

10 9 8 7 6 5 4 3 2 1

America's Publisher of Contemporary Romance

Printed in the U.S.A.

Amanda York
was born and raised in Liverpool, England,
where she married an American airman and
proceeded to fall in love with his country.
They have two sons and a daughter, of whom
they're incredibly proud. When not writing,
she loves physical activities—but there's always a story simmering on the back burner.

Chapter 1

A CLARINET PLAYED SOFTLY IN THE SHADOWED BAR, A SAD sweet melody evocative of long-ago partings. *No one to talk with . . . all by myself . . .*

Stale cigarette smoke hung in the air, mingling with the collective odors of food, booze, perfume, and rain-damp coats; muted now, with that 4:00 A.M. calm that came even to the Workin' Late Bar and Grill.

Ain't misbehavin' . . . I'm savin' my love for you . . . Ginny Hooper mouthed the words in silent accompaniment to the clarinet's insistent cry. She stood behind the vine-wrapped column separating restaurant from bar, straining into the smoky darkness to see who was playing the clarinet with such haunting precision.

The music faltered, then died. A male voice said, "Is someone there?"

Ginny answered without revealing herself. "I'm sorry; were you locked in when we closed up?"

"I'm waiting for Al."

The neon sign outside flashed a red glow, briefly illuminating tables and upturned chairs, the wiped-clean bar, and a tall, rangy figure with an untidy mop of hair. She had a quick glimpse of a faded Western shirt and jeans as the man stood up.

"Al must have forgotten; he's gone home. But if you wanted to talk about a job, I'd better warn you that the combo here plays strictly country-western."

Ginny reached for the light switch and flooded the tiled entry with butter-yellow light from a coach lantern attached to the wall. The clarinet player moved reluctantly toward her, blinking a pair of deep blue eyes that were heavy with fatigue but flickered over her abbreviated costume with undisguised interest. He said, "He's not at his apartment. Any idea where he might be?"

"No, I haven't, and even if I had, I'm not sure I'd tell a total stranger."

"My name's Tony. Al must have spoken of me."

The name meant nothing to her, although she noted he didn't give his last name. "Why don't you call Al tomorrow? I'd give him a message, but I won't be back; this is my last night here." Her last night of groping hands and the usual propositions. Her last night of going home to a house that was as neat as she'd left it that morning . . . of picking up the phone to be sure it wasn't disconnected, of waiting for a call that never came. Of wasting her life waiting for a man who needed to "find himself" more than he needed her.

She looked into the stranger's tired eyes and was tempted to add, *If you're a burglar, or a sadistic killer of lone cocktail waitresses, go ahead . . . finish me off. I'm really past caring.* But it wouldn't have been true, because an innate curiosity about what tomorrow might bring had always sustained her, even in moments of despair.

Tony said, "I'm not a professional musician; I just play a little to amuse myself. I guess I should have realized Al would duck out on me. Still, someone should tell him that pretty redheads with sensational figures shouldn't be left alone to lock up. A lot of weird characters pass this way."

"Tell me about it." Ginny slipped her arms into the raincoat she had been carrying, slung her bag over her shoulder, and stepped outside, waiting with key in hand. Tony left the clarinet on the bar and joined her. He took the key and locked the door, checked it, then handed the key back. She stuck it into the envelope she had ready, then slipped it under the door.

The rain had slowed to a misty drizzle, and the gravelly sand of the parking lot was already drying. In the distance the lights of Las Vegas lay under an amber halo created by the storm. There were two cars left in the deserted lot. Ginny's forlorn little VW bug and a sleek Jaguar that didn't seem to go with the man's trail-worn clothes, unless its owner was one of those men who ran the glittering hotels of the Strip.

As they crossed the parking lot she gave him a quick sidelong appraisal. He moved with a certain catlike grace, as though unwilling to trust the ground underfoot and wary of announcing his approach to others. The casual dress, she decided, was calculated to create a relaxed appearance, but it didn't quite come off. There was tethered energy behind that weary expression, and she imagined that women probably found it easy to misread those shattered eyes, seeing disillusion when they should be recognizing danger. Was he a gambler, perhaps? Although they didn't usually stop at roadside inns, not when the lights of Vegas were within view.

He stayed with her when she walked past the rain-misted Jaguar and approached the VW. Opening the door for her, he said, "You should lock it. You're liable to find an unpleasant surprise awaiting you in the backseat some night."

Sliding into the driver's seat, Ginny said a silent prayer that the engine would start.

The watching man commented, "Even rain has a make-believe quality here, doesn't it? As though some entrepreneur had it flown in and dropped from the sky to amuse us."

She put her key into the ignition. "In a few weeks the rain will bring a carpet of wildflowers in the canyons. There's more magic in the desert than the neon merchants can conjure."

He smiled at her through the open window. "Are you a poet or a conservationist in disguise?"

"No. I'm just what you see, a tired waitress on her way home. Guess fatigue has the same effect on me that drinking has on other people: gilds my tongue a little. Good night." She turned the key and the VW's engine grumbled, then died. She turned it again and there was an ominous click.

"You didn't tell me your name."

"Ginny." She flipped the key back and forth, trying to coax a response from the ailing engine. Or was it the battery again? Damn that Marc. The least he could have done was to get her car in running order before he decided to walk out on her.

"Sounds like your battery's dead," he said. "I've got jumper cables in my car; I'll get them and get you started."

Too weary to argue or to consider the consequences of trusting a stranger, she watched him stride across the parking lot. If he hadn't been here, what then? She wouldn't have had to go to her empty house. She'd have sat in the car and watched the storm clouds disappear over the distant mountains. At dawn she would've caught the bus returning to the California border with its cargo of sleeping day-trippers, their hard-earned wages left behind in the jaws of the one-armed bandits of the Strip. Ginny hated slot machines almost as much as she hated serving drinks to glazed-eyed men and hyperactive women, their brittle facades transparent as the plastic on the decks of blackjack cards—empty dreams, imaginary pots of gold under mirage rainbows, the good life hanging on the turn of a card or the spin of a wheel. In the early hours of the morning the people and paraphernalia became interchangeable, the gamblers turning into automated robots, while the machines acquired a deadly intelligence of their own. Of all the places on earth Marc could have abandoned her, he chose this one with a sadist's eye for detail.

Tony returned with the jumper cables, and she watched his face, although reason told her she should be watching his hands and learning that particular car-starting trick herself. Not really a good-looking face, but she supposed his features could accurately be described as arresting. Lean, like his body, without a spare fold of skin or ounce of flesh to be seen. Older than she'd first supposed—midthirties, at least. A little younger than Marc. She wondered if she was now forever condemned to compare every man on earth with Marc, the one who had deserted her.

The Jaguar engine purred to life. Tony called to her, "Get back behind the wheel; I'll let you know when to start her."

When her own car started, she revved up the engine, and the moment the cables were removed, yelled "thanks," and roared across the parking lot.

The rain had stopped, which was fortunate, as her windshield wipers didn't work either. Nor did the defogger. She traveled a couple of miles down the

highway before the small rear window cleared and she
noticed the following headlights. When she turned off
onto the dirt road leading to the house and the headlights continued to follow, she immediately thought,
Marc! He's come home! But, she chastised herself, any
rational woman would be worrying about prowlers.
Marc had once said that her incurable optimism was
like hot fudge sundaes for breakfast—sickening rather
than appealing.

The headlights didn't belong to Marc. They belonged
to Tony's Jaguar. As she got out of her car he rolled
down the window and called to her, "Just wanted to be
sure you made it home safely. Hope I didn't frighten
you by following, but you left too quickly for me to tell
you what I was going to do."

"Thanks again," she said uncertainly, all at once
aware of the remoteness of the tiny cinder block house,
hidden from the highway by a formation of boulders
vaguely resembling Quasimodo and the bells of Notre
Dame. She wondered if she should race for the house
and lock the door or if she'd be safer out in the open.
She knew every inch of the terrain and could easily lose
him in the open desert, but a door could be battered
down and there'd be no one to hear.

"Ginny, listen, I know it's an imposition and I hate to
ask, but I see a swing on your porch. Could I spend
what's left of the night there and go back to see Al
when it's light? I don't see any hotels or motels around,
and I sure don't want to miss him tomorrow."

"You're right. It's an imposition. You can wait for
him in the parking lot of the Workin' Late Bar if you're
so concerned about missing him."

He opened the car door and slid out. "Perhaps I
should be honest. When you turned off onto the dirt
road, I realized your house was hidden from the
highway. It would be a good place to park the Jag."

"Oh, God," Ginny groaned. "It's stolen. I should have known."

"Not stolen, just too identifiable. Please, trust me."

"Why should I trust you? I don't know you. Besides, my husband's inside asleep, and I don't think he'd like strange men following me home. He . . . uh . . . has a loaded shotgun."

He glanced toward the house, with the lamp burning in the front window. "He must be a sound sleeper—two cars and a conversation six feet away haven't wakened him." He started toward the house and, angry rather than scared, Ginny went after him.

"All right, there's no husband. Just who are you and what do you want with me?"

He stopped on the sagging wooden porch. "Open the front door, Ginny, or I kick it in. If Al's hiding out here, you'd better tell me now."

"Al? You think he's here? You're crazy." Ginny unlocked the door and gestured for him to enter. "Go see for yourself."

It took only a couple of minutes for him to search the three-room house, built as a vacation retreat way back when and abandoned by owners who couldn't take the suffocating sandstorms that blew up occasionally and all but buried the place. She and Marc had done most of the restoration work themselves, in happier times. She waited on the porch until Tony returned.

"How long have you worked for Al?"

"Couple of months." And before that there was a hash joint at the truck stop down the road. She hadn't had much choice of occupation in the dusty straggle of food and service stops along the desert highway. But she'd been so sure Marc would come back. She added, "But I'm not going to answer any more questions until you tell me just who you are and what you want from Al."

"My name is Tony DeLeon."

DeLeon! The family that owned not only the Workin'
Late Bar and Grill and several other restaurants and
nightclubs, but also the fantastic new hotel and casino
called The Sand Castle. Ginny felt her hackles rise. The
name DeLeon was synonymous with gambling.

He asked quickly, "What do you know about the
poker game Al's been running in the back room?"

"I served drinks to the players a couple of times.
Look, Mr. DeLeon, this is Nevada. Nothing illegal
about gambling here, as you very well know. Your
family sure made a bundle from it. Why would I think
twice about a private poker game?"

"Al's game was crooked. Last week's receipts
weren't deposited in the bank, and that's probably only
the tip of the iceberg. The bartender and hostess stalled
me with excuses that Al had to run into town and would
be back."

"So you thought that if they were in on it, I was too.
Surely you didn't really expect to find Al here?"

"It was a long shot, but you looked out of place, and
out of character, in that skimpy costume. There's a
certain innocence . . . honesty, about you that card
sharpers like Al find invaluable in plying their trade.
You'd make the perfect shill. You look like a college
girl, yet you've got a woman's figure and a way of
moving that spells sensuality. A combination most men
find irresistible."

She stifled an impulse to answer that she never made
it past her first semester in college and that two years of
living with Marc surely had left a few ragged edges
around her ingenue look. "Mr. DeLeon—"

"Tony."

"Tony, if you want to wait on my porch in hopes that
Al will go sneaking back to the bar, fine. But you'd be
better off leaving your car here and parking yourself in
that cluster of boulders by the highway. You could spot

Al's car going by from there. Now, if you'll excuse me, I have to finish packing. Today is the first day of my new life. Besides, the new tenants will be moving in later."

She went into the house because there didn't seem to be any way she could force him to leave, and if he'd wished her any harm, he'd had plenty of opportunity to perpetrate it. He followed. "Let me help you. It's the least I can do after forcing my way in here and accusing you. I'll catch up with Al eventually."

"I'm going to change clothes. You can haul those boxes out to my car, if you want to make yourself useful." The grocery store cartons were packed and waiting by the front door. She glanced about the small room, thinking of all the lonely hours she'd spent here, dying by inches. She didn't really have to give way to the new tenants until tomorrow, but all at once she was ready to leave. Even an eternal optimist had to eventually give up a lost dream. Marc wasn't coming back. She went into the bedroom and closed the door.

When she emerged a few minutes later, she was dressed in jeans and a cotton shirt, her hair tied back in a ponytail, her face scrubbed clean of makeup. Tony had taken the cartons out to the car and was making coffee. "Hope you don't mind. This is my second night without sleep."

"Help yourself." She had several hangers of clothes and a suitcase, and he came and took them from her. "You think all this stuff is going into that bug?"

"This is it. I'm leaving everything else."

She saw his eyes go to the framed photograph standing on the wicker trunk she'd used as an end table. Marc's restless dark eyes expressed impatience while his mouth smiled easily at the photographer, and Ginny nestled against his broad shoulder like a forgotten appendage. Tony's eyes asked the unspoken question and she said, "This was his house. He walked out on me six months ago."

"What are your plans now?" Tony asked when he returned from putting her clothes in the backseat of the Volkswagen. She was sitting on the couch, going through a box of papers. Bills, receipts, unanswered queries from family and friends who hadn't heard from her.

"Once upon a time and long ago, I wanted to be a dress designer. I even studied for a while at a design school. A man came to the bar a few days ago and asked about the costume I was wearing. It was one I designed and made myself because the ones Al had didn't fit right. In fact, I ended up making costumes for all of the waitresses and hostesses. Anyway, the result was that I was offered a job. The only reason I'm telling you this is because the man who offered me the job is the entertainment director at The Sand Castle."

"Julius," Tony said thoughtfully.

"Yes. You know, it strikes me as peculiar that a DeLeon is chasing down a crooked manager. Why didn't you just call the police?"

He brought two cups of coffee and sat down beside her. "The DeLeons prefer to handle these matters privately. You know, I noticed that costume you wore was a cut above the bunny-style thing cocktail waitresses usually wear."

"I don't know why I've told you so much about me and my life."

"Maybe because you haven't had an opportunity to tell anyone else?" he suggested softly. "I recognize loneliness when I see it. Where's home?"

"Oregon. A little town built around a lumber mill. Pretty, misty blue-green, gentle. Sometimes I think I dreamed it."

"You certainly substituted a harsh landscape."

"Oh, I love the desert too. There's a stark grandeur to it. A bare-bones-of-the-earth quality that strips away unessential clutter. But men like your father couldn't resist cluttering it up with casinos and bright lights."

Detecting the edge to her voice, he said, "For someone about to go to work at the largest hotel and casino in Vegas, you sound a trifle disapproving."

"I don't know exactly what Julius has in mind, but I expect I'll be working for the costume department and dealing only with the entertainment part of the business. Gambling causes a lot of misery to a lot of people."

"I'm sorry for the compulsive gamblers of the world, but most people know when to quit."

She stood up. "I have to check the cupboards. I hate to be rude, but isn't it about time you were getting back to searching for Al?"

"I think I'd better wait and see if that ancient bug outside starts again for you." He glanced at the photo of Marc again. "Was he a compulsive gambler?"

"None of your damn business." She grabbed the picture and dropped it into the box of bills, then went out to the car.

Along the horizon a brilliant streak of silver appeared as the dawn peeled back the night. A jackrabbit bounded out of Ginny's lettuce patch and disappeared into the shadowed chaparral that would soon reclaim her garden. The air was cool and sweet after the rain. It was going to be one of those sparkling February days when distant peaks seemed to be painted on the sky close enough to reach out and touch.

A lump came into her throat at the thought that she had to lose the house and garden, too, but Marc had taken everything of value, including a couple of months' rent money. He'd needed a stake, of course. He always needed a stake.

Tony DeLeon appeared silently at her side and opened the car door for her. She flung picture and box

on top of the clothes lying on the backseat. Damn,
damn, tears were stinging the backs of her eyes again.
Tony's hand cupped her shoulder and he squeezed
gently. "There are better days ahead, believe me. It's
the oldest cliché on earth, but sometimes things do
happen for the best."

She brushed her fist across her eyes. "If there's one
thing I don't need right now, it's some complete
stranger giving me advice. You don't know a thing
about me, or my life. And what I know about you I
already hate. I hate everyone, everywhere, who caters
to anybody's urge to gamble."

"My mother always told me I should have stuck to
my clarinet lessons." Tony paused, his eyes searching
her face in the predawn light. "You're a beautiful
woman, Ginny. After you get over the hurt, you'll find
someone else to love."

"Don't talk to me like a Dutch uncle," she said, her
voice ready to break. "You're not. We're not friends;
we're not even acquaintances. You're just walking
through my life and I wish you'd keep going."

He smiled, as though he could see something that
was hidden from her view. His smile transformed his
face, lighting it up the way moonlight brings texture to a
darkened landscape. He said quietly, "Good luck in
your new job, Ginny. I don't usually spend much time
at the Castle, but when I do, I'll drop in on you." Then
he walked over to his car.

She resisted asking him why he would bother, since
she'd made it clear she didn't want to pursue an
acquaintance with a DeLeon. It was the DeLeons of
the world who had catered to Marc's obsession and,
ultimately, taken him away from her.

Ginny still had several small loads to bring out of the
house and Tony stayed until her car was completely
packed and the engine was running. The Jaguar fol-

lowed her to the highway, but when she turned toward Las Vegas he went in the opposite direction, back to the Workin' Late Bar and Grill.

Forty minutes later she turned off the highway and drove through deserted suburban streets. It was too early for anyone to be up yet. A lean tomcat circled a couple of trash cans speculatively, and a newspaper blew across the road in front of her, the only movements in the sleeping city.

The apartment she'd taken was in the outer suburbs of the city. Ginny had spent the past few days scrubbing the floors clean. Since it was unfurnished, she'd scouted the thrift shops for a few odds and ends. These, along with boxes of dishes and pots and pans, had been delivered the previous weekend by Al, who'd been sorry to lose her and had been kind to her, even if he had cheated his employer and run a dishonest poker game.

Al had brought the furniture and boxes over for her when she confided she hadn't saved enough money to hire a moving van. She wondered what would happen to poor old Al when Tony DeLeon caught up with him and briefly regretted being civil to the man.

Grabbing an armload of clothes, she walked toward a garish orange-painted front door, telling herself that this was just a temporary place to crash; that when she owned her own boutique, she'd have a place out of town, perhaps even move back to the little house she'd just left.

In a couple of hours she'd be starting an exciting new career. What did it matter where she lived? She supposed lack of sleep tended to kill enthusiasm, but all she could think of was that she wanted to go home to their little house in the desert and crawl into Marc's arms and have him tell her that he was back to stay.

Inside, the apartment smelled of fresh paint and

detergent. She dropped her clothes on the bed and sat down to catch her breath, thinking of the things she had to do.

One of the cardboard boxes lying on the floor had been opened and retaped. She stared at it, puzzled, knowing she had never wrapped two strips of strong nylon-reinforced tape around each end of the box.

The razor blade she had used to scrape paint from the window lay on the ledge in front of her and she picked it up and slit open the retaped box.

Lying on top of her carefully packed starter set of china—a shower gift from her mother—was a shoebox, also tightly sealed. Moments later Ginny was looking down at stacks of slightly soiled and wrinkled hundred-dollar bills.

Chapter 2

"I KNEW NOBODY COULD BE AS INNOCENT AS YOU MANAGE to look." Tony DeLeon's voice came from the open front door. He crossed the small living room and stopped at the bedroom door.

Startled, Ginny jumped to her feet, still clutching the shoebox packed with money. "I swear I didn't know about this. I just found it."

There was both anger and disappointment in Tony's eyes as he snatched the box from her hands and riffled through the contents. He jammed the lid on the box and tossed it to the bed. "When do you expect Al?"

"I don't expect him, I mean, I didn't until I found that money. Oh, God, please, you've got to believe me. I'm not involved in any skimming. Why would I give up my house if I was going to share in that kind of money? Why would I jeopardize my new job?"

He shrugged, unmoved. "A smoke screen, maybe? Who's going to suspect a young waitress down on her luck, struggling to make an honest living? How many of the other DeLeon employees are involved? Was this apartment going to be the drop point? I suppose Al arranged your meeting with the Castle's entertainment director so you'd be handy for picking up loot there. Is Julius involved too? God knows, my father pays him a small fortune, but there's no figuring how greedy people can be."

The room revolved dizzily around Ginny's head. She collapsed weakly to the bed, horrified that circumstantial evidence could pile up so swiftly. "No, I swear that Julius just happened to drop in. I didn't know Al was skimming. If there's some sort of ring stealing from you, I'm not a part of it."

He regarded her silently for a moment and she felt like a butterfly pinned to a collector's board. The cold appraisal stirred a seed of anger in her that quickly grew. She rose slowly to her feet. "If you hadn't followed me here I'd have turned that money over to the police. I'm not guilty of anything. But you are: breaking and entering and . . . intimidating. I don't care if your name is DeLeon; you've no right to harass me. Now get out of my apartment before I . . ." She broke off. Before she called the police? The phone hadn't been installed yet.

Surprisingly he said, "Okay, Ginny. I'll give you the benefit of the doubt for the time being. We'll sit down and wait for Al to come pick up the money."

"I can't. I'm supposed to be at The Sand Castle this morning. Julius is expecting me. Besides, I think you should let the police handle this. What are you going to do, make a citizen's arrest? Don't you have to have hard evidence like serial numbers of bills or something?"

He paused, considering, then said, "Okay. I'm going to trust you to go to the Castle. I'll wait here for Al. Don't say anything to anybody, including Julius, about this."

Ginny left the bright morning sunshine and stepped into the dim Casino, hearing the metallic clamor of slot machines and tinkling coins as small jackpots coaxed reluctant gamblers to continue feeding them.

She crossed the crowded lobby and took an escalator to the floor above where the dinner theater was located. Dressing rooms, offices, and workrooms were hidden from view behind the theater, reachable by an EMPLOYEES ONLY door.

Julius was seated behind a monstrously large desk in his private office, the walls of which were covered with an abstract design of red and black that was dramatic but unsettling. Black carpeting covered the floor, and the desk was painted red. Since Julius was on the phone when she was shown into his office, Ginny waited, observing him as unobtrusively as possible.

The man was as flamboyant as his surroundings. Huge in both height and girth, he wore a caftan of black linen. He had shaved his balding head, adding a vaguely Mongolian aura to his already imposing presence. Neither his size nor his baldness disguised the fact that he was still a comparatively young man.

The use of a single name, Julius, indicated an ego about the size of his body, Ginny decided. Still, he was giving her the opportunity she'd dreamed about, although she knew the best she could hope for was a job as alteration girl. Julius had been so impressed with the costumes she'd designed for herself and the other waitresses, he'd asked to see sketches of any other designs she'd done.

Ginny knew that the costumes for the shows were designed and made when the show itself was conceived, usually in Los Angeles. A local costume rental company supplied items such as tights, bodysuits, and so on. There would be a wardrobe mistress, and seamstresses to take care of minor repairs and alterations.

Still, if her designs interested Julius, perhaps she would meet someone through him who could offer her a job as a designer. At the very least, she'd be working with beautiful fabrics and exciting costumes. She was gratified to see the folder of designs she had given Julius lying on the desk.

Replacing the receiver, he looked up at her, his incongruously cherubic pink face breaking into a smile. "My dear Miss Hooper. Please, sit down."

She sat in a black leather armchair as Julius flipped through her designs until he came to the middle of the folder. Ginny felt a twinge of nervousness. The two pages were covered with seven or eight sketches of show costumes, and she wondered if he'd guessed at what had inspired her.

The night she made those sketches came back to her in vivid detail. Marc at the gaming tables, his expression blank and hard, oblivious of her presence. She had wandered away and found herself caught in the throng of people going to the early show. The revue had been good, fast-paced, well-choreographed, the comedian amusing, the singer talented. But the costumes had been uninspired. Later, to pass the time while she waited for Marc to run out of money, she'd sketched new designs, making subtle changes, varying color schemes. Damn, why hadn't she remembered to remove those pages from the folder? Julius must have realized what she'd done, and what she'd done was to criticize costumes he'd approved.

He closed the folder and spread his hands over it.

Several diamond rings glittered on manicured fingers. "With your talent, Miss Hooper, why have you been working as a waitress?"

Ginny cleared her throat. "I—we never stayed long enough in one place for me to plan on a career. But that part of my life is over now."

"You have a family, presumably, somewhere?"

"In Oregon. But they . . . I haven't been in touch with them for some time. They didn't approve of the man I was living with." She wondered whether to add that Marc had charmed them at first but that they were old-fashioned; they had expected them to get married. And so had she, for two alternately wonderful and excruciatingly miserable years. But she decided a man like Julius wasn't likely to be interested in the story of her life.

"Have you had any training or experience, other than doing the waitress costumes at the Workin' Late?"

"A year of art school. Fashion drawing, dress design. Plus my own sewing machine since I was eight years old."

"There's a certain freshness to your approach to resort clothes and sportswear that has promise. But it takes a great deal more than a bright idea to produce the finished product, and still more expertise to market it."

Ginny listened silently, unsure what to say, since although his words seemed to praise her designs, there was an underlying tone of reluctance, perhaps even resentment.

Julius leaned back in his chair, surveying her with small calculating eyes. "I've been thinking of investing in a boutique. Something classy, along the lines of the Rodeo Drive places. There's certainly enough money in this town to support one. I'd offer a woman a total look—when she left my boutique she'd be outfitted from head to toe, from her silk teddy to her accessories. Many women simply don't know how to pull an outfit together with the right shoes, belts, jewelry, and so on."

"Designer clothes?" Ginny asked, holding her breath.

"Naturally. I'd go with big-name designers to begin with. I've already talked to several. What I need is someone with a flair for clothes. A combination fashion coordinator, sales wizard, and designer. How would you like to find suitable premises and run the boutique, under my direction? You could do a little designing on the side. We could test-market your clothes. If your designs are successful here, we could market them nationally.

Ginny felt a pleasant golden haze surround her. "I—don't know what to say. I'm overwhelmed."

"Of course," Julius went on smoothly, "I'd own the designs, not you."

"Oh" was all Ginny could think of to say. "I don't know—"

"You realize, of course, you're a totally unknown quantity? I'm taking an enormous chance on the strength of a few sketches and the waitress costumes you did. Allowing you to display your designs next to the big boys' clothes is an opportunity most young designers would kill for."

"But if we market my designs under your name, if I ever wanted to strike out on my own, I'd have to start from scratch. Building the name of a line is the tough part."

He folded his ring-bedecked hands and nodded. "True. The Julius label would always belong to me. But without me, you're a cocktail waitress with little hope of a career as a designer. You can still have the job as alteration girl, though, if you wish. Although there is the small matter of your being accepted into the union first. It's a tough one to crack, and I can't help you there."

Ginny blinked, trying to bring everything into focus, wishing she weren't so tired, or that Tony DeLeon weren't waiting for Al back at her apartment, or that Marc hadn't left her. At length she said, "I'll design for a Julius label and be glad to run the boutique."

Ginny spent the rest of the day in an exhausting search for a suitable shop to use as a boutique. She didn't return to her apartment until late afternoon, sure that by then Tony DeLeon would have left. She hoped Al had shown up and cleared her of any complicity in his skimming operation.

The Jaguar was still parked in front of her apartment, and as she reached the front door she heard the soft strains of a clarinet playing "Stardust." The music stopped as her key turned in the lock.

Tony was sitting on her only chair, clarinet in hand. He stood up and with a sweeping gesture offered her the chair. She looked around, but he appeared to be alone. The apartment was filled with the unmistakable aroma of pizza. She sniffed the air, realizing she was hungry.

"I sent out for pizza—pepperoni, no anchovies. There's a bottle of wine too."

Ginny remained standing. "How long do you intend to camp out in my apartment, waiting for Al to show up?"

He gave her a frankly conciliatory smile. "Al was here this morning, shortly after you left."

"And?"

"He admitted he stashed the money with your stuff on impulse and that you didn't know anything about it. He had a key made to the apartment when he delivered your furniture and intended to slip in and pick up the cash while you were gone."

"Is he in jail?"

"No. I let him go with a warning."

"Why didn't you prosecute?"

"Because I believe Al was only one link in a whole chain involved in stealing from my father. I want all of them. By letting him go he might lead me to some of the others."

"So why are you still here?" Ginny asked, making a mental note to get her lock changed.

"To apologize for accusing you. To make amends."

Ginny collapsed into the chair. She kicked off her shoes. "I'll be glad to share the wine and pizza with you, then we'll call it quits."

His eyes held hers for a long moment, and the undisguised admiration in his gaze might have soothed her wounded pride had she allowed it to.

Tony disappeared into the kitchen and returned with an orange crate and a tablecloth. Ten minutes later the steaming pizza, cut into wedges of heroic proportions, and two glasses of an excellent burgundy were on the improvised table in front of her.

He raised his glass in a toast. "To beginnings. Our friendship, your new job at the Castle."

"I'm not your friend," Ginny said, sipping the wine nevertheless. "And I'm not going to be working at the Castle after all."

He looked at her sharply. "Why not?"

She hesitated. One of the conditions Julius had imposed on their partnership was absolute secrecy as to her true function. She'd thought it wouldn't bother her to let people believe she was merely a salesclerk in his boutique, and he was the designer, but all at once she longed to tell Tony the truth. Why, she wasn't sure. Perhaps because she was afraid he still harbored some suspicions about her honesty; maybe she just wanted to impress him. She asked herself sternly why she would care what a man like Tony thought about her and said aloud, "I'm going to be managing a boutique Julius is opening instead."

He passed her a paper plate sagging under the weight of the thick-crusted pizza. "What happened to your ambition to become a designer?"

She bit into the pizza and swallowed both the cheesy crust and her pride before answering. "I'm not ready yet. I need some experience."

They ate in silence for a while, although Tony continued to watch her with an appraising scrutiny she found disturbing. As he refilled their glasses he said, "Are you hanging around here hoping Marc Noland will come back to you?"

She felt herself freeze. "I never told you his name."

"Why don't you go home, Ginny? Back to that misty-blue town in Oregon and your family."

"Not that it's any of your business, but I doubt they'd have me back."

His expression softened slightly. "I see. I guess I can understand that situation. I've been somewhat estranged from my family for some time."

"You checked on me," Ginny said. "You found out about Marc, yet you still think I was involved with Al's crooked games."

"Marc Noland was well-known at all the casinos. He's a compulsive gambler. Right now he's in Jersey City. You were going to be married, but instead you ran off together and, as far as I can determine, never actually tied the knot."

"Get out," Ginny said. "Now." When he didn't move she stood up and grabbed the wine bottle. "Get out!"

In a split second he was on his feet, the bottle was out of her hand, and she was enclosed by unrelenting, muscular arms. "I'm sorry, that was unnecessarily cruel. Excuse my bluntness; it comes with my job."

"Your job," Ginny panted, struggling to free herself.

"Your noble profession, catering to the obsessions of sick people like Marc. Damn you, you're as bad as a drug dealer."

"It's true that my family owns casinos, Ginny," Tony said. "But they're run by my father and brother. I don't work for DeLeon Enterprises. I'm a private investigator."

Chapter 3

TONY PARKED THE JAGUAR IN FRONT OF AN OFFICE BUILD-
ing that resembled an oversize ice cube, with its box
shape and all-glass walls glittering coldly in the sun.
Ginny Hooper was still very much on his mind as he
took the elevator up to the tenth floor.

There had been plenty of women in his life, including
one who hadn't cared enough to wait when he went to
Vietnam. After that taste of heartbreak he'd promised
himself no more serious involvements.

Why, then, did Ginny Hooper inspire protective
instincts in him? His attraction to her had caught him
off guard and he concentrated on all the reasons he
should fight it. She was probably involved in the
skimming ring, and she was obviously still carrying a
torch for her gambler friend, Marc Noland.

At the tenth floor the elevator doors opened into the reception area of the Sutcliffe School for Private Investigators. Tony greeted the young woman at the desk and asked, "Is he in?"

The receptionist grinned and winked. "Yes, but you'd better knock before you go in. Hoshi is with him."

Tony wondered, somewhat cynically, if Brad Sutcliffe's fiancée was aware that his life was already pretty full. Maybe there'd be room in it for a wife, but Tony doubted it. "Tell them I'm here; I'll go get a cup of coffee."

An instructor ushering a small group down to the firing room in the soundproofed basement greeted him as he went by. Tony made his way past the familiar rooms to the lounge, poured a cup of coffee, and sat down. An intense-looking young woman waited on the couch opposite his, staring, mesmerized, at a magazine.

"Relax," Tony said, as she looked up. "He won't bite."

"I heard the first interview is the worst. That Mr. Sutcliffe tries to weed out people he thinks won't make it."

"There are a lot of misconceptions about private investigators."

"Sounds like you've already taken this course."

The receptionist's head appeared around the door. "Tony, Brad says to go right in."

"Take the young lady first. Tell him I can wait."

The prospective student flashed him a smile of thanks as she went by. Tony leaned back and closed his eyes, his mind wandering back to his first meeting with Brad Sutcliffe. Then his thoughts meandered back to the chaos of Saigon in those last frantic days, whirring chopper blades, desperate people mobbing every American uniform and begging for help to escape. The incredible amounts of money, black market goods, graft, and corruption all whirled around in his memory like particles in a crazy kaleidoscope.

Saigon memories inevitably brought back the pain of Lonnie's death. Lonnie had been a lanky, soft-spoken Southerner whose courage and integrity had deserved more than a knife in the back in a seedy Saigon alley.

The Three Musketeers they'd dubbed themselves, Lonnie, Brad, and himself. Each so different, bringing to their friendship qualities the others felt they lacked, but most of all a sense of surrogate family. "Someone to cover my ass" was the way Brad Sutcliffe had once defined his feelings about Lonnie and Tony. But it was much more than that.

It had been Brad who had come to the rescue when Tony, in the blind rage of grief, decided to root out the rats' nest of black marketeers he knew were responsible for killing Lonnie. Brad hadn't wanted Tony to act on his own, but he showed up anyway, in time to save Tony's life.

Back home, the DeLeons couldn't understand why Tony, after returning from a year of hell to a fiancée who'd married someone else, was subject to bad moods, disillusionment, and a sudden aversion to his family's wealth-insulated life-style.

Brad had returned to the investigative agency in Los Angeles where he'd started out as an operative, but a few months later he visited Tony in Las Vegas and announced that he was going to open a school for investigators.

"Supply and demand, old buddy," Brad had said. "This town uses more security personnel than any other. Oh, I'll take on some investigations too—for a price—but mostly I want not to get shot at personally from now on. Well, hell, I might as well come clean— you're a DeLeon—your old man owns enough casinos that if I can get the contract to supply his security personnel, I'll have it made."

When Tony explained that he and his father weren't getting along too well and he had no intention of being part of the DeLeon gambling empire, Brad suggested, "Why don't you come to work for me? I'll teach you the ropes, then we'll get you a license, and later on, if you don't care for the work, you can be an instructor."

But Tony had never become an instructor. He'd been too successful as an investigator. Within a few years he had opened his own agency and had several operators working for him. He took only selected, usually well-paid cases, and was almost embarrassed by the amount of money he made. Sometimes he wondered if having everything turn to gold was a DeLeon curse.

"Old buddy, why are you hiding out back here?" Brad's voice cut into his thoughts like a honey-covered blade. Brad stood in the doorway, his arm draped casually over the shoulder of a petite Nisei woman with waist-length dark hair.

"Hi, Tony," Hoshi said.

Tony stood up as he returned her greeting, recalling their first meeting a few months earlier when he had been so overwhelmed by her Oriental beauty that he had bowed and addressed her in Japanese, only to be told, with a grin, "Gee, that's sure nice, Tony, but I'm about as Japanese as a McDonald's hamburger. I was born and raised in L.A."

Brad's quarterback-size shoulders and chest seemed to puff out even more than usual when Hoshi gazed up at him adoringly. Tony supposed that was because she was so different from the women Brad usually ran around with.

Brad was one of those golden people who somehow manage to breeze through life impervious to the small and large catastrophes that overtake others not so favored by the gods. Vietnam had left him untouched; he'd built a successful business, enjoyed romantic liaisons with a succession of beautiful women, and now was going to marry the loveliest of them all, who worshipped him. His good looks, athlete's physique, blond hair, and happy-go-lucky personality had perhaps guaranteed him a charmed existence.

"Tony, you promised to find a nice girl in town who'll stand up for me at the wedding," Hoshi reminded him, a trifle wistfully. Her family and friends disapproved of Brad, because he was not of her race, and Tony knew Hoshi had been lonely since coming to Las Vegas.

"As a matter of fact, I did," he answered quickly. "How about a cozy little dinner sometime soon, the four of us, and you can meet her?"

"Hey, great," Brad said. "Now run along, princess, and I'll pick you up for lunch. Old buddy and I have business to discuss."

After Hoshi left they went into Brad's private office and closed the door. "Well?" Brad asked.

"Nothing on your missing operative yet. Apparently her work at the Castle was routine stuff—you said yourself there was nothing in her reports to indicate trouble. I'm betting on a jealous husband or boyfriend someplace. But you were right about security being lax there. I checked on some of my father's other operations, too, and it was worse. The manager of a roadhouse out of town was running a crooked game and skimming. I put a stop to that but let him go. His name is Al Vernon. Put out the word to keep an eye out for him, in case he shows up at any of the tables in town."

Brad gave him a half-quizzical, half-lazy smile, "Your old man have anything to say about you nosing around?"

"My father hasn't been well lately. I guess my mother's death hit him pretty hard. Dad stays pretty much in the background nowadays. My brother is in charge."

Brad raised his eyebrows. "The kid?"

"Vince is twenty-five now," Tony said shortly, not

wanting to think about how immature and pleasure-
seeking his younger brother really was. Maybe the
responsibility would make him grow up.

"Who's the woman you're going to introduce to
Hoshi? I don't want her mixing with any chorus girls on
the make."

Tony gave him a pained look.

Brad chuckled as Tony wondered if he could get
Ginny Hooper to come to dinner and meet his friends.

Ginny was sewing a length of jade-green silk in the
back room of the boutique, hoping to have at least one
of her own designs ready before opening day, when
Tony arrived.

He picked his way through an obstacle course of
boxes and cartons in various stages of unpacking. A
pretty young girl, who had probably come to town with
show business hopes, was alternately unpacking boxes
and arranging costume jewelry on a black velvet bed in
the front of the window. Jumpsuits and dresses lay in a
heap on the counter, waiting to be hung on racks or
placed on mannequins in the window.

"Lynn," Ginny called, as the doorbell tinkled, "Is
that the cash register man?"

"Yes, ma'am," Tony said. "What seems to be the
problem? No money in the till? Maybe it would help if
you got rid of that CLOSED sign."

Ginny stopped sewing and looked up at him. "We're
not open for business yet. What do you want?"

Tony, who had kept his right hand behind his back,
now brought a small bouquet of flowers into view.
"You were right. Those wildflowers in the canyons
were about to open."

The desert flowers were as brilliantly colored and
delicate as first love. Ginny looked at them and felt her
eyes mist slightly, both at the fragile beauty of the
flowers and the thought that this man, this stranger,

had gone into the desert to pick flowers for her. She got up and went to one of the cupboards, found a glass jar, and filled it with water.

Tony watched as she carefully arranged the flowers. She said, "They're so fresh you must have picked them very recently."

"An hour ago in the canyon near the little house where you lived. Did you know the new people didn't stay? It's vacant again."

"Makes no difference to me."

He rested his weight against the edge of her work-table. "The desert was beautiful at dawn. Still and silent. I always feel a desert sunrise is like a litany: it renews hope, faith."

Ginny didn't look at him. She didn't want to let him know how pleased she was to see him. "I'm glad you have the time to go and watch the sun come up."

"Like the fool on the hill, you mean? Why haven't you returned any of my calls? You can't spend all of your time working. You'll shrivel up and blow away with the dust if you do."

"I have to get ready for our grand opening. There's a lot to be done."

"You make all this stuff?"

"Lord, no. Julius bought it from various designers and wholesalers."

"What exactly is a boutique, anyway?"

"A small store specializing in high-fashion clothes and accessories for women. We hope to create a total look."

"Bully for you. Come on, it's nearly noon; let's have lunch."

Ginny glanced through the open doorway to where her assistant stood, watching them with undisguised interest. She knew what she ought to do—stay and work—but she'd make an exception this time. "Lynn, this is Tony DeLeon. We're going out for a while. Take

care of things, will you? And if Julius calls, tell him
we'll be ready for the opening."

She picked up her purse, and they went out into
sparkling spring sunshine. A warm breeze hinted of
journeys through sagebrush, and in the distance the
mountains carved a purple-hued horizon on a sky of
infinite blue.

A covey of tourists went by, the women giggling and
giving Tony sidelong glances. Ginny couldn't stop
herself from smiling. He moved with controlled grace,
and his chiseled features were tanned, emphasizing his
deep-blue eyes. If the eyes were indeed the mirror of
the soul, then Tony's revealed a searching quest for
truth, as well as a sense of humor. Ginny wasn't sure
how easy it would be to resist such a man. She'd have to
concentrate mightily on remembering Marc's betrayal
and abandonment.

"There's a sushi bar nearby," Tony said, ignoring the
tourists.

"The idea of raw fish—" Ginny began.

"Don't knock it if you haven't tried it. Come on,
here it is."

They stepped into a tightly packed café, and Ginny
looked around with some relief at the tables, which all
appeared to be taken. Perhaps they could now go get a
hamburger somewhere. Across the room a strikingly
pretty Japanese girl dressed in a white dress that set off
her dark hair and delicate coloring raised her hand and
waved. "Tony! Over here."

Tony took Ginny's elbow and led her to the table.
"Ginny, this is Hoshi, who is going to marry my best
friend. Hoshi, say hello to Ginny."

Hoshi shook Ginny's hand with an astonishingly firm
grip. "I was afraid I was never going to get to meet you.
Tony talks about you, but he said you were busy getting
ready to open a boutique. I wondered if you could help
me find a wedding dress. We just decided to get

married next week, so there's not much time for shopping around."

Ginny sat down. She was mildly taken aback by the woman's direct and friendly approach. Since Las Vegas was the land of instant weddings, it wasn't surprising that Hoshi hadn't bought her bridal gown yet. Before Ginny could reply, Hoshi went on, "And please—no old family wedding kimonos, or anything ethnic. But I would like something different. Either modern, or *really* antique."

Ginny relaxed, smiling, feeling drawn by Hoshi's warmly outgoing nature and at the same time flattered that Tony had evidently told his friends a great deal about the boutique and Ginny's abilities as a designer.

By the time they'd finished lunch, which to Ginny's surprise she enjoyed very much, she felt as though she and Hoshi were old friends. So much so that when Tony mentioned that Brad and Hoshi were having dinner at his place that night and suggested Ginny join them, she immediately agreed.

Hoshi had offered to stop by her apartment and pick her up and Ginny wondered if perhaps Tony had arranged this in advance, to be sure she didn't back out. She speculated, too, about how different everything might have been had she met Tony before she knew Marc. But there was no need to dwell on that. Just so long as she reminded herself that Tony DeLeon was a casual encounter and she was never going to allow him to be anything more. The trouble was, she kept remembering the wildflowers he'd made a trip into the desert to gather for her.

Chapter 4

HOSHI WAS APOLOGETIC ABOUT THE LIMOUSINE IN WHICH she arrived to take Ginny to Tony's house for dinner. "It's ridiculously ostentatious, but Brad is going to be late and he insisted. He doesn't like me driving by myself at night."

"Please, don't apologize! I've never had a ride in a limousine," Ginny said, as the chauffeur closed the door. "How far do we have to go?"

"Tony has a house way out of town." Hoshi wore a flaming vermilion silk dress, and her long hair was fastened on top of her head with ivory combs. Her almond eyes went over Ginny with wistful awe. "Your dress is stunning—it's the color of lemon sherbet. I wish I had your figure so I could wear a scoop neckline; I'm just too flat."

"You're gorgeous." Ginny assured her sincerely, "I'm pleased you like my dress, though. It's one of my own designs."

They talked about clothes for a while, but in the back of Ginny's mind hovered the thought that it would have been wiser to turn down this dinner date with Tony DeLeon. There was no doubt in her mind that he still suspected she had something to do with Al's crooked operation and was probably keeping an eye on her.

As they left the bright lights of the Strip behind, Ginny asked, "Does Brad live out of town too?"

"No. He has a penthouse apartment right in the thick of things," Hoshi replied. "But I'm hoping after we're married he'll get a place like Tony's."

The streets they traveled grew more deserted, the houses wider spaced. There were now so few cars on the street that Ginny glanced at the sideview mirror, then back over her shoulder. "You know, that Mustang has been back there for quite a while. Are we being followed, do you think?"

Hoshi looked back and sighed. "It's entirely possible. Brad sometimes gets a little paranoid. I suppose it's the business he's in."

"What business is that?"

After Hoshi had explained, Ginny thought the precautions seemed a little excessive, considering the fact that Brad only ran a school for private investigators, who then went out on their own. He also supplied various hotels and casinos with security personnel whom he trained, and who remained in his employ, working on a contract basis. Hoshi had said he no longer took on private investigations but turned them over to his former star pupil, Tony.

"Is he afraid somebody will try to kidnap you?" Ginny asked.

"Not exactly. But my family aren't thrilled about my marrying him. Brad's been afraid they'll spirit me away. Or maybe one of his student investigators is following us as a training exercise. Who knows?"

"Look, there's Tony's house ahead," Hoshi informed her.

Tony's house was a rambling ranch-style structure built of redwood and surrounded by a pleasing conglomeration of palms, olive trees, and cacti interspersed with rock formations. It appeared that the builder of the house had cleared only the ground necessary for construction, augmenting the natural chaparral with shade trees, so that the house lived in harmony with its setting.

"Tony designed and built this place himself," Hoshi said as the car drew to a halt.

Ginny thought again that Tony DeLeon was a fascinating paradox and a younger Ginny would have been bowled over by him. He was obviously a man in tune with nature, a talented musician, someone with the endearing gift of focusing on exactly what a woman needed at a particular time, whether it was a flattering remark or a bunch of freshly picked flowers. Yet there was that underlying toughness and even an occasional glimpse of cynicism. She found herself wondering if, like herself, he'd once been hurt by someone and had learned to hide his vulnerability.

Looking back, Ginny noted that the following car continued past the house and disappeared into the dusk.

Tony came to the door himself, dressed casually in dark slacks and a gray shirt. Ginny wondered if he realized that that particular shade of gray made his eyes seem as fathomless as mountain lakes. He kissed Hoshi's hand and then hers in a charmingly courteous way that didn't seem at all contrived. "Thank you both for coming. Brad called; he'll be later than he thought, so I'll have you both all to myself for a while."

Slipping their arms through his, he led them across a

slate-tiled entry hall to a wood-paneled room where a log fire in a brick fireplace warded off the night chill of the desert.

"Hoshi, why don't you take Ginny on a quick tour of the house while I fix some drinks and check on my barbecued salmon. I'll meet you back here in five minutes."

Hoshi gestured toward an inner courtyard beyond a sliding glass window. "The house is built around an atrium. All the rooms open either to the atrium or to the garden. Spanish-style, I guess." She led Ginny through an arched doorway to a tiled corridor. "Bedrooms this way; we can dump our wraps."

"Doesn't he have a housekeeper or anything? Is he really fixing dinner for us himself?" Ginny whispered as they went into a large bedroom dominated by what appeared to be an authentic Spanish Colonial bed.

"Yup, he lives alone, does all the cooking, laundry, and you name it. I believe he has a woman come in once a week to clean. Boy, does he need a wife." Hoshi gave her a mischievous sidelong glance. "And since he's Brad's best friend, do I need him to have a wife I like."

The innuendo surprised Ginny and made her wonder what exactly Tony had told Hoshi about their relationship. She decided to give a somewhat offhand reply. "I hope he finds someone you both approve of, then. Has he ever been married?"

Looking disappointed at the response, Hoshi said, "Brad said he got a Dear John letter while he was in 'Nam. That's where they met." When Ginny didn't comment on this, Hoshi added, "This is the spare room. Come and see Tony's bedroom."

Hoshi led the way down the hall to Tony's bedroom, which was even larger, but perhaps more spartan. It, too, had a massive bed of antique mahogany. Ginny had to drag her eyes away from the bed in an attempt to rearrange her thoughts to eliminate the image of Tony's lean, muscular body lying there naked. She didn't usually have carnal thoughts about casual acquaintances. Her commitment to Marc had been too complete to separate sex from love, and she was disturbed that she found Tony so physically appealing.

Forcing herself to look at a matching Spanish Colonial dresser, Ginny caught her breath at the magnificence of the carvings in the wood. She moved closer so she could trail her fingers across the surface, feeling the subtle spell of the strongly masculine furniture. Solid, mellowed wood, worn to a fine patina, suggested both strength and endurance. Something like the owner, she decided, as her eyes drifted to the items on the dresser.

Lying on a valet tray was a key ring, some coins, and a leather wallet that had obviously been hastily dropped there, because the contents had partially spilled out. Ginny found herself looking down at a photograph of a beautiful blonde woman, who gazed back at her with a cool smile of possession.

"Hoshi . . . is this the woman he was going to marry? He must really be carrying a torch if he's still got her picture in his wallet after all these years."

Hoshi came to her side and nudged the picture with her fingernail. "The woman he was going to marry was a well-known model. I've seen her picture dozens of times on magazine covers. No, this isn't her. I don't know who this is."

"I suppose," Ginny said slowly, "she must be the current love of his life."

"If so, he sure keeps her hidden," Hoshi said, and the regret in her voice matched Ginny's feeling of disappointment. But then, why should she assume that a man as attractive as Tony wouldn't have a woman friend? She kept that in mind as they went back to the living room, although she knew that deep down what bothered her was that whoever and wherever she was, that woman in the picture didn't know that Tony was actively pursuing another woman. It was, Ginny decided, men's small infidelities and omissions that were hardest to bear.

Despite her silent resolve not to be charmed by Tony DeLeon's undeniable attractiveness, Ginny found herself laughing and talking animatedly with him and Hoshi during a leisurely meal.

It was clear that Tony and Hoshi enjoyed kidding each other in a good-natured way that said they had established an easy friendship. Hoshi was strictly a big-city girl with the usual misconceptions about the desert, like expecting rattlesnakes under every rock, while Tony hadn't reconciled her fragile Geisha-like beauty with an all-American upbringing. Occasionally Hoshi would mischievously affect a phony Oriental accent, while Tony would tell outrageous stories about Gila monsters and giant scorpions invading desert homes. Tony spoke to Ginny in the same easygoing manner, but the expression in his eyes changed subtly when he looked at her, and Ginny found it difficult to assess just what that look expressed.

The barbecued salmon was delicious and was served with a tasty vegetable mixture that included translucent wedges of cactus in a garlic-butter sauce.

After dinner they arranged themselves comfortably around the living room fire and Hoshi said, "Play for us, Tony. Please."

He grinned. "Thought you'd never ask. Remind me to give you the money later."

Turning to Ginny, Hoshi said, "I'll never understand why a man who plays the clarinet like Tony isn't doing it for a living."

"Maybe because music would lose its charm for him if it became part of the daily grind," Ginny suggested.

Tony took his clarinet from its case and held it

lovingly. "When you two have finished discussing me as
if I weren't here, I'll let you be the first to hear one of
my own compositions."

His eyes were fixed on Ginny as he raised the
instrument to his lips. The first slow haunting bars of
the piece seemed to surround and engulf her, filling all
the space around her and driving every image and
sensation from her mind except the sound of the music.

Sad at first, like a broken love affair, the music then
picked up tempo to express the beginning of hope
again, the certain knowledge that life will go on. Ginny
realized the music had so much power she was telling
herself a story from it and the story was hers.

When the notes of the clarinet faltered and died, she
knew it was unfinished and felt keen disappointment. It
was like reading a wonderful novel that had no conclu-
sion.

"That's all I've done so far," Tony said into the
silence that fell when the music ended.

"Oh, Tony, that's beautiful. You've got to finish it."
Hoshi exclaimed, clapping her hands. "What do you
call it?"

He was still staring at Ginny, with a look in his eyes
that sent a slow ripple along her spine. He said, "I hope
you don't mind . . . I've called it 'Ginny's Song.' There
aren't any words, but . . ."

Ginny couldn't look away: her eyes were locked with
his and she felt a yearning for physical contact that
almost propelled her toward him.

"Hey, you guys," Hoshi said, "Don't mind me. I can
go into the kitchen and whip up some octopus pie or
something."

Before either of them could respond, the doorbell
chimed. Hoshi jumped to her feet. "That'll be Brad;
it's about time. I'll get it."

They heard her high heels click across the slate floor
of the hall and the sound of voices—Brad's deep laugh,

Hoshi's lighthearted giggle—then a pause that indicated they were probably kissing. And still Ginny and Tony stared silently at each other.

At length Tony returned his clarinet to its case. "I should have worked on it some more. It's pretty clumsy, I know."

"No," Ginny said quickly, "No, it was beautiful. I'm just a little . . . taken aback, I guess. No one ever wrote any music about me before."

"Don't let it go to your head," Tony said, grinning.

Ginny disengaged her eyes from his reluctantly and looked into the dancing flames of the fire. "I didn't realize I came across as being so sad. I didn't used to be."

"The piece isn't finished yet, and neither are you. You did seem pretty down that first time I saw you. But there's a resilience about you that I admire. You'll be okay."

Ginny was battling several conflicting emotions. She had been touched by his going into the desert to gather wildflowers for her; even more deeply moved by the composition of the music. But a warning voice told her to consider his motives. He's got seduction on his mind, she told herself, along with surveillance.

Knowing that, it was incomprehensible to her that a glance from Tony DeLeon and a few bars of music could render her a romantic fool, painting illusions of sweet surrender on her mind like patterns scratched into desert sand. And just as fleeting. There was no doubt in her mind it would be dangerous to her emotional well-being to get to know him too well. She might just get to liking him too much.

Fortunately at that moment Brad and Hoshi came into the room. Hoshi looked even more petite beside a brawny blond man with handsome features and a toothpaste-ad smile. As she was introduced to Brad Sutcliffe, Ginny found herself wondering about his friendship with Tony. The two men were so completely unalike. Brad was obviously extroverted and perhaps a little blustery, an always-onstage type of person, quick with the banter and a trifle pouty if someone else took center stage. Tony, however, although possessing a wry sense of humor, was a more reflective personality, not as flashily handsome or athletic-looking, yet curiously giving the impression of greater strength and stamina.

"The salmon is cold," Tony said. "You want me to throw it into the microwave? It would be better not to, but—"

Brad slapped his shoulder. "No, thanks, Mom; I grabbed a sandwich before I left." He picked Hoshi up and sat down, placing her on his lap. "Sorry, I'm so late, babe. I should've called, but I got tied up."

Watching them, Ginny felt like an intruder. They were so very much in love it seemed a radiant aura hung about them. It was only after a moment that she realized that it was Hoshi who generated that feeling of love. She obviously worshipped Brad, and he wallowed in it. Ginny felt a twinge of alarm, recognizing in Hoshi the echoes of her own blind devotion to Marc. She wanted to warn Hoshi, to cry out Don't wear your heart on your sleeve like that—hold a little something back. But perhaps, Ginny told herself, she was just reading her own experience into the situation.

Feeling Tony's eyes on her again, she noted with some satisfaction that although he was not as conventionally handsome as Brad, his face was much more interesting. She was glad she was with him, if only temporarily.

"You scared Ginny with that tail you put on us," Hoshi said. "Was that really necessary besides the chauffeured limo?"

Brad looked blank. "What tail?"

"You didn't have one of your operatives follow us in a dark-colored Mustang? I figured you were doing some on-the-job training or something," Hoshi answered lightly.

"If you were followed," Brad said, his voice suddenly serious, "you'd better tell us all about it."

Tony had straightened up, too, his eyes alert. Hoshi said, "I didn't really see the car until we were a couple of blocks from here. Maybe it was just taking a shortcut to the freeway."

Brad and Tony exchanged glances. Ginny said in a faraway voice, "That's probably right. It was just that the Mustang didn't pass us, and we were going so slowly."

She wondered if it was Marc, maybe he was back but afraid to face her. The car had pulled out right after they'd left her apartment. There'd been a time when her heart would have rejoiced, but now all she felt was alarm. Several things clicked into place in her mind, not least of which was the fact that Marc had spent a lot of time at the Workin' Late Bar, and had been friendly with Al.

If Marc were prowling around waiting for her, it would be better to see him and tell him it was over between them as soon as possible. She didn't want to jeopardize her position with Julius and, more importantly, didn't want any kind of confrontation between Marc and Tony.

She stood up, wanting to get out of Tony's house and back to her apartment before Marc in his hotheaded fashion decided to come and ring Tony's doorbell. Was he driving around the neighborhood right now, waiting? He'd taken off in a Chrysler, but that didn't mean anything. Cars, any kind of possession, lasted only until they needed to be converted to a gambling stake. "It's been a lovely evening," she said. "But I've an early start tomorrow."

Tony rose too. "I'll take you home."

"No—" Ginny broke off, hearing the sharp command in her voice. "I mean, that's really not necessary. I can call a cab." She felt uncomfortable under their polite but surprised scrutiny, feeling guilty of an incredible social blunder yet unable to stop herself from compounding it. "I'd prefer to go home alone. I've enjoyed meeting with you, Hoshi, Brad—but I . . . really don't belong here. Tony, I'm sorry, if I gave you the wrong idea . . ."

Hoshi said, "Would you like us to take you home, Ginny? Brad and I could drop you off—"

"No, thanks," Ginny said in rising desperation. "Forgive me, but I want to go by myself." She turned to Tony. "Would you mind calling a cab for me?"

"Yes. I would. I'll get your wrap and drive you home," he answered shortly and left the room with long angry strides.

Hoshi uncurled herself from Brad and crossed the room. She asked, "May I call you tomorrow?"

Ginny nodded, feeling a little like a child who finds itself surrounded by adult disapproval and unsure how to put things right again.

Brad was regarding her with what seemed to be a knowing look, but all he said was, "It was nice meeting you, Ginny. I hope you'll come to our wedding."

Tony came back wearing a suede jacket, Ginny's shawl over his arm. Ginny said, "I won't get into your car with you, so either call a cab for me or I'll start walking."

"What the hell did I do?" Tony exclaimed, patience snapping.

"Nothing. I told you, I don't want you to take me home, that's all." *If Marc's waiting for me I don't want you to be there.*

Brad reached for a telephone on the table beside him and dialed a number. "You heard the lady, Tony. Let's not get into a brawl over it. Sit down, Ginny. I'll get you a cab." A moment later he said into the receiver,

"Yes. I need a cab; how soon can you get one out here?"

It took less than ten minutes, but by the time Ginny left, she felt as if she had roasted slowly on a spit for hours. But there was simply no graceful way to explain why she wanted to go home alone.

The cab driver waited until she unlocked her door and went inside before driving away, a little courtesy that reminded her that her apartment was in a slightly seedy neighborhood. Before she had a chance to reach for the light switch, a tall shadow separated itself from the darkness and a man's arms went roughly around her.

Chapter 5

"DON'T SCREAM; DON'T MOVE A MUSCLE," A STRANGE male voice ordered. Ginny was being held from behind, and in the darkened apartment all she knew for certain was that no man of her acquaintance used as pungent a cologne as the intruder.

Several possibilities, all equally frightening, flashed through her mind, along with regret that she hadn't allowed Tony to bring her home.

"Al Vernon left a package here. Where is it?" the man asked. "And where is he?" His arm tightened around her throat.

"Someone else . . . picked it up." It was difficult to speak with the pressure against her larynx. "Please, I can't breathe—"

The pressure eased slightly. "Who? Who picked it up?"

She hesitated, wondering why she felt it would be a betrayal to tell him Tony's name. The grip tightened again and she gasped, "I don't know; I never saw him before. He came and got the box and sent me out of the apartment while he waited for Al. . . . I don't know what happened, honestly—"

All at once he released her, and she staggered against the wall. He muttered, "Tony DeLeon."

Ginny remembered the Mustang that had followed them to Tony's house. She groped along the wall, seeking the doorknob, but was too shaken and disoriented to find it.

The man snapped, "Okay—you were with DeLeon tonight. Where's Al? Why wasn't he charged?"

"He . . . he was given a warning. That's all I know. I think he left town."

There was a muttered curse, then the door was flung open. Ginny had a quick glimpse of a muscular back clad in a dark jacket before the door slammed.

She slid the bolt, then ran to the window, raised the shade and peered outside. The man had vanished among the rows of parked cars. Still shaking, she flipped on the light switch and looked at the wrecked remains of her furniture and clothes.

The phone was on the floor, and the line hadn't been cut. With shaking fingers she began to dial Tony's number, then stopped. Gambling money . . . Al . . . Tony, yes, and Marc too—all of them belonged in her past and that's where they were going to stay. Perhaps a scare like this was what she needed to make her come to her senses. She dialed a different number and when a languid voice answered, said, "Julius? This is Ginny. I'm sorry to bother you so late, but I just had a great idea."

"I'm looking at your new sketches. They're not bad. Tell me about your idea."

"Well, as you know, it takes me an hour and a half, sometimes more when the traffic's heavy, traveling to and from my apartment every day. I could use that time more productively if I lived downtown, and since the Castle is the closest hotel to the boutique, I wondered if you could get me a room there at a reasonable rate?"

There was a pause. "And you'd be on hand if I needed you after business hours, wouldn't you, my sweet? What a wonderful idea. Pack your things and come over first thing tomorrow."

The grand opening of the Julius Boutique brought a bevy of showgirls, as well as passing tourists. Ginny and her assistant, Lynn, were kept busy packing items into red-and-black plastic bags bearing the distinctive Julius logo, the J of which formed a fire-breathing dragon. Ginny had persuaded him that decorating the interior of the shop in red and black would not set off the clothes to their best advantage, so he had contented himself with several abstract paintings in red and black against neutral walls.

Ginny had visited a couple of designers and numerous wholesalers in Los Angeles and had stocked the boutique with simply designed clothes that could be mixed and matched. Julius had been generous with money, so she had invested heavily in accessories with which to take an off-the-rack outfit out of the ordinary and into the designer category.

After she and Lynn were finished putting together a blouse and skirt, they cinched it together with the right belt and a necklace or scarf. Some of their selections were on hangers on the racks, others pinned to the walls or draped artfully on a series of small daises, so that hats and shoes could be added. As a result, purchases were invariably for the entire ensemble.

Just before closing time Hoshi appeared. She looked at the depleted racks and disorder of a rush of business and gave Ginny a happy smile. "Looks like the Great One is a success—all thanks due to you two, I'm sure, I bet you worked your buns off."

Ginny pushed a strand of hair out of her eyes, grinning at the incongruity of Hoshi's speech. Hoshi looked as if the tragic aria of *Madame Butterfly* should come from her lips instead of some current American-ism. Somehow her presence caused the strain of the day to fall from Ginny's shoulders. "I'm glad you came. I've been meaning to call you, but it's been frantic. Come and see what I found."

She led Hoshi into the back room, where a white lace dress hung over the back of the door. "It's an antique," Ginny said, "I found it in an antique clothing store on my last buying trip to L.A. It's at least a hundred years old. The lace had yellowed, but the cleaners have a new process they used. Isn't it lovely? If you like it, I can easily alter it to fit."

"Gosh, it's beautiful," Hoshi breathed, fingering the delicate lace. "And the high neck and ruffles will disguise the fact that I'm built like a boy."

"You are not! You have a perfect figure, and you know it."

Hoshi turned and looked at her. "You *will* come tomorrow? You promised."

"I'll be there."

"I guess I sort of led you to believe we were getting married in a wedding chapel, but Brad has his heart set on getting married in Tony's house."

Ginny digested this news silently. Tony hadn't called her since the night she'd left so abruptly. Still, she could hardly back out now, since Hoshi had no one else. "Well, if you don't mind that the best man and maid of honor will probably ignore each other . . . Now, slip on the dress while I go and lock the front door. We've a lot of work ahead of us tonight.''

Hoshi looked radiant in the antique wedding gown, carrying a simple bouquet of red roses, which she handed to Ginny just before Brad slipped the wedding ring from his pocket.

Ginny wore a full-length gown of deep blue she had found in the same antique clothing store. They looked, they had decided earlier amid giggles, like two nineteenth-century women who probably knew a little bit more about men than they were supposed to.

As the minister spoke the words of the marriage ceremony, some of Ginny's earlier gaiety faded as she listened to the solemn vows. Once she had been so sure that she would make those same vows to Marc. She felt Tony's eyes on her but didn't turn in his direction.

He had been polite but distant since her arrival. Not quite in the manner of a man meeting a woman for the first time. Perhaps more like a man tolerating a friend of a friend, of whom he disapproves.

Ginny felt an unreasonable resentment about this but had vowed to herself she wouldn't explain anything to him, although she was still arguing with herself as to whether she should have told him about the intruder in her apartment. The trouble was, even if she'd wanted to, there'd been no opportunity. She had been so busy moving into the hotel and preparing to open the boutique, she'd barely had time to work on her own designs, and she was anxious to get some of her clothes before the public eye.

Tony's living room had been decorated with flowers and ribbon bows, and the bride and groom stood under an archway trailing orange blossoms. The house was packed with people, all of them Caucasians, friends of Brad, Ginny assumed. She was saddened that Hoshi could not share this most special of days with any of her own family and friends.

Ginny could easily emphathize with Hoshi's isolation and alienation, as it certainly paralleled the last couple of years of her own life. Ginny had left home with Marc against her family's wishes, had moved from one gambling town to another, never making any lasting friends or putting down roots. So many times Ginny had longed to have a close friend to confide in, and pride had kept her from admitting to her family that they'd been right about Marc. So she'd worn a brave smile and pretended that Marc and her life-style suited her just fine. Looking at Hoshi, whose eyes were shining with love, Ginny fervently hoped that in time Hoshi's family would accept Brad.

Turning her head, Ginny became aware that Tony was watching her. His expression had changed slightly and seemed to acknowledge that he knew what she was thinking and not only agreed but perhaps now also understood Ginny a little better. Never having known a man whose mind seemed able to reach out and touch hers, Ginny was more than a little disoriented.

Caterers had been hired to provide a wedding feast, which would follow the ceremony. Ginny decided that as soon as Hoshi left the festivities to change into her traveling suit, she would unobtrusively depart. She didn't want to risk any kind of confrontation with Tony. She had a feeling that the emotionally charged atmosphere of the wedding might cause her to respond to him in a way that might horrify her tomorrow.

He looked particularly appealing in his white dinner jacket, but Ginny didn't allow herself to dwell on that. She looked around for the woman in the photograph he carried but didn't see anyone resembling her.

Hoshi and Brad were declared husband and wife, and after they kissed, Ginny hugged Hoshi and wished her happiness, gave Brad a peck on the cheek, then stood aside to allow the other guests to do the same.

A moment later a voice at her side said, "Will you come outside with me for a moment, before it gets dark?"

She looked into Tony's eyes and saw that the acutely aware gaze he'd worn during the ceremony had now been replaced by the expression she'd noticed the first time she'd met him. An ice-thin veneer of nonchalance over a well-deep mass of pain—disillusionment—whatever it was that made him hurt inside. It occurred to her suddenly that she was probably the first woman he'd shown that part of himself to for a very long time, and he wasn't pleased with himself for having done so. He added, "There's something I'd like you to see."

She nodded and he opened the sliding glass door for her. It was that most beautiful time in the desert, the beginning of sunset, and the sky was streaked with gold and purple and flame. She followed him past a gnarled olive tree, around a rock garden of cholla and barrel cactus, to a gravel-strewn slope that fell away from the rear of the house. Just below the edge a cluster of spiky leaves formed a nest around a tall magnificent blossom.

Ginny gasped with pure pleasure. "A century plant! It must have bloomed just today . . . and it's almost pure white. I've never seen a white one; they're usually yellow." She moved closer, admiring the waxy perfection of the tall column of flowers.

"An omen for Hoshi's happiness, I hope," Tony said.

"And Brad's, of course."

"Brad is always happy, no matter what. It's Hoshi I worry about; she's giving up everything. Brad still has everything he had before *and* Hoshi."

Ginny looked at him curiously. "What a paradox you are. So sensitive in some ways, so—" About to say "so tough in others," she broke off, remembering her resolve not to start anything with him. She added lightly, "I thought Brad was your best friend."

"He saved my life. I owe him a great deal. I still worry about Hoshi. She's lonely without her family. I'm glad you and she are friends. Tell me, how are things with you and Julius?" The hard look was back in his eyes, and Ginny turned to look at the century plant again.

"It's taken fifteen to eighteen years to produce this blossom, and now it's already dying. Things are fine with Julius. We had our grand opening yesterday and just about sold out our inventory."

"Julius doesn't have a very good reputation with women in this town. I hope you know what you're doing."

She looked at him in amazement. Surely he didn't imagine any relationship between her and Julius other than a professional one? But before she could speak, Tony said, "I know, I know, it's none of my business. What is it about you, Ginny, that makes me want to protect you, even from yourself? I don't suppose you'd care to stick around after everyone leaves so we could talk about it, would you?"

In the rapidly fading light he was a silhouette, his stance relaxed, easy, yet there was a certain inclination of his arms, curving toward her, that was both inviting and disturbing. It had been a long time since Ginny had slipped into the comforting warmth of a masculine embrace.

The sheer physical spell this man seemed to cast over her was in such violent contrast to her feelings about him otherwise that she found herself blurting out, "I don't want to start anything with you, Tony. You're a DeLeon, and even though you play at being an investigator, you're still part of the DeLeon gambling millions. You know how I feel about that."

"I don't share in any gambling profits. Besides, it's unfair to blame the DeLeons because your . . . friend is a compulsive gambler."

"It's not just that. I—" Ginny looked away, across the shadowed sweep of desert stretching to the dark-red horizon. She was thinking of the photograph Tony carried but could hardly say to him, I don't want to be one of a pack. Any man in my life has to be faithful; I couldn't go through the pain Marc inflicted with his infidelities again. The pattern with Marc had been quickly established: When he was gambling and losing, broke, he was all hers, attentive, contrite, faithful. But when he was on a winning streak, he needed the adoration of more than one woman.

"I finished 'Ginny's Song,'" Tony said suddenly. "Would you like to hear it?"

The memory of the music flooded through her mind, and she turned to look at the man who had created it and found that his face was only inches from hers. Behind his head the last blaze of glory of the sunset faded and the stillness of the desert surrounded them. As if in a trance, Ginny swayed closer. Tony's arms went around her and his lips touched hers, tentatively at first, then claiming her mouth in such complete possession that she lost all awareness of anything but the magic of his kiss.

For an endless moment as he explored her mouth and she felt his heart pound against hers, it was possible to believe that the two of them had come together in a brand-new dream of love, untarnished by old sorrows. But then the spell was broken by Brad's voice, calling from the house behind them.

"Tony? Ginny? We're ready to go. You want to come to the airfield with us?"

Tony released her lips but still held her close. "They're using my private plane. Let's go and see them off, then come back here."

Ginny struggled to return to reality, unwilling to let go of the exciting tension of the kiss or the promise of Tony's lean body pressed to hers. She could only nod silently, and he kept his arm around her waist as he led her back to the house.

It took over an hour to drive to the airport and back and when they arrived, some of the guests still lingered, drinking the last of the champagne. Tony ushered them firmly to the front door, while Ginny curled up in a chair beside the fireplace and wondered what she was doing there. Too much champagne, too much romantic ambiance spilling over from the wedding, too much of Tony DeLeon's understated charm. Luckily the ride to the airport and back had cooled some of Ginny's ardor. At least to the point that she was back in control of her emotions.

When Tony returned from saying good-bye to the last of the guests and asked, "Would you like a drink? Something to eat?" Ginny answered, "No, thanks. I'd like to hear the ending to your composition, though. I'm curious about how it came out."

He picked up his clarinet and flipped off lights as he came toward her, leaving only a Spanish *triángulo* of red lanterns in a wall sconce to cast their soft glow over the room. The bridal arch still stood, just to the right of a grand piano, and the air was heavy with the scent of orange blossoms. In the instant before he began to play Ginny thought, *If ever there was a scene set for seduction, this is it.* But she wasn't sure who the seducer would be, in view of her own instincts whenever Tony was near.

The opening bars of "Ginny's Song" seemed familiar and dear as an old friend, and Ginny closed her eyes and lost herself in the music. When he reached the point he had left off the last time he played for her, she was surprised by the sudden vigor of the tune. Her eyes flew open, and she watched as he flung back his head and the melody poured out, darting like quicksilver in several directions before returning to a slower, more peaceful refrain. Then, just as she began to relax and feel the tension slip away, the pace changed again, to a throbbing, insistently disturbing beat that spoke of desire and fulfillment.

Ginny squirmed in her chair, feeling not only as if her own passionate longings were revealed but also as if she were an unwilling witness to the composer's fierce desire. She stood up, whispering, "No . . . no, stop it. I don't want—"

Instantly he laid the clarinet down and came to her. She tried to evade his arms, but they went around her and he pulled her close, his breath warm against her hair. "Ginny, don't tell me you don't want me as much as I want you. Don't rationalize away what we feel for each other. It doesn't have anything to do with anyone else but *us*, don't you understand? There's no connection to any other time but *now*. Let me make love to you, Ginny."

How easy it would have been to slip her arms around his neck, let her fingers play with his tousled brown hair, give in to the exciting pressure of his body, allow herself to melt into that beckoning molten pool of surrender. But a faraway voice tugged insistently at her conscience, warning that capitulation without emotional commitment would leave her more devastated than ever. She placed her hands on his chest and pushed him away.

"No! I can't. It's too casual. I'm sorry. I'm not a one-night-stand type of person."

"Why are you assuming that's all we'd have? Ginny, listen to me. I know I should wait for your wounds to heal, but I'm not a very patient type. I want you too much to let you keep me at arm's length much longer."

She felt buffeted by several conflicting emotions. A

push-pull between the strong physical desire she felt and her fear of again being burned.

She said, "Tony, I like you, I really do, but . . . well, I'm not ready to get that deeply involved with anyone just now. Apart from any other considerations, I honestly don't have time." It was almost true. And it certainly sounded a lot less revealing than admitting to him that she needed time to heal her wounds—time to decide whether a love affair with Tony DeLeon would be worth the possible price she'd have to pay. She'd learned caution, at least, from her experience with Marc. To temper the refusal a little, she added, "I'd still like to be friends with you and see you once in a while."

He was silent for a moment, then a mask slipped over his features that hid what his reaction might have been. He said, "Maybe I'm rushing you. At least give me enough time to offer you a little companionship. How about a picnic in the desert next Sunday? You haven't seen the wildflowers yet, and I just bought a Jeep I want to try out in the back country."

She hesitated, thinking how beautiful the canyons would be now, and Tony pressed his advantage. He raised one hand solemnly. "I swear, no hands. Strictly a nature tour. Come on, Ginny, don't look so damn serious. Say yes, and I'll pick you up at your apartment about ten-thirty."

"If I can get away, I'll call you Sunday morning," she answered. It occurred to her that he didn't know she'd left her apartment and was living at The Sand Castle. Perhaps she'd keep quiet about that. After all, if they were going out into the desert, it would make sense for her to meet him at his house—it was on the way. Besides, he might wonder why she was living in his father's hotel and again start suspecting she was part of the skimming operation.

Chapter 6

TONY LOOKED AT THE PAIN-LINED FACE OF HIS FATHER, still tanned but gaunt and ravaged against the white of the hospital bed. The old man's eyes rolled slowly in his direction, recognition flickering in the steel-gray depths but no welcoming warmth.

"How are you feeling?" Tony whispered, reluctant to disturb the aching silence of the room. He placed a pot filled with cacti, each small plant having had a pair of dolls' eyes fastened to it so that the cactus resembled a portly audience of gray-clad people all waiting for the entertainment to begin. In the flower shop the whimsical offering had seemed lighthearted fun, but now he wasn't so sure.

His father mumbled something in a heavily sedated

voice. That he was fine or some such nonsense. There
was accusation in his gaze now. Tony could have recited
his father's thoughts for him. You're my firstborn son,
and you let me down. You didn't become what I wanted
you to become. You're spoiling my immortality for me.
Where are the grandsons I wanted? Where is the
comfort of a multigenerational family for my old age?
The old man coughed, cleared his throat, the tube
running from an IV bottle shaking alarmingly.

"Would you like some water?" Tony asked, feeling
helpless.

"You been to the Castle? You check on Vince? Is he
running things right? A ship needs a skipper, Tony, you
know that. Vince thinks if you hire enough people the
job gets done. But it doesn't . . ." His voice broke into
another paroxysm of coughing.

"Vince is doing a great job," Tony lied. "He's
settling down. Don't worry. I'll go over there this
afternoon and—"

"You should be running DeLeon Enterprises. It's
your responsibility, not his. He's still a boy. Should
have time to play a little—shouldn't have been put in
that position at his age . . ."

Tony bit back the retort that when he was Vince's age
his life was directed by the whims of old men in
government who were determined to impose their will
on other governments at the expense of the youth of
their countries. He said, "You just concentrate on
getting well, okay?"

His father's eyes closed, and Tony was about to tiptoe
from the room when the old man asked, "You get
yourself a nice girl yet?"

Tony thought about Ginny and felt his blood heat.
Even days after seeing her, her face was still so clear in
his mind he could almost trace with his fingers the
lovely contours of her delicate cheekbones, the vulner-

able tilt to her hazel eyes, the full curving lips that were made for kisses and laughter. He answered without thinking, "Yes, as a matter of fact, I did. You'll meet her as soon as you get out of here. Can't have her thinking I come from a long line of invalids, can we?"

His father sighed contentedly. "It's about time. Maybe there's hope for you yet. Now get out of here, and let me sleep."

Vince was strolling among the blackjack tables of the Castle when Tony arrived. His younger brother wore a tuxedo the way other men wore jeans and T-shirts, as though that were the most comfortable way for him to dress. There was an exotic-looking dark-haired woman at his side, several years his senior. He circled the tables, greeting the regulars. Going through the motions of running the hotel and casino.

"Hey, Tony," he exclaimed, catching sight of his brother. "Say hello to Gilda."

Tony nodded in the woman's direction, then turned to Vince. "I need to see you privately; won't take a minute."

"Sure. Let's go up to my office."

He started toward the elevators, but Tony said, "Let's walk up."

As they went up the wide red-carpeted staircase Tony asked, "You check on your personnel department like I suggested?"

It was obvious from Vince's rambling response that nothing had been done since Tony's last visit. Tony restrained himself from commenting until they were in what used to be their father's private office. Vince looked as out of place behind the Chippendale desk as a flamingo in a snowstorm.

Tony went to a leather-topped bar and reached for a bottle of soda water, ignoring his brother's request for a bourbon. "Look, Vince, you've got to screen the people you hire. I've seen at least one pit boss here who was fired from every other casino in town. Get rid of that personnel director and do the job yourself for a while. There's definitely a skimming operation and God knows how many of your employees are involved."

"Hey, bro', lighten up." Vince gave his boyishly engaging grin. "You're not supposed to even be involved in our little problems with the help. Brad said he'd take care of things. If the old man knew what you were doing . . ."

Tony leaned on the desk, feeling the solid bulk of the wood beneath his hands. The office was furnished with genuine Chippendale and Sheraton pieces, and Tony had acquired his father's appreciation of the lasting beauty of classic designs. "I didn't tell you the last time I was here, but I had a phone call late one night from one of Brad's security officers, a Paula Phillips. I'm pretty sure she'd uncovered a skimming ring and was afraid the people involved knew she had."

"She called you? Why?"

"She'd tried to reach Brad, but he wasn't either at home or his office. She didn't know when he'd get the message she left on his answering machine, so she called me to see if I could find him. Said she had to talk to him right away, it was urgent."

"And?"

"I made a few phone calls, but nobody knew where Brad was. So I came over here to the casino to see if there was something I could do for her. By the time I got here she was gone—she hasn't been seen since."

Vince squirmed uneasily. "Well . . . you know how these chicks are. They breeze into town and out again like migrating—"

"She has a two-year-old son at home." Tony reached

for his wallet. "I'd like your permission to show this to
some of your people—see if I can get a line on her. I
feel responsible for her disappearance since I was the
last one to talk to her." He laid the picture of the
blonde woman with the cool smile on the desk in front
of his brother.

Vince studied it. "Why, sure, I remember her. She
was only here a few days. Come on, let's go down to
personnel for starters."

They were crossing the lobby toward the ground
floor personnel office when Tony caught a glimpse of a
long-legged redhead, her burnished hair flying around
her shoulders as she ran up the stairs with the grace of a
gazelle. Tony stopped and turned to watch her, his
expression showing his surprise.

Vince chuckled. "I share your opinion, bro; but I
think Julius has already put his brand on her. She's
running the boutique he opened, and he set her up in a
suite near his. Her name's Ginny Hooper."

"You didn't tell me you'd moved to the Castle,"
Tony said to Ginny as soon as her customer left the
boutique. "Is that why you suggested we meet at my
house on Sunday? So I wouldn't know about your living
arrangements?"

Ginny regarded him silently for a moment, trying to
read all the hidden meanings behind his words and the
anger in his expression. "Your house is on the edge of
town; it didn't seem logical for you to drive all the way
downtown to get me. Besides, I thought I'd tell you
about my move to the Castle when we were away from
everything. I didn't want you to go rushing about
putting the arm on people, or whatever it was you did
to Al to make him leave town."

Tony's eyes narrowed. "What are you talking
about?"

She explained about the man who had broken into her apartment and her hasty departure to the hotel the following day.

"Why didn't you tell me? Why didn't you call me that night? Don't you realize what danger you were in?"

"You're not my keeper. I just wanted to . . . to disassociate myself from everything connected with gambling money."

"So you moved into the Castle, let Julius set you up in a suite. How long before you move into his suite?"

"No, you're wrong. I work for Julius. Good lord, you don't imagine he and I—" Ginny broke off. Then anger took over. "Damn you, Tony DeLeon, why am I defending my actions to you? Get out of here, and don't come back."

He reached across the counter separating them and caught her hands in his. The censure in his expression had been replaced by genuine concern. "Listen to me. You don't know Julius like I do. There have been some particularly unsavory episodes with women. I don't know why my father ever hired him—or kept him on."

Ginny felt some of her resentment evaporate. But she still felt he was treating her like an unsophisticated schoolgirl. She said, "I have a professional relationship with him. Nothing more. But even if I had, it's none of your damn business."

Tony regarded her with a slightly serious, half-conciliatory but uncomfortably knowing look. "I just punched all the wrong buttons, didn't I? Look, I know you're perfectly capable of taking care of yourself, but I can't seem to stop worrying about you. I suppose mainly because you're so open and aboveboard yourself that I find it hard to believe you have any conception of how devious some people can be. Julius is a case in point."

Ginny was silent, unwilling to speak in case she

revealed too much of herself too soon to a man whom
she wanted to continue treating her in a rather appeal-
ingly protective manner. Tony was so different from
Marc in every way, and Ginny was reluctant to dispel
any of Tony's illusions about her. He seemed to think
she had emerged from her relationship with Marc
totally unaware of the dark underside of some people's
personalities. Devious! Compared to Marc, Julius was
an open book. But for now it was nice that Tony
thought she was still so sheltered.

"Okay, Tony," she said, giving him a warm smile.
"Don't go away mad. I'll watch out for Julius, I
promise. And our Sunday picnic in the desert is still
on."

Ginny wore jeans and hiking boots, a long-sleeved
cotton shirt, and a bush hat. There was a rucksack over
her shoulders. Tony surveyed her gravely. "Dr. Living-
stone, I presume?"

"What a day," Ginny said, hands gesturing toward
the desert vistas beyond his house, each detail vivid in
the brilliance of the sunlight. The clarity of the air made
the distant mountains seem deceptively close, and the
breeze whispered of cool canyons waiting to be explored.

Tony took her rucksack and threw it into the back of
the Jeep parked next to his Jaguar as Ginny reached
into the back of her VW for a second rucksack. She
handed it to him. "Your share of the lunch and water
flasks is in here. I didn't know if you had one." He
glanced at it briefly before placing it beside hers in the
Jeep. Ginny said defensively, "I bought it yesterday. It
didn't belong to Marc, if that's what you're thinking."

His hand went to her arm, trailed up her shoulder,
and came to rest against her cheek. "Just for today . . .
let's make a pact. We won't talk about anybody but you

and me." He helped her into the Jeep, swung himself into the driver's seat, and started the engine.

As they set off down the street toward the open desert, Ginny said, "There's a canyon I'd like to explore. We'll have a pretty strenuous climb to get into it, but we're not likely to meet any other hikers. You're not wearing a beeper or anything, are you? I mean, you're not on call to anyone? I'd hate to have civilization intrude."

"No. I'm off today. First day off I've taken in weeks."

"You're working on a case, I suppose?" She tried to keep her tone only mildly interested. The picture of the blonde woman he carried in his wallet had been passed around to Castle employees with instructions to call Tony if anyone knew of her whereabouts. Ginny felt mildly embarrassed that she'd assumed Paula Phillips meant more to Tony than an investigation of a missing person, even though he was unaware of her assumption.

"I usually am. But I've got other people working on it too. Here comes the turnoff. Which direction to your canyon?"

An hour later they parked the Jeep in a dry wash and climbed a rocky slope. On the highest ridge they paused to drink in the stark beauty of the desert below, mysterious as a lunar landscape. Tony pulled a flask of water from his backpack and handed it to her. "You're not even breathing heavy. How can you be so tough yet look so fragile?"

She took a long swallow of icy water. "I learned that strenuous exercise is the best cure for depression. You can't feel sorry for yourself when you're pushing your body to its limit."

"They say your brain releases certain chemicals when you exercise, too, don't they? That give a sense of well-being." He drank some water, replaced the flask, then slipped his arm around her waist. "Are you over him yet, Ginny?"

She looked up into his eyes. "Yes. I'm over him. But when he left, he took something from me that I miss. I'd like to have it back."

"What's that?"

"My trust. My belief that people—men—are basically decent and caring. That they aren't all self-centered, deceiving, unfaithful."

He pulled her head down on his shoulder and held her, catching her hat as it fell. "I felt the same way for a long time. The woman who was going to be my wife found someone else while I was away—someone who could give her the career she wanted. She married the owner of a big modeling agency and divorced him a year later when she'd become a top model. Funny how long it took me to realize what a lucky escape I'd had. It never ceases to amaze me how we pine for the people who hurt us most, instead of being glad they're no longer around to torture us."

His finger went under her chin, and he tilted her face up so that he could kiss her. The breeze came rustling up the canyon and ruffled her hair. His lips were cool from the icy water and tasted a little like wild sage. She wrapped her arms around him, inhaling the fresh clean scent of the chaparral on the hillside that clung to his clothes.

As his lips and tongue sought the response she wanted to give, she pulled away, still wary about yielding to desires that could make her feel vulnerable again. "Let's try to get into Lost Canyon before lunch," she said shortly.

He looked at her, puzzled. "What's the matter?"

"You're rushing things again. You promised a no-hands picnic, remember?"

His eyes flickered over her. "I seem to forget a lot of

things when I'm around you. Why do you suppose that is?"

"Oh, come on, let's go. I don't feel like being analyzed today." She slipped her arms through her backpack and started through the pass leading to the canyon.

The downhill journey was more difficult than the climb, with shifting rocks and loose gravel. They concentrated on their footwork rather than conversation. Several boulders as big as two-story buildings blocked the entrance to Lost Canyon, and Ginny pointed to the barely discernible toeholds they would use to climb over them.

Tony shook his head slightly as he prepared to go first.

"It'll be worth it, I promise," Ginny said. "There's even a small stream and a waterfall in there. Except for the midday heat, you'd never know you were in the desert."

Half an hour later they reached a meadow of wildflowers, bright yellows and blues and reds, gentle mauves and pinks, determinedly thrusting fragile stems through the sand.

Ginny sank to her knees to touch the petals of a verbena. "And waste its sweetness on the desert air . . ." she quoted. "Gray was wrong. Sweetness such as this is never wasted." She sat back on her haunches. "Let's have lunch here, shall we? I'm starving."

Tony unhooked his backpack and cocked his head to one side, listening. "I can hear water."

She took his hand. "Over here. See where the manzanita and desert orchids are thickest?"

A shallow stream traversed a rocky path down the canyon wall, dropping several feet in a rushing white spray of water. Ginny pulled a couple of apples from her pack and put them into the water to chill them, wedging them between two rocks to keep them from

floating away. She had insisted on providing lunch
herself, cold chicken and French bread and cheese,
homemade cake.

They ate with hungry abandon, then stretched out in
the sun, sated and content.

Tony asked, "Are they worth a penny?"

"I was just thinking that it's nice to be with a man
who enjoys the same things I do."

"Funny, I was thinking that I don't know another
woman in town who would spend the day hiking in the
desert with me. I wouldn't even ask most of the women
of my acquaintance."

He rolled on his side, looking down at her. She lay
with her head resting on a backpack in the shade of an
overhanging rock. With one finger he pushed a strand
of her hair back behind her ear.

She smiled up at him, thinking how much she liked
the way his mouth went up at one corner and his eyes
searched her face as though he were committing it to
memory. The lazy warmth of the midday sun crept
through her body, and she raised her arms above her
head to stretch with sheer catlike pleasure.

The next moment his face was close to hers, his lips
touching her temple, moving to close her eyelid, then
his breath was warm against her cheek. Her arms went
around his neck, and her mouth sought his, her lips
feverish with need. This time she knew there would be
no holding back. There was an almost desperate hunger
in her response to his kiss, to the way her flesh
throbbed under his caress. Yet he moved slowly, almost
leisurely, unbuttoning her shirt, pausing to express his
wonder at the perfection of her breasts.

When he bent to take her nipple in his mouth, she
clasped his head and tried not to moan aloud with the
sweet agony of wanting him. She would have flung off
her clothes and made love to him on the spot, oblivious

of the unyielding sand beneath her, but he stood up and slipped his arms under her shoulders and knees. He carried her to the banks of the stream, where the grasses were softest, and placed her down with reverent care.

Within the sheltering walls of the canyon he cast off his restraining clothes, revealing the lean muscular lines of his body, emphasized by broad shoulders and strong pectoral plains. She watched him, thinking that everything that had ever been said or written about masculine beauty could not come close to describing the pure pleasure she felt at the sight of his tanned body.

Kneeling beside her, he helped her remove her clothes. The sunlight felt even more erotic than moonlight on her naked flesh, and her desire was heightened by the way his eyes drank in every inch of her.

"God, Ginny, you're beautiful . . ." he whispered before he began to trail kisses down the length of her body.

She had never been so aroused. Wherever his fingertips and lips touched, it seemed molten flows of lava erupted along her veins. Unable to lie still, she moved her hips, felt her fingernails sink into the hard smooth flesh of his back as she pulled him to her.

The sun blazed over the granite walls of the canyon, and she closed her eyes against the glare, mindless of anything but the pressure of his body against hers and the promise of fulfillment. Then he was part of her and they were climbing to new plateaus of pleasure, flesh fused and moving in rhythms as old as the mountains shutting out the rest of the world.

Somewhere on the edge of her consciousness was the wondrous knowledge that for the first time she was making love, not sex, and the man who so carefully controlled his own desire to synchronize with hers was equally enthralled. When release came, almost simultaneously, they held each other, panting and laughing with joy and awe.

She placed her hand on the back of his head to guide his face toward her so she could kiss his mouth, afraid that if she spoke she would tell him she was falling in love with him.

Chapter 7

As Ginny was closing the boutique the following day, the phone rang and Hoshi's voice squeaked over the line. "Hi, Ginny. The honeymooners are back in town. Where've you been? I tried to call you all day yesterday."

Ginny felt a warm rush of sensual memory suffuse her entire body. She still basked in a rosy haze each time she thought of the afternoon of lovemaking in the desert. "I . . . uh . . . went out with Tony, believe it or not. We sort of . . . got together . . . while you and Brad were away."

"Hey, that's great."

"Where did you go on your honeymoon?"

"Tahoe . . . it was beautiful, except . . ." Hoshi paused.

"Anything wrong?" Ginny asked.

"Not really. I guess I didn't expect Brad would let business intrude on our honeymoon. I've a hunch he's taken on a case . . . you know he swore he wouldn't do any more investigating, that he'd concentrate on the school and the security personnel."

"What makes you think he's investigating?"

"He disappeared several times . . . oh, not for long, just a couple of hours, but . . ."

"Well, you know how men are. They have the idea their work is a part of their lives that can't be isolated."

"You're right. I suppose I just wanted him to concentrate on me every second. Ginny, before I forget why I called, one of the women who was at the wedding wanted to know where I got my wedding dress. Her name is Vera, and she's in the chorus line at one of the shows—a friend of Brad's, naturally. Anyway, she wants to wear her mother's wedding dress and wanted you to alter it and fix it up for her. I told her to come see you. Is that okay?"

"Oh . . . yes, sure."

"How about coming to dinner tomorrow night—you and Tony? I need you to admire what I've done to Brad's apartment. It used to look like a nineteenth-century bordello. Now I've got a horrible feeling I've made it look like a twentieth-century bordello."

Ginny laughed. "I'll check with Tony, but I'm sure it's a date."

Replacing the receiver, she picked up her briefcase and went through the door to a mauve-tinted twilight. The parking lot still reflected the heat of the day, but a cooling breeze was coming in with nightfall.

A vintage Jaguar was parked just out of sight of the boutique windows, and Tony perched on the hood, waiting. As she turned after locking the door and saw him, he jumped lightly to the ground and came toward her.

She felt a surge of surprise and pleasure. "Tony! You should have come inside. How long have you been waiting out here?"

"Didn't want to interrupt that last-minute frenzy you had going." In the rapidly fading light she hadn't noticed that he held one hand behind his back. Now he withdrew it and solemnly presented her with a huge lollipop.

"Thank you," she said, taking it.

"Not to be eaten before dinner," he cautioned, "And from now on I want you to remember not to take candy from strange men."

"Oh, you're not so strange. Just a bit odd."

He picked up her hand and kissed each of her fingertips, his eyes fixed on her face. "I know you said you had to work tonight, but I thought we could have dinner together at least. I had to see you tonight, Ginny, or I wouldn't have been able to work tomorrow. I spent most of the day thinking about you. Figured maybe I could get you to remove the spell you'd cast; it interferes with my reasoning abilities, which are essential to my trade."

Ginny felt a certain shyness that perhaps had its origins in her memory of their lovemaking in the desert. Their two naked bodies coming together with a frenzy seemed as far removed from their workaday selves as the glitter of Las Vegas was from the real world. Unaccountably Ginny experienced a fleeting longing that she'd met Tony somewhere else.

Though her briefcase bulged with unfinished sketches that she'd planned to work on, she answered, "Dinner would be lovely." She slipped her arm through his as they walked over to his car. "The Jaguar is magnificent. It must be at least fifty years old. It's interesting that you have both a new Jag and an antique."

"This one belongs to my father. But he lets me play

with it when I've been good. Well, the truth is the old man's been sick, and I had some work done on the car while he was in the hospital." Tony opened the door for her, and she sank onto smooth leather.

"I hope it's nothing serious?"

"No, just had the engine tuned."

She let him have an elbow in the ribs as he settled in front of the wheel. "I meant your father, you idiot."

"He'll be fine. He's as tough as they come."

"So I've heard." Like father, like son, she thought as the car glided away. Only they'd channeled their considerable drive in different directions. Or had they, really? Would the day come when Tony would step into his father's shoes and run a gambling empire? And how did she feel about that, having experienced the misery gambling caused?

Tony drove more slowly than usual, and Ginny felt the tension of the day slip away. He took her to a tiny café tucked away on a quiet street. "Set your watch back to 1932," Tony said as he pulled out a chair for her.

The decor was old-fashioned, the food wholesome and unadorned, the wine mellow. Forgetting her urgency to work on her designs, Ginny leaned back in her seat and surveyed the man opposite her. "I know this place can't be as old as it looks—it's an illusion, like everything else in this town. But I don't know when I've enjoyed a meal more, or felt so relaxed."

"How about yesterday afternoon in the desert?" Tony asked, a carnal gleam in his eye. "Or am I not supposed to mention that? I don't want to act like a cad or anything, but, Ginny, yesterday was very special to me."

"To me too, Tony." She didn't trust herself to say any more and reached for her wineglass.

His hand moved across the table and touched hers. It

seemed the most natural thing in the world for her to turn her hand over, exposing the palm so that he could caress it, then run his forefinger lightly over each of her fingers. They were separated by the table, joined only by the lightest touch of their hands, yet Ginny felt closer to him than she had ever felt to any other man, even Marc, whom she'd believed she'd loved.

"Too bad you have to work," Tony said. "They're showing an old Bogart movie at a theater that runs vintage films. Bogie as Sam Spade might just convince you that private investigators are tough yet gentle, glamorous and mysterious—you know, the sort of image I strive to project."

She smiled. "I love Bogie. Going to see him in your father's vintage car would be perfect, but—"

"Don't mention that word *work*," Tony warned her. "Tell me about how you've always wanted to be courted by a dashing private eye."

They talked about wonderful fictional private detectives, about books and films. Ginny felt comfortable and at the same time stimulated by his conversation, his way of watching her intently with those deep blue eyes of his, by their entwined fingers on a checkered tablecloth.

What was it about Tony DeLeon that made her feel she must grasp this moment and wring from it every drop of pleasure? The pleasure of his touch, his presence, the strongly masculine appeal of him. Was it the knowledge that he'd entered her life at the wrong time, when she was still trying to recover from a love gone wrong? Or his background, and her dislike of gambling tycoons, that cast a gossamer web of fragility over their relationship? She felt that one false move by either of them would destroy all those delicate threads.

Unaware of the passage of time, she realized with a start that they were the last and only patrons in the café. A yawning waiter hovered nearby, and Tony said, "Do you suppose we ought to let these people go home to their families?"

"How could we possibly have talked for so long?" Ginny exclaimed, glancing at her watch. "I'd no idea it was so late. Do you realize we could have gone to see the Bogie film?"

"We'll go tomorrow night instead."

"Oh, I almost forgot. Hoshi and Brad are back, and they want us to go to dinner. I gave her a tentative yes."

"Tomorrow? That's Tuesday. I think maybe Hoshi's forgotten that Brad always has a staff meeting at the school on Tuesday evenings. We'd better check with her before we show up for dinner."

Something in his tone disturbed her. "Why do you assume that Brad wouldn't cancel the meeting if his bride wanted to have a dinner party?"

"Brad won't change his life-style one iota. I know him too well. He believes—mistakenly—that Hoshi is like the Oriental women he knew in 'Nam. That she'll always defer to his wishes."

Ginny hoped there would be more give and take in the marriage, but the following morning when she called Hoshi, she was told apologetically that the dinner would have to be postponed until the following Friday.

Tony picked Ginny up at the boutique again that evening and they went to see the Bogart film. Emerging from the theater into the warm spring night, Tony slipped his arm around Ginny's waist and asked, "Are you hungry?"

She shook her head, so aware of his arm around her body that she wanted to turn and be totally enclosed by his embrace, unmindful of the people around them. Despite the fatigue of a long working day, there was nothing on earth she wanted more than to have him make love to her, but the practical side of her voiced objections. Where would they go? Tony's house was so far out of town she'd have to spend the night and have a long traffic-battling journey back tomorrow morning. She didn't want to take him to her room at The Sand Castle. Apart from the fact that his family owned it, there seemed to her to be a tawdry predictability about inviting a man to a hotel room.

Before he could say anything else, Ginny said quickly, "I've really got to go back to the boutique for a little while. I was supposed to work last night, you know."

"Don't turn into a workaholic, Ginny. Believe me, your work won't keep you warm at night."

"And you will?"

"Try me." His hand went to cup her face and turn her toward him. He kissed her lips lightly as they walked along the neon-bright street. "How about coming out to the house tomorrow night? I'll throw a couple of steaks on the barbecue."

"Not tomorrow—I have to go to L.A. on a buying trip. Thursday?"

"You've got a date."

She was still tingling from his kiss when she left him, and in a romantic haze went back to work on the wedding dress she was altering for Vera, which had to be done on Ginny's own time.

As she worked she allowed her mind to wander, imagining how it would be to spend the whole night with Tony. The imprint of his kiss seemed to linger on her lips, and her finger drifted to her mouth as though to seal the memory. It took all her self-discipline to concentrate on the dress and to try to ignore a nagging voice at the back of her mind that asked if perhaps the fever-pitch of her feelings for Tony was a danger signal. Hadn't she sworn, after Marc, never to be that vulnerable again?

The next two days went by in a flurry of activity, and Ginny rushed to get caught up so that she could leave the boutique early on Thursday and wash her hair before Tony came to pick her up.

She was just about to step into the shower when her phone rang. "Ginny?" Tony's voice sounded slightly strained. "I'm really sorry about this, but I'm going to be tied up this evening. I don't know for how long. I hate like hell to cancel at the last minute, but something came up. I'll tell you all about it tomorrow night."

"Oh . . . there's no need," Ginny said in a distant voice. It's beginning, she thought; the broken promises, the places to be that are more alluring than being with me. Oh, Tony, not you too. "As a matter of fact," she said more briskly, "I really should work tonight. Don't forget we promised to have dinner tomorrow night with Hoshi and Brad."

Hoshi conducted Ginny on a tour of Brad's penthouse suite, regaling her with descriptions of its former interior decoration. "And he had these samurai battle flags draped over the bed—mirrors on all the walls, and a picture that I think showed two tigers coupling. . . . I'mnotsurebecauseIranawayinfrightwhenhetried to get me into the bedroom, and I never got a real close look at it. . . . Anyway, I called up Goodwill and told them to pick up *everything* in the bedroom while we were gone."

Laughing, Ginny surveyed the sleek simple lines of the ultramodern furniture that now stood in the bedroom. The effect would have been sterile had it not been for masses of plants in multitextured containers, standing or hanging everywhere.

"I always had this fantasy about a Great White Hunter on safari . . ." Hoshi said dreamily.

"Well, you certainly turned this room into a jungle," Ginny responded. "And Brad looks the part. Did you get him a leopard-skin loincloth?"

They were giggling when they rejoined the men in the living room, and Ginny noted that neither Tony nor Brad looked up questioningly. They continued to speak to each other in low, urgent tones, as though getting some important conversation out of the way that they didn't want to share with the women.

Ginny had not had an opportunity to speak privately with Tony since his arrival, and it was obvious that he was preoccupied. She felt acutely his sudden change of mood. It was almost like witnessing a man doing battle with himself. Occasionally she looked up to see him watching her in a loving, longing way that said he wanted to get her alone. Then, without apparent reason, she would catch a flash of calculating assessment in his eyes, and he seemed to retreat from her.

What could possibly have happened since last evening to produce such a change in him? Perhaps, she decided, she had been a little cool with him when they met, since she was still slightly stinging from the broken date.

"Oh, they're still talking business," Hoshi exclaimed. "Come and see the kitchen. I didn't do a thing in there because Brad has the most formidable cook-housekeeper you ever met." She lowered her voice to a whisper and added, "A sort of cross between King Kong and Julia Child, if you can imagine that. I think she expects me to sit on the floor and pour sake all the time. I'm going to have to broach the subject of my doing some of the meals . . ."

Tony watched Ginny and Hoshi disappear in the direction of the kitchen, then said to Brad, "I'm going

to have to take her in to look at mug shots. I don't want
to, but—"

"What else is eating you?" Brad inquired. "No,
don't give me any bull—something is."

"I don't like her living under Julius's nose. I guess I
don't like her working for him. I'd like to get her to
move out of the Castle, but . . . well, I found out that
she's only paying a fraction of the rent on the room she
has. Julius is picking up most of the tab."

"So you imagined the worst? Hell, she's making such
a success of that boutique of his, why wouldn't he throw
in some fringe benefits?"

"You forgetting Julius's history? Can you really see
him passing up a woman as beautiful as Ginny? And
you know what his methods are."

"So warn her. Tell her about him."

"I tried to," Tony said gloomily. "But she didn't
want to listen. I don't want to pressure her."

"They'll be back in a minute. Listen, don't say
anything about Al Vernon until after dinner, okay?
Hoshi worked hard on getting the place ready for
tonight, and you're our first dinner guests."

Tony nodded as the two women returned. Ginny was
giving him a wary look that worried him. He wasn't
sure why the tense edginess in her gaze had returned,
other than the fact that he'd broken their date last
night. Surely that wasn't a capital offense? Especially
when he would explain why. No, she'd undoubtedly
picked up on his own tension, and not knowing the
reason for it, reciprocated in kind. It was both a
testament to their closeness and a reminder of the
distance between them that needed bridging.

Brad's housekeeper, who was built like a linebacker,
announced that dinner was served. Everyone meekly
trooped into the dining room.

Taking his place opposite Ginny, all Tony wanted to

do was to stare at her. She looked particularly lovely tonight, her auburn hair gleaming under the lights of the chandelier, her dark-green satin dress shimmering and bringing out the sparkling green flecks in her hazel eyes. She had the milky complexion of the true redhead but somehow managed a peach glow after a day in the sun, rather than a mass of freckles.

Everything about Ginny Hooper, he decided, was designed to drive a man wild. In those rapturous moments of making love to her, he'd believed that there was nothing more he could ever want from her—nothing beyond being with her, talking to her, touching her. She had given her body to him with an abandon that had surprised and delighted him. *Why wasn't it enough?* He knew the answer, of course. Because he wanted her to love him the way she'd loved Marc Noland. Completely, unconditionally, without fear or reservation. But would that ever be possible for her again? More to the point, did he, Tony, want that from her only because it represented an impossible challenge?

"Tony, you'd better eat your salad, or I'm sure you'll get it in your eggs for breakfast," Hoshi said, and he realized that he hadn't touched his food.

Brad dropped his napkin on the table. "Tony's got something on his mind, babe. Listen, old buddy—we're obviously not going to be able to do a thing with you tonight. Why don't you take Ginny into the next room and tell her what you know you've got to tell her. Then maybe we can all decide whether we want to eat dinner or not."

"Tell me here," Ginny said quietly. "I've a feeling it's going to be something unpleasant, from your expression."

"I suppose there's no point in putting it off," Tony answered. "I have to take you to police headquarters

later to look at mug shots and see if you can pick out
the guy who broke into your apartment that night
asking for Al."

"Now?" Ginny asked incredulously. "Couldn't it
wait until morning? Why the sudden urgency?"

"Last night . . ." Tony said slowly, his expression
grim, "Al Vernon's body was found buried in a shallow
grave in the desert."

Chapter 8

GINNY, STILL GROGGY FROM SEVERAL HOURS OF PORING over police photographs, insisted that Tony say good night to her in the lobby of The Sand Castle. "I'm beat; I just want to crash. I'm sorry I wasn't more help, but all of those men looked the same to me."

Tony looked down at her with a faintly quizzical expression. "I couldn't identify him," Ginny said defensively. "I told you, I didn't really see his face."

"I've *never* been invited into your room here," Tony responded, apparently oblivious of the proximity of several late-night gamblers feeding silver dollars and quarters to slot machines.

"I know. I suppose because I don't consider it home. It's a hotel room and too impersonal. I'm afraid I'd feel like a . . ." her voice trailed off.

"Sure, I understand." The expression on his face said that he didn't understand and was hurt by her inference, but before she could make amends he bent and kissed her lips lightly and said, "Good night, Ginny. I'll call you tomorrow."

She went wearily to the elevator and rode up to the fourteenth floor, which, as was the custom in most hotels, was really the thirteenth floor. As a gesture of his gratitude for the success of the boutique, Julius had found her a spacious suite of rooms for the same rent she had paid for the single room. Still, Ginny was determined that as soon as she could afford a decent place in the suburbs, or better still, out in the desert, that's where she'd live.

Placing the key in her door, she was surprised to find it not only unlocked but slightly ajar. A light was on in the living room and the unmistakable black caftan flowing over the bulk of Julius's body was visible above the arm of her sofa.

"Ah, my dear Ginny, you're here at last. I was afraid the champagne would be warm if you didn't come soon." He rose majestically, reaching for a serving cart that held an ice bucket and a crystal bowl filled with fresh strawberries.

Ginny stood on the threshold of the room, trying to control her anger. "I feel . . ." she said slowly, "that this may be just a suite in a hotel, but it's my private residence. How dare you just let yourself in here and—"

The champagne cork popped, and Julius's booming laugh rang out. "Darling, I knew you weren't home— I'd been calling you all evening. I didn't want to miss you. I promise I'll never violate the sanctity of your room again, although I'd love to violate your sweet body. Now, now, don't give in to that redheaded urge to kill. I have news that simply couldn't wait until morning . . . a small celebration had to be held to-night."

"I don't care—" Ginny began.

"Oh? You don't care that the largest chain of department stores in the country has expressed an interest in marketing a Julius line of sportswear?"

Ginny sat down weakly on the nearest chair.

"Are you in shock?" Julius inquired, placing a glass of champagne in her hand. Chuckling, he picked up a fat strawberry and said, "Open wide."

She almost swallowed the strawberry whole, gulped a little champagne, and tried to comprehend what he was saying. "Julius, there is no line of sportswear yet. Just my sketches."

"Which I showed to several buyers. I did perhaps exaggerate how close we were to production, but frankly I didn't expect they'd react quite the way they did. They're already talking about a promotion campaign—not only ads in all the glossies, but TV commercials too."

"When do they want to see samples?" Ginny asked, taking another sip of champagne.

Ignoring the question, Julius filled her glass again. "I want you to hire someone else to help Lynn at the shop—you, my love, are going to concentrate on designing our new line and supervising the production."

The room revolved dizzily, and Ginny gripped the edge of the chair with her free hand, suddenly aware that she and Tony had left for the police station without eating dinner, and champagne on an empty stomach was a very bad idea.

Julius pushed the serving cart close to her, dragged another chair over, and lowered himself into it. Ginny took several more strawberries, hoping they'd counteract the effects of the champagne. It was only after she'd swallowed several that she realized they'd been dipped in a liqueur. Julius continued smiling and talking about advertising campaigns and spring showings.

"Naturally, you'll need a proper place to work. A nice studio, I thought, with good light—"

"Yes, and a raise in salary so I can move out of here," Ginny heard herself say.

He laughed again and refilled her glass. "But, of course, whatever you want. Within reason."

Her head cleared a little at the prospect of a house with a studio . . . he did mean a house? She drank some more champagne and leaned back, feeling slightly nauseated. Something was very wrong. Surely a little champagne and liqueur-dipped strawberries wouldn't be having this effect on her?

Julius's face floated toward her like a ghostly moon. She felt his hands close around hers, and he drew her to her feet. As the room spun dizzily she realized that he must have put something into the champagne. She found herself suddenly enveloped by yards of black caftan, crushed against the rolls of fat it concealed.

Julius's face danced blurrily in front of her, his manic chuckle seeming to echo all around her head. She felt him panting excitedly, and his hands swept from her back to cup her breasts. "Just think, you'd still be a cocktail waitress if I hadn't walked into your life. How grateful to me you must be."

The thin satin of her dress gave under his fumbling hands in the instant she leapt backward, pushing him away from her. Shock sobered her, and she backed behind the chair. "You'd better get out of here, Julius. I'll be charitable and put your actions down to the champagne . . . but I'm warning you—"

Still giggling, he advanced toward her. "You really don't know what you're missing. Julius is the last of the truly great lovers."

Ginny turned and stumbled to the door, wrenched it open, and found herself looking into Tony's eyes.

"I came back to tell you the police have picked up a guy they think—" He broke off, his gaze dropping to the tear in the décolletage of her dress, then moving to find Julius standing behind her.

The onslaught of morning sunlight on her closed eyelids awakened her. She remembered opening the drapes last night and standing looking down at the neon-lit city wondering what on earth Ginny Hooper was doing in fantasy land.

She sat up slowly, groaned, and pressed her fingers gingerly to her brow. She had a headache that stretched all the way to her toes. Strangely it wasn't the news that her designs were to be marketed nationwide that came to her first but rather Tony's stunned expression at finding Julius with her.

The bits and pieces of last night's events mixed together in her mind to form a crazy jigsaw. Her own reaction had been a tipsy rage at the injustice of the accusation in Tony's eyes. This morning she vaguely remembered screaming that they were both to get out and leave her alone.

Julius had swept past her, chuckling in that insane way, and for an instant she'd been afraid Tony would take a swing at him. She had stepped between them, and Tony's steel-blue eyes sliced into her unmercifully. Would she have offered any explanation, she wondered, had he not growled at her, "You'd better go sew your damn dress. You're in no condition to view a lineup anyway. I'll call you when you're sober."

She reached for the telephone on the nightstand and dialed a number with shaky fingers. "Lynn . . . ?"

"Hi, Ginny. Not to worry, Julius has already called me, and he said he'd get in touch with the employment agency. We're not too busy, so I'll manage. Hey, what great news . . ."

Lynn rattled on until Ginny was able to extricate herself and call room service. She ordered coffee and toast, since she wasn't sure she had the strength to go into the kitchen and make it for herself. Recalling the look on Julius's face the moment before Tony arrived, she shuddered and vowed never to let Julius catch her alone again, and certainly never to let him offer her a drink.

An hour later, after eating, drinking several cups of black coffee, and taking a hot shower, she felt considerably better. She called Julius and said, "Ginny Hooper. I want an advance against my new salary—this morning. I'm going to look for a place to live, and I'll need first and last month's rent and probably a deposit too. You can send a bellboy up here with the check."

There was a moment's silence and then Julius responded in his usual suave tones, "Certainly, my dear. Consider it done. Now, when can you have about a dozen new sketches for the line in my hands?"

"I'll let you know after you swear to me that there'll never, ever be a repetition of last night's nonsense."

"What an ingenue you are! But we'll play by your rules until you grow up a little. Believe me, the time will come when you'll be begging for—"

Ginny wrinkled her nose at the phone but reminded herself to keep a reasonably civil tongue in her head, since the man was her employer. She interrupted, "I'll call you after I get the advance check."

After she ended the conversation she sat on the bed staring at the phone for a minute or two, wondering whether to call Tony and apologize for ordering him to leave last night without any explanation. No, better not, that would put her on the defensive. He should call her.

She prowled the room for a few minutes, willing the

phone to ring, then stopped pacing and slid open her closet door to select a dress to wear.

Damm it, she wasn't going to fall into that trap again. She wouldn't wait around for Tony to call her—even though she assumed that the police wanted her to see if she could pick the intruder in her apartment out of a lineup. Instead of calling Tony, she rang the police, who asked her to come in as soon as she possibly could.

She was just about to leave for the police station when her phone rang. Hoshi's voice, sounding worried, came on the line. "Ginny . . . it's me . . . you don't happen to know where Tony is, do you?"

"No, I haven't seen him since last night. Why, is something wrong?"

"It's just that . . ." Hoshi sounded suspiciously close to tears. "I called Brad's office, and he isn't there. He hasn't been in this morning."

"Perhaps he had to stop off at one of the hotels to check on his security personnel," Ginny suggested.

"You don't understand . . . oh, Ginny, he didn't come home all night."

Chapter 9

GINNY'S COURAGE FALTERED A LITTLE AS SHE LOOKED AT the directory sign at the entrance to a small complex of professional offices. Under the *D*'s was listed DELEON, ANTHONY, INVESTIGATIONS. Most of the other tenants were attorneys and insurance agents. She squared her shoulders slightly and headed for Suite Seven.

She could have called—Tony had given her his office number—but she wanted this to be a face-to-face confrontation.

The receptionist was staring at a computer screen. She was middle-aged, with hennaed hair, outsize glasses, and a dismayed expression. " 'Morning. May I help you?"

Before Ginny could respond a door to the rear of the reception desk opened and a young man stuck his head out. "Frances, baby, hurry it up, will you? And how about some coffee?"

"Get your own damn coffee," Frances growled. "And you'll get your profile when your profile is good and ready."

The man winked at Ginny and disappeared. Frances said, "I remember the good old days when they just went door to door and asked questions, instead of hanging around the office playing with machines."

"Don't they go door to door anymore?" Ginny asked, feeling some sort of comment was necessary.

"Oh, sure—after they've squeezed every bit of data out of one of these babies. You here about a missing person?"

"No. I'd like to see Mr. DeLeon. I'm a personal friend. My name is Ginny Hooper."

"Well, why didn't you say so?" Frances hit a button on her phone. "Tony said if you phoned to put you right through. Mr. DeLeon? Miss Hooper is here to see you. Yes, sir, in the flesh."

She grinned at Ginny as she replaced the receiver. "First door on your left; go right in."

Ginny opened the door to Tony's office and almost collided with him. He said, "I was just coming to get you."

"I've already talked to the police lieutenant," Ginny said. "And seen the lineup. I couldn't identify the man who was in my apartment, but I told them if they picked up a man wearing the same cologne, I'd remember it until the day I die. It's sort of a combination of Raid and Black Flag roach killer, with a touch of sour lemon."

Tony laughed and slipped one arm casually around her shoulders as he led her into his office. "Ginny, am I glad to see you. After I got home last night I started thinking about how you looked—your dress torn and your face all flushed, and I realized how wrong I was. I know how Julius operates—spiked liquor. I should

have warned you. Anyway, this morning I went over to
the Castle to see him. I guess I was going to pound him
to pulp—but he told me about your promotion to dress
designer and how you'd be moving out . . . also that
you'd more than taken care of yourself when he made a
pass."

Ginny carefully unfastened his arm from her shoulder. "Sit down, Tony; I want to talk to you."

"Yes, ma'am." He went to his desk, perched on the
edge of it, and waited expectantly. "I deserve to be
bawled out, but be gentle, okay?"

Ginny had worn a cream linen suit but was already
feeling too warm for the jacket. She took it off and
tossed it onto a chair. Tony murmured, "Uh-oh. She's
getting ready to punch me out."

"I suppose I was going to give you a piece of my mind
for jumping to conclusions about Julius and me, but
you've forestalled that. I do have a couple of other
things on my mind, though. First, about canceling our
date on Thursday. I assume it had something to do with
the Al Vernon murder. I think you might have told me
that, rather than just saying 'something came up.'"

A metallic gleam appeared in his eyes. "I prefer to
keep my work as separate as possible from my social
life."

"I assumed as much. That's why I decided to come to
see you here in your office. To tell you I think it would
be best not to see each other again. I don't want to be
kept around just for social purposes."

He slid from the desk and came to her, placing his
hands lightly on her arms, as though to keep her from
running away. "I didn't mean that the way it sounded.
The only reason I don't want to talk about my work to
you is that I don't want you involved in some of the
situations I have to deal with at times."

"When we first met, you believed I was involved in a
skimming operation. Is that why you don't want to talk

to me about your investigations? I don't like the feeling
that you don't trust me."

"If you're asking if I still suspect you, the answer is
no, I don't. Look, let me tell you a little about what I
do, most of the time. See that stack of files on my desk?
Those are all current missing persons cases we're
handling. The bulk of my business consists of tracing
lost people."

"Paula Phillips—the blonde woman in the picture
that was shown around The Sand Castle—she's a
missing person?"

"Yes. Unless it's a child under twelve, the police
don't do any massive searches for missing persons.
They simply haven't the time or manpower. Paula
Phillips was one of Brad's security personnel. She
disappeared after working a few days at The Sand
Castle, leaving a two-year-old child in the care of a
baby-sitter. I'm trying to find her, and I've an uneasy
hunch her disappearance may be connected with the
skimming ring."

"And Al Vernon was part of it, and he's dead,"
Ginny said, shivering.

Tony pulled her close to him and pressed his lips
against her hair. "Promise me that if you ever smell
that cologne you told me about on anybody, anywhere,
you'll call me? And Ginny, from now on if I have to
break a date, I'll be sure to tell you it's because of my
work. Only I can't promise I'll give you details, okay?"

Ginny put her arms around his neck and laid her
head on his chest. "Funny how every rational thought
in my head tells me to run from you, Tony, but my feet
won't obey."

He placed a finger under her chin, raised her face for
a kiss, but she pulled back and said, "There's something else I wanted to tell you. About your friend
Brad."

She told him of Hoshi's frantic phone call and Brad's

staying out all night without explanation. Tony's brows knitted together in a worried frown, but he didn't comment, and Ginny went on, "I called before I came over here and Brad's in his office now."

"What do you want me to do about it, Ginny? Chastise him? It's none of my business, and if I were you, I wouldn't get involved either."

Ginny turned to look out the window. His office had an uninspired view of the jammed parking lot of one of the major hotels across the street. Sunlight reflected on windshields with blinding intensity. Ginny pondered about the differences in men's friendships and those of women. There was no way she could remain indifferent to Hoshi's troubles.

Tony moved behind her, slipped his hands around her waist, and kissed the nape of her neck. "Don't worry; Brad cares about her, in his own way. They'll work things out. What we have to do is concentrate on each other."

Ginny felt herself tremble slightly, and she turned to offer her lips. His kiss was long and hard, so full of promise that for an instant she was afraid they'd both throw caution to the winds and make love right there among his files of missing persons. At last, breathless, she pulled away.

Tony smiled. "I'd like to continue that later, if it's okay with you."

"I'd love to, Tony, but I'm house-hunting again. I decided to move out of the Castle."

"Good. I'll help. I know this town like the back of my hand."

She hesitated, all at once aware of the implications of what she had in mind. She replied evasively, "Oh, I've already narrowed it down to a couple of places. I was even thinking of going back to the little cinder block house where I lived before."

"Don't go back there, Ginny, please," Tony said.

"Why? It would be a wonderful place to work—isolated, no distractions."

"I'm sorry now I told you the place was vacant again. Seeing it will just open old wounds for you. Besides, it's a lousy place to work; it's too far from town. Think of all the commuting you'd have to do."

"It's not definite yet. As I said, I have a couple of ideas in mind."

He regarded her silently for a moment, and neither of them mentioned what was really on their minds. Ginny wanted to say, *I'm over him. I don't pine for Marc Noland anymore.* But she knew that if she protested too much, Tony wouldn't believe her.

After a while he said, "By the way, after you get moved into your new quarters, I'd like you to meet my father and brother. My father's out of the hospital, and I want to try to make peace with him. We've been at odds for years. I'll be honest with you; he'll be easier on me if you're along. He has an old man's morbid desire for grandchildren, so don't be surprised at anything he might say."

"I'd be honored to meet him," Ginny answered.

The telephone on his desk rang with shrill insistence. He picked it up, listened for a moment, then said, "I'm on my way." To Ginny he added, "Somebody contacted Paula Phillips's baby-sitter and said they were going to pick up Paula's son and take him to her. I'd better get right over there. Ginny, I don't know how long this will take—"

"That's all right," Ginny said quickly. "I'll call you when I know where I'm going to be living."

Ginny turned the wheel of her VW sharply and negotiated the turn around the Quasimodo-shaped boulder marking the dirt road leading to the little cinder block house. Bumping over the rocks and gravel, she felt a blinding flash of nostalgia, déjà vu, so fierce that she braked sharply before the house came into view.

Staring at the tumbleweeds lining the narrow road like an advancing army, she thought of the first time she and Marc had come to look at the house. They'd had dinner at the Workin' Late Bar and Grill down the highway, and Al Vernon had told them about the house. "Place's been vacant for years—hell, you could probably live there for months before the owners know you've moved in."

Al had been most helpful after Marc had dropped most of their stake in his slot machines. "If we decide to take the house," Ginny had responded, "we'll get in touch with the owner before we move in."

Marc had at first laughed when he saw the state the house was in. "No way, baby! Plumbing is shot; broken windows; roof is probably bad. Why should we fix the place up just to rent it?"

"Maybe the owners will let us live rent-free for a month or so if we do the repairs. And we could clear some of the land; grow our own vegetables."

How long ago it all seemed now, how blurred the images, almost as if it had happened to someone else. She got out of the car and walked up the rutted path to the garden. The jackrabbits and gophers had finished off everything she'd planted, and wild mustard was already sprouting.

Sand dusted everything, including the sagging front porch of the house. The tenants who had moved in when she moved out had evidently thought better of the decision almost immediately.

The front door was unlocked, and she went in. Sand everywhere but memories of stardust too. Of imagining herself in love. Was she doing it again, with Tony? Shouldn't she be heeding the warning signals—of missing him when he wasn't near, of feeling her senses quicken when he appeared?

Funny, she barely recalled what Marc looked like. Oh, she remembered that he liked to sleep until dusk and then bask in the bright lights all night. "You only come to life when everything is ending," she'd told him once. "The daylight dying—the sun going down. You miss all the promise of dawns and new days."

His moods always swung from highs to lows. The lows were all for her . . . the highs he shared with other women.

She sat down on the couch, wanting to laugh out loud with the sheer relief of realizing that her pain over Marc had ended. She wished him well, but he'd lost his power over her. It was almost as though a spell had been lifted. She was aghast now to realize what a willing victim she'd been and promised herself never to let it happen again.

"Ginny . . . ? Oh, God, I hoped it was you when I heard a VW bug out on the road."

For a split second she was sure she was dreaming, that she'd imagined that voice from the past. Her head swiveled slowly in the direction of the door leading to the bedroom.

He was gauntly thin, his face shrunken and pallid, his dark eyes feverish. His jeans were tattered, shirt stained, and his feet bare. Clutching the door to support himself, Marc Noland gave her a ghost of a smile.

Chapter 10

For a moment Ginny couldn't speak, or move, then she stood up slowly. "How long . . . have you been here?"

"Couple of days—weeks—I'm not sure." There were beads of perspiration on Marc's brow, and he leaned against the door, shaking visibly. "Ginny, don't tell anyone I'm here, please . . . it's a matter of life and . . ." His eyes rolled upward, and he slid to the floor.

Ginny flew to him, dropped to her knees, and rolled him over. He was burning with fever, but his eyes blinked open almost immediately, and he whispered, "Weak . . . that's all . . . can you . . . help me back to bed?"

The effort to get him back into the bedroom exhausted both of them, as Marc was considerably bigger and heavier than Ginny. She pulled the blankets over him and looked around the room. The floor was littered with empty bottles and cans, some opened and containing molding baked beans. His clothes lay in crumpled heaps, along with several racing forms and newspapers.

He had evidently spent all of his time in the bedroom, leaving the rest of the house undisturbed. He could have been living here undetected for some time—he'd certainly come prepared, as there were a couple of cardboard cartons of canned foods standing in the corner of the room. A half-empty bottle of whiskey stood on the floor near the head of the bed, within easy reach.

There was no telling how long he'd been back. The old lady who owned the house lived in Reno and never came here. Besides, the house had stood empty more than it had been occupied for the past several years.

She turned to look down at Marc, feeling pity for his suffering, but no other emotion. She said, "I'm going to bathe you—try to find some clean clothes—then drive you into town to see a doctor."

His hand came up and clutched her wrist, and there was terror in his eyes. "No! For God's sake—no doctors. Ginny, I've got a couple of guys after me who'll kill me if they catch up with me."

"You're exaggerating, Marc; you always did dramatize everything. Who are they, loan sharks? They're not going to be able to get near you in the hospital, and you won't be able to pay them back until you're well. How long have you had this fever?"

"Not long . . . please, Ginny—"

She went into the bathroom, then remembered that the water would have been turned off when the last tenants moved out. She went back to the bedroom. "What have you been doing for water?"

He nodded in the direction of the closet and she

opened the door to find several plastic bottles. She found a reasonably clean shirt, wet the corner of it, and went to bathe his brow.

"Ginny . . . I'm sorry I left without a word. I—didn't have any choice. I didn't want them to hurt you . . . I wanted to lead them away from you."

Once she would have been pathetically grateful to hear that, but now it didn't really matter what kind of excuse he came up with, because she knew she didn't want him back in her life.

"I'm not going to leave you here, and that's final. You need someone to take care of you, and it's not going to be me."

"Please . . . get me some aspirin and more drinks—bring me some fresh water. I'll be back on my feet in a few days, and I swear to God I'll get out of your life and never bother you again, if that's what you want."

The way he looked at her indicated clearly that he didn't think that was what she wanted. He'd actually thought she would be waiting here for him, after all these months.

"How did you get here, anyway? I didn't see a car," she said, wiping his cracked lips with the wet shirt.

"Hitchhiked. A truck dropped me down the highway at Al's bar."

The thought flashed through her mind that since he referred to the Workin' Late Bar and Grill as "Al's bar," he had evidently not talked to anyone there or found out that Al was dead. "Why did you come back? If there are loan sharks after you, why didn't you stay wherever you ran to?"

"Had to come back to you, Ginny . . . I love you . . . I couldn't stay away . . ." His eyelids slid down, and his breathing became deeper. "But you weren't here . . . and then I got sick . . ." He was drifting off to sleep.

Ginny looked down at him, wondering what to do.

Unless he cooperated, there was no way she could carry him out to the car. There was no phone. She could go down the highway to the gas station and call for an ambulance, but was he really that sick? He wasn't faking the fever, but with Marc there was no way of knowing if he was exaggerating the rest of it. Could she get a doctor to come out here?

Marc was now sleeping soundly. Ginny began to pick up the litter and sort Marc's clothes, trying to find some that were unsoiled. There was a pair of lacy black panties protruding from the pocket of one of his jackets, which she shoved back inside, amazed that she really didn't care.

When the room was reasonably tidy, she went out to her car and drove to the gas station adjacent to the Workin' Late Bar and Grill, which wasn't open at this early hour of the morning.

The gas station attendant ambled over as she got out of her car. "Do you have a phone? And can you tell me if there's a doctor near here—someone who'd make a house call?"

He pointed to a pay phone partially hidden by a pile of used tires. "Ain't no doctor—no nothing near here, 'cept the bar and an eatery."

The first two doctors' offices in Las Vegas she called couldn't see any patients for a couple of weeks, and no, they didn't make house calls to strangers—only to patients already on their books. The third doctor said he made house calls within the city limits only. They all suggested she take the patient to a hospital emergency room. Ginny thought for a moment, then dialed again.

"Hoshi? It's Ginny. I need your help. I've got to get a doctor to come and see someone—but there's a couple of hours driving involved. Do you think Brad knows a doctor who'd come? . . . And Hoshi, the fewer people who know about this, the better. The sick man is on the run."

There was a moment's pause, then Hoshi replied, "Brad's out of town, but I'll see what I can do. If I can find someone, where shall I send him?"

"There's a roadside inn—it's called the Workin' Late Bar and Grill—I'll meet him in the parking lot. Right now I'm in a gas station. I'll give you the phone number here, and maybe you can call me back?"

It took Hoshi nearly forty-five minutes, but she eventually called to say she'd found a doctor. He needed a rundown on symptoms, so he'd know what to bring. Ginny breathed a sigh of relief and promised herself that this would be her last act of service to Marc Noland.

Hoshi accompanied the doctor, a young Japanese man she introduced as Dr. Shigero Ayusawa. While the doctor ministered to Marc, the two women waited in the living room.

"You shouldn't have come," Ginny whispered. "But I'm glad you did. I'm also grateful you found Dr. Ayusawa."

"I have to confess I appealed to him on the basis of our mutual national origins," Hoshi answered with a grin. "Used my maiden name and everything. But I was shot down when he tried to speak to me in Japanese. Still, he agreed to come anyway. He's with a tour group from Japan, staying at the Castle. I remembered Brad mentioned the Japanese tour group were all doctors . . . I sort of led him to believe the patient was a Japanese national down on his luck."

Ginny admired Hoshi's ingenuity but decided that it would take a man already suffering from rigor mortis to refuse any request the exquisite Hoshi made.

When the doctor emerged from the bedroom, he bowed and said in hesitant but precise English, "The gentleman has, I believe, influenza, with an accompanying ear infection. I've given him an injection of antibiotics, and I'll leave some capsules he should take every six hours. He should also take aspirin and plenty of fluids. You must get his own physician to look at him as soon as possible."

Hoshi said, "I'll walk out to the car with you. We're very grateful, Doctor."

When she returned a few minutes later, Ginny was sweeping the sand from the living room floor. Hoshi asked, "What now? We can't leave the poor guy all alone here—who is he, anyway?"

"I'm going to stay with him until he's better," Ginny said. "Would you make a few calls for me? To the owner of this house—she knows me—tell her I want to rent it again. And I'll need to have the utilities turned on as quickly as possible."

"Ginny, is he a relative?"

"Please, don't ask me questions about him; it's not that I don't want to tell you, but I don't want to involve you any more than I already have."

"Have you given any thought to what Tony is going to think about you living here with another man, sick or not?"

"Tony isn't my keeper. I make my own decisions." Ginny hesitated. "But I'd appreciate it if you didn't tell Tony about this—or Brad, in case he tells him. I'll keep my suite at the Castle for the time being and pretend I'm still living there. It will only be for a few days, until Marc's better."

"Marc . . ." Hoshi repeated. Ginny had told her she had been involved with another man before Tony but had not gone into detail. Still, Hoshi completed the name. "Marc Noland. The man you were going to marry. Oh, God, Ginny. Do you know what you're doing?"

"How did you know about Marc?"

"Brad told me. Don't be angry. He and Tony are investigators. They root out information the way the rest of us read cereal boxes when we don't really care to know what we're eating. It's sort of second nature."

"There's another call I'd like you to make," Ginny said. "Would you call Julius and tell him I'm going to hole up somewhere private until I've finished the sketches for the sportswear line, and I'll be in touch later this week."

Hoshi regarded her with solemn eyes. "And what do I tell Tony? You know he'll hightail it right out here to see you."

"Don't tell him where I am—please. Tell him the same thing you're telling Julius."

Hoshi shook her head sadly, sending her silken curtain of dark hair dancing. "I hope you know what you're doing," she said again.

Two days later Marc's fever had broken, but he had developed a cough that was wearing him out. They now had water and electricity in the house, and Ginny had cleaned everywhere thoroughly. The telephone had not yet been installed. She left a prepared meal in the refrigerator and drove to town to get something for his cough.

Dusk was beginning to shadow the streets and neon signs blink into gaudy life as she reached the outskirts of Las Vegas. She went to a drugstore and bought some over-the-counter cough medicine and throat lozenges. Not having any clothes other than those she was wearing, she decided to slip into the Castle to go to her room.

Ginny was caught in the lobby by Julius. His eyes went over her as though searching for something. "Ginny, love, it's about time you reappeared. But I don't see a portfolio under your arm. Where are the sketches?"

"They're almost finished," Ginny lied. She hadn't even thought about the new designs. "I needed some notes I have up in my room. How's Lynn doing at the boutique? I hoped you've checked on her stock." As soon as she could, she raced for the elevator.

Her room had been meticulously maintained by maid service but already had a cold, empty look. Ginny went to wash her hands and comb her hair. She peered at herself in the bathroom mirror. Two days out in the desert had brought a healthy glow to her cheeks, since between caring for Marc she had spent every moment outside, weeding and clearing the encroaching chaparral.

The telephone rang, and she jumped, not having heard one for two days. She drew a blank when a female voice said, "Hi, this is Vera. I just wanted to tell you that everybody was wild about my dress." Of course, the woman who had been a guest at Hoshi's wedding for whom Ginny had altered her mother's wedding dress.

Vera went on: "I have a friend who wants an antique-looking dress but wants you to make it—new— for her. She thinks all the modern dresses look alike. She's in show biz and wants to keep the design of her dress a secret." Vera mentioned the name of a headliner at one of the shows on the Strip.

Several thoughts flashed through Ginny's mind. She had agreed to design sportswear for Julius, not wedding gowns. There had been little creative satisfaction in finding an antique gown for Hoshi and remodeling Vera's gown. It would be fun to design an "antique." Julius would be furious if he found out Ginny wasn't working on his sportswear twenty-four hours a day, but she had a right to do whatever she chose on her own time. "Give me her phone number. I'll call her," she told Vera.

She went into the kitchen to see if she had any cold drinks. Her sketch pad was lying on the breakfast bar, and as she sipped a soda she began to draw the figure of a woman, then a dress, not really thinking about what she was doing.

A moment later she was looking down at a wedding dress design vaguely reminiscent of the Queen Anne period. Vera had been right about the boring sameness of most bridal gowns. Besides, there was a wonderful sense of adventure in designing a dress for the most special day in a woman's life. Looking at her sketch again, she dotted seed pearls on the bodice and added a dramatic floating panel.

The sportswear line for Julius had been inspired mainly by her own desire for clothes that were both comfortable and attractive, an alternative to the ubiquitous blue jeans. She had been able to come up with culottes and pants that fastened without the necessity of zippers and buttons that became hot and bit into tender flesh, but for sheer drama, designing a dress to be worn only once presented the ultimate challenge.

While the creative part of her mind took over, she momentarily forgot Marc and every other problem in her life as she let her imagination seek out something wonderful for a bride to wear . . . oh, yes, and for the bridesmaids, and mothers of brides and grooms, who surely were tired of polyester crepe. Ginny was filled with an excitement she hadn't felt before.

When someone knocked on her door, she almost jumped out of her skin after being so wrapped up in her thoughts of fairy-tale wedding clothes that she had forgotten everything else. Opening the door, she was instantly swept into Tony's arms.

He kissed her with a hunger that matched her own feelings. She had missed him so—how many times during the past couple of days had she thought about him, holding him, touching him!

He picked her up, kicked the door shut behind them, and marched into the bedroom, kissing her all the way. They collapsed on the bed, a warm tangle of arms and legs and mouths that wanted to keep kissing but needed to talk.

"Where have you been?" Tony demanded, then imprisoned her lower lip between his so she couldn't answer. "I've been going crazy trying to find you. I threatened to turn Hoshi into chop suey if she didn't tell me where you'd gone. She wasn't amused."

Ginny laughed, wriggling her arms free so she could wrap them around him. "How did you know I was here? I've only been back a little while."

"I've got an operative here, trying to come up with a lead on the skimming operation. He phoned me when you arrived."

"I'll think about that later," Ginny said, kissing the corner of his mouth. "And probably get mad. I don't like being watched."

"Then, don't vanish into thin air on me," Tony said, bending his head so his lips could find the warm hollow of her throat.

"What happened with Paula Phillips?"

"Not a thing. Someone had already picked up her kid by the time I got to the baby-sitter. And that's it for business. Do you realize this is the first time I've been allowed into your room?" Tony looked down at her with her hair spread out on the pillow, his blue eyes alight with warmth.

Ginny was filled with elation, a surging happiness at being in Tony's arms again, but the memory of where she'd been the past couple of days nagged her conscience. The mere fact that she was beginning to feel she had to tell Tony everything about her life caused an inner conflict.

He raised his head again, and she looked into his eyes, speaking from her heart rather than her head. "I've missed you too . . . so much."

"You didn't answer my question about where you've been. I thought you were moving out of here."

"I've been busy," she answered, looking away. It certainly was no lie. "I do still intend to move out of here in a few days."

"You're not thinking of going back to wherever you've been?"

"I have to—for a couple of days."

"Why? Look, if it's peace and quiet to work you want, move into my house. I'm gone all day—but we could relax together in the evenings."

"Tony, I can't."

"Why, Ginny? What is it you're not telling me? I feel like a door just slammed shut in my face."

Ginny felt a knot of tension clamp together between her brows. If she told him about Marc, would he understand?

"I don't want to move in with you. I don't need to give reasons, do I?"

It was so wonderful being with Tony again, why spoil it with a probably lengthy and tense discussion about Marc? He'd be out of her life in a few days. For right now, this moment, all Ginny wanted to do was to make love.

Her body ached with need, and ignoring Tony's questioning look, she pulled his face down so she could kiss his mouth, then began to unfasten the buttons of his shirt to feel the hard warmth of his flesh.

When he tried to speak, she smothered his words with her lips until at last he groaned. For a moment he was baffled by her ingeniously designed pants, which wrapped and stayed closed with only a tiny square of Velcro concealed in the waistband. Laughing, Ginny took them off herself.

Moments later they were both naked and straining together to get so close that it seemed each felt what the other was feeling, enhancing each's own passion. For Ginny this time was even more special because she was able to allow all her emotions to flow outward toward this man, holding none of herself back from him as she had before. At that moment she didn't realize that her feelings for Tony were no longer shadowed by the hurt Marc had inflicted, that seeing Marc again had released her from the last bonds of the past. That realization would come later. For now she knew only that magic that she and Tony miraculously created when they were together.

As if sensing the subtle change in her, it seemed that Tony was even more tender, more loving, more concerned with her pleasure than his own. She thought wonderingly that the joy of making love was not simply in receiving sensual pleasure but in giving so wholeheartedly of oneself that the love that was returned was increased a thousandfold.

She pressed her mouth to his chest, to the flat male nipples that hardened as she encircled them with her lips, then moved downward, fondling him with her hands, touching him with her tongue. When he could no longer hold back, he swung his body over hers and they soared together to that pinnacle of delight, hovered in dizzy anticipation for a second, then went crashing over the edge.

For several minutes they lay in each other's arms savoring the floating-to-earth sensation. Tony stroked her hair back from her forehead and pressed his lips to her temple. "If staying away from me for a couple of days earns me this kind of pleasure . . . I may leave for a month. But on second thought I couldn't stand not seeing you for that long. Now . . . tell me you were kidding about going into hiding again."

"Shut up," Ginny murmured. "I don't want to talk right now. I just want to glow."

"If I promise to shut up, will you let me ask one question?"

"If it's the right question." Damn, she hadn't meant to say that—it must have slipped out of the golden afterglow of passion.

There was an awkward pause, then Tony replied, "Nothing important. Before you become incommunicado again, I was going to ask if you'd drive to Tahoe with me Sunday to meet my father?"

"Sunday . . ." Three days away, Ginny thought; by then Marc should be back on his feet. "Yes, I'd love to meet your father on Sunday."

Chapter 11

THE FOLLOWING SUNDAY MORNING GINNY DRESSED CARE-
fully for her meeting with Tony's father, selecting a
simple celery-green dress in a cool crisp linen. She was
feeling a little drained, both from taking care of Marc
for several days and finishing the sketches for the Julius
line of sportswear.

She also experienced a profound sense of relief.
Marc Noland was finally only a part of her past. She
had even been able to see through his back-to-the-wall
declaration that he had at last realized he was a
compulsive gambler and intended to start attending
Gamblers Anonymous meetings.

Leaving him enough money to buy food and a bus
ticket out of town, she had told him she never wanted
to see him again. His mouth had twisted into an ugly

117

grimace when he asked who the new man in her life was, and that assumption had drawn her only heated response. She was taking care of herself, she told him, and didn't need a man to fulfill her dreams for her.

Reflecting later on that statement, she wondered if anyone's life could be complete if they always traveled alone. One part of Ginny's practical nature yearned for the stardust of an intensely romantic affair with a man like Tony—perhaps even like Marc in the beginning— because they were so different from her. But whereas Tony showed both a tough and a tender side to his personality, Marc had merely played the roles that suited his needs at the moment. Remembering the heartache of Marc, she was reluctant ever to allow Tony to have that kind of power over her.

When Tony arrived to pick her up, he whistled softly. "You're so beautiful you literally take my breath away." Ginny smiled and returned his kiss.

She was uneasy that she hadn't confided in him right away that Marc was back and now didn't know how to tell him without seeming guilty of a serious omission. "Tony . . ." she began.

He gave her a reassuring hug. "I know, you're feeling intimidated about meeting the old man. Don't be. Come and sit down and relax for a minute." He took her hand and led her to the couch, and they sat side by side, Tony holding her hand.

"Let me tell you a little about him. He's one of a very few old-time gamblers and entrepreneurs who made this state synonomous with gambling. He's also probably the last to resist being taken over by corporations and public stock issues."

Ginny didn't interrupt to tell him what she had been going to tell him. She reasoned silently that Marc would not stay around for long now that he was well—not if loan sharks were after him.

Tony went on, "He started out with a small club at Tahoe back in the thirties, and when gambling was legalized, he put in six slot machines. In those days hardly anybody went to the lake in winter. Then he traded some lakeside land he owned for land on the California-Nevada border—Las Vegas didn't exist in those days—and built the DeLeon Saloon and Gambling Hall. It's still there.

He was already in his forties when he married my mother. After World War II he started operations in Vegas, and in the sixties built one of the first high-rise clubs at Tahoe. I guess that's when he and I began to quarrel. He couldn't understand why I thought the lake should have been left as it was. I felt all the casinos should be concentrated in the cities, leaving the natural beauty of the lake for future generations. He'd say that I wasn't doing anything to ensure there'd be any future generations."

He paused, his eyes looking beyond her to some point in his memory. After a moment he said, "You know about Vietnam—about the woman who didn't wait. My father seems to think I should marry any reasonably healthy woman who comes along, just to assure him that there'll be a DeLeon to inherit his empire."

"What about your brother? Maybe he'll have children."

Tony gave a short laugh. "Vince? He's the playboy of the Western World. Besides, my father's getting well on in years; he has a sense of urgency and figures he won't be around to see Vince's children."

"How do you feel about it, Tony? Have you been soured on the idea of marriage?" Ginny asked softly.

He didn't look at her. "Let's just say it isn't something I'd want to rush into. But I like the *idea* of the constancy of two people becoming a couple. I suppose I need to learn to trust somebody, completely, again. Just like you, Ginny. Maybe that's what drew us together."

Raising his hand, he cupped her cheek, holding her face in a touchingly reverent way that was without passion yet so beautifully tender that Ginny felt herself melting all over. He didn't speak but looked deep into her eyes. She was struck again by the strangely fatigued quality of his gaze, as though his spirit sought to triumph over some impossible quest and knew it was beyond mortal endeavor. Those eyes had looked into hell, but they had a vision of heaven too. Ginny wanted to pull his head down to her breast, to cradle it there, and stroke his tousled hair.

Instead the two of them sat quietly, his hand on her cheek. At last he let his fingers slide gently down her throat and come to rest on her shoulder. "You filled an empty place in my life, Ginny, that I didn't even know was there. For the first time in years, I find myself waking up in the morning with a sense of anticipation."

"Yes," Ginny said softly, "I feel it too. I didn't realize how quickly the time passes when we're together until these past few days when I didn't see you."

His fingers played with a strand of her hair. "You realize that I'm spending too much time thinking about you and not enough chasing bad guys?"

She smiled and laid her head down on his shoulder, thinking how wonderful it was to be with a man who didn't hesitate to express his feelings when the mood and the moment demanded it yet was strong and capable in dealing with every other aspect of his life. There had been tragedy in Tony's past, she was sure, and it was something more than a faithless fiancée.

"Tony . . . Vietnam scarred a lot of men. You don't talk about it much. Is it an experience you've been able to put behind you?"

There was a fraction of a second's hesitation before

he replied, "It was over a long time ago. Hey, look at the time, we'd better make tracks. The old man doesn't like to be kept waiting."

Ginny reluctantly relinquished the warmth of his arms and stood up, making a mental note not to mention Vietnam again unless he brought it up. She said, "I'll just get my purse."

When she came out of the bedroom a moment later, Tony was standing beside the breakfast bar that divided the kitchen area from the living room, staring down at something. When he raised his head, he looked at her strangely.

Moving closer, she saw that she had left the sketch of the wedding dress she had made for Vera's friend. With the veil, headdress, and trailing bouquet of flowers, it was obviously a picture of a bride.

Tony's jaw moved slightly. "Ginny . . . don't get the wrong idea, just because I'm taking you to meet my father. It isn't synonomous with a proposal."

Color flooded her face. She was assaulted by several different emotions at once, not least of which was a fierce disappointment that the romantic mood between them had instantaneously been destroyed. She heard again the nagging echoes of Marc's derision at her obsession with legalizing love with a piece of paper.

Her insides curled into a tight ball consisting of equal parts of humiliation, embarrassment, and anger, erupting in a lava flow of words that defended by attacking. "Why you arrogant . . . conceited . . . vain—that sketch is part of my *work*—I'm thinking of designing bridal gowns."

In her acute embarrassment at his misinterpreting the reason for the sketch, Ginny couldn't stop lashing out at him. "Did you actually think I was dreaming about wearing it *myself*? Of being *married* to *you*? You're crazy! You think I'd marry somebody even remotely connected with gambling?"

"Ginny—" Tony tried to interrupt, his face stricken, but she was too angry to stop.

Perhaps too many hurts about the delicate question of commitment had been inflicted by Marc, but now Tony had to bear the brunt of the defense mechanisms she had devised. "I don't want to marry you, Tony DeLeon. You occupy the same place in my life that I do in yours. My career comes first, and if it takes me to New York or Paris or London, I'll go with never a backward glance."

She stopped, aghast at the diatribe that had come from her lips. But it had been the only way she could deal with her own sense of humiliation at both his assumption and his rejection, for that's what it had been: there was no other way of labeling it.

Tony's expression froze. He looked at her through half-closed eyes, as though he were an unwilling spectator of a stranger's rage, and that was even harder for her to bear. He said stiffly, "Ginny, I'm sorry for making an assumption I shouldn't have, and for my clumsiness in handling it. Put it down to a few women in my past who tried to maneuver me into marriage."

"It seems we're both prisoners of our past, Tony," Ginny answered, suddenly feeling drained, defeated in some way she didn't yet understand. "I wonder if we'll ever sever the bonds."

They watched each other warily for an endless minute, as two tigers meeting in neutral territory, each wondering whether to claim it for its own.

At length Tony asked in a voice that was deadly quiet, "Did you mean what you said about being able to leave without a backward glance?"

No, she thought, I didn't mean it, but if I admit that to you I'll lose face again, and I just can't stand that right now. She shrugged. "I should think that would be exactly what a gun-shy male would want to hear—that there are no designs on him."

Tony stared at her for so long that she felt perhaps he'd probed her thoughts, but perhaps that resigned look on his face merely meant that he recognized the rift he'd caused. After a while he said, "My father will be disappointed if we don't show up. I'd appreciate it if you'd come to Tahoe."

"Of course we'll go. You didn't think I'd refuse just because you're not about to propose to me? Believe me, I wouldn't be interested." She wondered, as she turned toward the door, if that declaration rang as false to him as it did to her. But then, there was no way he could know the hurt she felt.

Chapter 12

STANDING IN THE PINE-SCENTED AIR LOOKING ACROSS THE tranquil surface of Lake Tahoe, Ginny felt much of her tension dissipate. The deck of Tony's father's cabin was shielded by tall trees, hiding other buildings and giving the illusion that this part of the lake was theirs alone. The mountain peaks here were still snowcapped and the air brisk.

At her side Mr. DeLeon, bundled in a plaid blanket and seated in a wheelchair, said, "Where did that son of mine find a girl like you, anyway?"

"Waiting tables at your Workin' Late Bar and Grill," Ginny answered.

The old man's face crinkled into a satisfied smile. "I like you, Ginny; you're the first honest woman either of my boys has brought home."

His "boys" had been ordered to stay and visit with each other inside the house while he showed Ginny the view. He added, "And prettier than a summer day. Always did like red-haired women with long legs. I thought maybe you were a showgirl when you walked in here. You carry yourself like a dancer. You think you can get Tony to forget all that private-eye nonsense? Yeah, I know, I'm not supposed to call him a private eye. You know, I figured he was just doing it until he had enough capital to invest in his ranch, but hell, when I offered to finance it if he'd settle down and run DeLeon Enterprises, he turned me down."

"His ranch?" Ginny asked, surprised.

"He didn't tell you? He wanted to buy land in the Carson Valley—raise cattle and buffalo. Seems like he always wanted to do the opposite of what I wanted."

There was a certain amount of pride in his tone, Ginny noted. "Yessir, that number one son of mine always knew what he wanted, even when he was a kid. And didn't give a damn what anybody thought. If he wasn't fooling with his clarinet and writing music, he was out riding with any cowboy who'd put up with him. Never would have figured he'd get into police work."

He sighed. "He changed after Vietnam. After that buddy of his got killed. Maybe if it'd been by the enemy, the Vietcong, you know, but he got knifed in the back. I think that's what drove Tony into police work."

"Perhaps," Ginny said, a sudden vision of Tony astride a horse, rounding up cattle, taking shape in her mind. Yes, he was an outdoor sort of man; it did fit. But he'd never mentioned becoming a rancher; perhaps this was another boyhood dream that his father had clung to, rather than Tony. More significant was the news that Tony's friend had been killed so brutally in Vietnam.

She said, "Tony never told me he'd lost a close friend in the war."

"Southern boy named Lonnie. Killed just a few days before the last chopper left Saigon. He and Brad and Tony were the three musketeers. I don't know if it was Lonnie's death or that Tony found out he'd been involved in the black market that shook him up so bad. Tony wrote to his mother describing Lonnie as a cross between George Washington and that priest who took care of all the reform-school boys, I forget his name. Anyway, it seems Lonnie was forever helping the Saigon street kids and orphans—"

"Okay, Pop," Tony's voice cut in. "You've monopolized Ginny long enough. Besides, it's too cold out here for you." Tony walked across the wooden deck and took hold of the wheelchair.

"You leave me be," his father said. "I'll go back inside when I'm damn good and ready. Ginny and I were just getting to know one another." He had begun to wheeze.

Tony pushed the wheelchair toward the sliding glass doors leading to a solarium. "You can admire the view from in here and still get to know Ginny. That is, if you give her a chance to get a word in edgewise. She tell you she's going to be a famous dress designer?"

Ginny followed, amused by the old man's colorful threats as to what he'd do to Tony if he didn't take his damn hands off the wheelchair, which Tony ignored.

The old man peered at her with watery eyes. "You design that dress you're wearing?" When she nodded, he said, "Nice, real nice. Classy—simple, a real lady's dress. Who do you work for now, Ginny? I take it you're not waitressing for me anymore?"

In the same instant Ginny opened her mouth to reply "Julius," Vince stepped into the room and said, "Don't tell him!" But it was too late. The old man spat out the name as though he'd taken a mouthful of venom.

"Julius! That fat pervert! I made Vince fire him and

good riddance. What's he doing still hanging around town? Ginny, you don't want to work for that scum." He was becoming so agitated he was shaking. Tony shook his head at Ginny in a silent warning not to say anything else.

Vince said quickly "I'll get the nurse," and disappeared through the door to the house. Tony knelt beside the wheelchair rubbing his father's hands as he fought for breath. Ginny watched, not knowing what to do or say. Obviously Vince was supposed to have fired Julius but hadn't. No wonder Julius was so anxious to open the boutique. She could tell by the set of Tony's jaw that he was angry, but he spoke in soothing tones to his father, calming him.

A moment later a white-uniformed nurse appeared, took one look at her patient, and said, "He needs to get on his breathing machine. Bring him to his bedroom."

While Tony and the nurse were taking Mr. DeLeon to his room, Vince returned. He gave Ginny a sheepish grin. He was a younger version of Tony in looks, but without the interesting character lines that experience had etched into Tony's face, or the sinewy hardness of his body. "Tony will raise hell with me now," Vince confessed. "He didn't know I was supposed to find a replacement for Julius. I've been looking, but I haven't found anybody. I was just keeping him on until I did."

"What did Julius do to make your father so angry?" Ginny asked.

Vince glanced toward the door, as though assessing the possibility that Tony would return. "Julius has a bad habit of slipping mickeys to unsuspecting young ladies and . . . well, some of his sexual preferences are on the unusual side. He got a couple of under-age tourist gals up in his room one night. They wouldn't press charges; I guess he bought them off. Don't tell Tony, okay? He doesn't know—oh, he knows Julius has a bad reputation—Tony and my father had a falling out, and Tony swore he'd never set foot in the Castle. He didn't, either, not until the old man got sick."

"But your father obviously thought you'd fired Julius. What are you going to do about that?"

"I couldn't fire him until I found somebody else, could I?"

Tony came back into the solarium, and Ginny noted that Vince moved almost imperceptibly backward, away from his brother. "Now, Tony, don't start . . . okay? Hell, you've stayed away for years—it's a bit late to start trying to run things now."

"I don't want your job, Vince. I never did. What about Julius?"

"I'll get rid of him first thing tomorrow. The ice revue looks like it will be good for a long run, so maybe we can get by without an entertainment director for a while."

Tony regarded his brother with an exasperated expression. "You realize it's entirely possible that Julius is part of the skimming operation? That he may be responsible for the disappearance of Paula Phillips? Maybe even Al Vernon's murder. Yet you kept him on."

"Brad said that Paula Phillips probably took off to escape a jealous husband. It makes sense—somebody came and got her kid. And Al's killing could have been a random one. But listen, bro', I want you to start a complete investigation. I want to hire you to do it."

"Unfortunately you don't have the authority," Tony said. "And the old man is still adamant that he doesn't want me to investigate DeLeon employees."

"Oh, for Pete's sake! Still? Why?"

Tony shrugged, "I suppose he feels it would be encouraging me to continue with a profession he doesn't approve of. Besides, he thinks that getting rid of Julius will fix everything."

Ginny asked, "Is your father all right?"

"Yes. But I think we ought to go." Tony turned to Vince. "I'll call you tomorrow. I'll ask Brad to put one of his operatives into the Castle. And Vince, keep in mind that Al Vernon was probably killed to keep him from implicating anyone else. We're not dealing with petty pilfering. This is a well-organized ring. I believe they're operating in several casinos."

"You really think Julius is behind it?"

"I haven't been able to pin anything specific on him, but . . ." Tony glanced at Ginny. "Where did he get the money to open the boutique and go into the rag trade? With his life-style I can't believe there was much left over from his salary."

On the drive back to Las Vegas Ginny silently watched the mountains and tall trees give way to desert vistas. She was reliving that searing scene in her apartment after Tony found her sketch of the wedding dress.

Now that they were again alone, stripped of the insulation of other people, there were feelings to be faced and decisions to be made. Where exactly were they, she and Tony? She didn't know, and the uncertainty caused a numbing ache in her.

To break the silence, she said, "I liked your father. I hope we didn't upset him too much."

Tony glanced at her sideways. "Do you like me enough to forgive that incredible blunder I made this morning?"

Ginny felt her breath slowly leave her body and realized she'd probably been holding it, waiting for this discussion to begin. Tony's tone was light, as though he'd accidently stepped on her toe, rather than the newly woven fabric of her emotions. One part of her wanted to tell him her feelings and another, more stubborn side urged that a cool, unperturbed response was in order. She answered, "I overreacted, Tony. I suppose it's funny really, that you'd imagine I had marriage on my mind."

He was silent, staring at the highway unfolding in front of the car, but Ginny saw with some satisfaction that a slow flush was creeping up his face. He said, "All day I've been trying to think of a way to tell you how I feel about you, how special you are to me."

She reached across the space between them and squeezed his arm lightly. "You don't have to put anything into words. This morning you expressed your feelings very well. They also happen to be mine. We're having a wonderful time together. Let's not ask for anything more than that. If we start analyzing our actions and reactions, it'll just get too complicated. Neither of us wants that."

From the way his shoulders slumped slightly, she knew her words were having the desired effect on him. Funny how empty a victory that seemed. But it was too late to take back the establishment of boundaries she'd just imposed on their relationship.

He said, "I wanted you to have enough time to find yourself, to get over your sense of loss and betrayal, to make some headway with your career." He paused. "I suppose I'm trying to tell you that I just felt it was too early to talk about the future. And if I'm honest, I'll admit I need to learn how to trust a woman again."

"Tony, it's all right. You don't have to hold a postmortem on what you said this morning or try to make me feel better about it. Honestly, I was angry then, but now I think it's probably just as well we had that misunderstanding. It gave us an opportunity to define where we are with each other."

"What about where we're going, Ginny? Do you want to talk about that?"

She leaned her head back against the car seat and

closed her eyes, because she was afraid he'd turn and see a sudden unexplained tear glistening there. There was nothing on earth more important to her than where they were going, but he hadn't said he wanted to talk about it; merely asked if she did. She said, "No, I'm content just to be with you."

The following morning Ginny awoke to the muffled roar of traffic on the street below her window and realized that she was back in her hotel suite. Since she had finished the sketches Julius needed, she decided to use the day to find herself a studio apartment. Somewhere with good light and enough space to spread swatches of material around. So far she had left most of the actual fabric selection to Julius, giving him notes and suggestions as to textures and colors. But this arrangement left her unsatisfied, rather like an artist making a charcoal sketch and allowing someone else to fill in the oil paint. She had just finished breakfast and was ready to leave when Julius called to ask her to meet him in his office.

When she entered the black-and-red room she saw that Julius was emptying the contents of his red-enameled desk into cardboard cartons. His usually-cherubic countenance was livid. He flopped back into his outsize leather chair when he saw her. "I've resigned. I'm getting out of here—right now. Be a love and finish packing for me, will you, Ginny? I'm quite exhausted."

Picking up a stack of her own sketches, Ginny asked, "Where are you setting up shop, at the Julius Boutique?"

His small eyes narrowed. "You don't seem surprised that I'm leaving the Castle."

She'd known that Vince was going to fire him, so she said quickly, "No, of course I'm not surprised. You're going to put a Julius line of sportswear into a major department store chain; obviously you won't have time to handle the entertainment here."

He relaxed slightly, a pleased smirk on his face. "Yes, yes, the Julius line. We'll have our work cut out for us this summer, getting ready for a fall showing. I've got a lead on a building we can convert to a production center. I'm thinking of leasing another storefront too—the shop we have isn't really large enough. For the time being I will have my office there; however, when I get the building, I'd like you to have a studio on the premises. In the meantime, no more running off to hide. I want to know where to find you at all times."

"I'm looking for an apartment in town," Ginny answered, wondering where he was getting the money to finance not only another boutique but a factory.

What if he was behind the skimming operation? If she was to work closely with him, perhaps she could find out? She'd be out of a job, but if he was stealing from the casinos, there wasn't much of a future for her with the Julius line anyway, since she had no doubt that Tony would eventually break up the ring. She added, "And I think it would be a good idea for me to have a studio close to your office."

"Good, good. Now help me carry a couple of these boxes down to my car, will you, dear? I've hired an assistant, but he hasn't arrived yet. His name is Lou Mando, by the way, so you'll know who he is if he calls."

They had just left the elevator when Ginny caught sight of a familiar figure walking slowly along an aisle of slot machines, in the manner of a man running a gauntlet. She felt a sick sense of inevitability, but there was no way she could avoid being seen by Marc. Apart from the fact that she hadn't wanted him to know where she lived and worked, she also felt a keen sense of disappointment that despite all his lofty promises to stop gambling, he was back in his old haunts.

Brad poured drinks and handed one to Tony, then returned to his desk, sipping from his glass before speaking into the intercom. "No calls—okay?"

"So stop with the Cheshire cat grin, and tell me the good news," Tony said.

Brad picked up a lavender envelope and handed it to him. The letter was addressed to Brad at the office, marked PRIVATE AND CONFIDENTIAL, and bore a San Francisco postmark. Tony pulled out a single sheet of matching notepaper and read the feminine scrawl.

Dear Mr. Sutcliffe:

Sorry I left in such a hurry. I should have given you notice, but I was afraid my ex would find me again. Would you please pay my baby-sitter and my landlord the salary I have coming? I owe them. Thanks.

Paula Phillips

"See?" Brad said. "Didn't I tell you? Now will you please stop chasing the poor girl and concentrate on pretty Ginny?"

"Paula Phillips was only one aspect of the case," Tony answered, folding the note and slipping it back into the envelope. "I'd heard rumors of a skimming operation before she called me that night. And I caught Al Vernon red-handed. You know the police let the suspect in the Vernon killing go for lack of evidence?"

"Tony, old buddy, why do you want to get involved with a murder investigation, or, for that matter, anything to do with the casinos? I thought you swore you'd never set foot in another casino? That you'd concentrate on finding missing people."

"They're hitting my father's casinos, Brad. His philosophy and mine may not agree, but I'll be damned if I'll let anybody steal from him, especially now that he's sick and not able to take care of things himself."

"I don't like it, I'm worried about you. I don't want them to find your body in a shallow grave in the desert. You haven't done this kind of work for some time, and you're out of touch."

Tony grinned. "You telling me I'm getting too old for it?"

"Maybe. Look, there's no need for you to personally stick your neck out. I'll put several of my young hotshots on the case. I can send them in disguised as ordinary security people and gamblers."

"Good," Tony said. "I can use all the help I can get."

"You'll stay out of it personally—promise?"

"You're worse than my mother used to be. What is this? Marriage turning you into a parent or something?"

Brad smiled. "Marriage is the best thing that ever happened to me. You should try it yourself. How about pretty Ginny?"

"The world is full of matchmakers. Ginny and I need a little time to get to know one another."

"You're still afraid to take a chance. You never were much of a gambler, were you, old buddy?"

Tony stood up to leave. "Say hello to Hoshi for me."

"Wait a minute. I've been meaning to ask you, are you still in the market for a ranch in the Carson Valley?"

Tony was surprised. "I haven't talked about that for years. What made you think of it?"

"Oh, a conversation I had with Vince the other day when I was over at the Castle. Anyway, when I was in Reno, I heard about some property that might be available soon. You interested?"

Tony hesitated, unwilling to resurrect old dreams,

old longings. The pain of relinquishing them was always too great. "Not right now. Not until either my father's back on his feet, or Vince is minding the store properly. And certainly not while somebody is stealing from them."

"Yeah, well, you wait too long and Ginny Hooper is going to be so wrapped up in her career she won't want to move out to some ranch with you. Keep that in mind, old buddy."

Tony reached for the door, feeling an overwhelming need to see Ginny, talk to her. To make her understand how important she was to him. To explain that he'd been wounded but had survived and so would she . . . but he knew better than to rush the process.

But was he being really honest with himself? Was that truly the reason he'd shied like a startled pony when he thought Ginny had wedding bells on her mind? Perhaps his father and Brad were right: If he couldn't trust a woman like Ginny, then there was no hope for him.

Leaving Brad's office, he drove to the Castle. A tour bus was parked outside and a covey of senior citizens were alighting, their expressions livelier than their feet. Tony waited until they were all through the doors and lined up at the check-in counter before heading for the main staircase leading to Vince's second-floor office. Better find out if he'd fired Julius first, before calling to see if Ginny was in.

Halfway up the stairs he caught a glimpse of a familiar head of burnished auburn waves. Ginny was seated at a table in one of the cocktail lounges adjacent to the blackjack tables, talking to a dark-haired man whose face Tony could not see.

He stopped, looking over the ornate balustrade of the staircase, feeling the first deadly pangs of jealousy. Who was the man? More important, what was he to Ginny? She hadn't wasted any time: it was only yesterday that they'd somehow got off the track with each other. But maybe he was jumping to conclusions; perhaps the man had something to do with her business?

As Tony started to climb the stairs again the dark-haired man raised his head to motion for a waitress. Although he looked a lot thinner and somewhat older than in the photograph Tony had seen in Ginny's little cinder block house in the desert, there was no mistaking who he was. That handsome face had been indelibly etched into Tony's memory because of all the pain its owner had inflicted on Ginny. Marc Noland was back in town, and Ginny was back at his side. Tony resisted the urge to smash his fist into the teak banister, unsure if his rage was at himself for believing Ginny cared about him, or at her for being such a fool as to go back for a second helping of heartache.

Chapter 13

"I DON'T WANT A DRINK, MARC," GINNY SAID. "AND I'VE
got to go—"

His hand snaked across the table and caught her
wrist. "No, please, not yet. Look, I told you I came
looking for you. I didn't come to gamble, no matter
what you think."

She looked down at his hand imprisoning her wrist,
feeling a fury that surprised her. "Let go of me. Right
now."

His hand retreated immediately. "I'm sorry, but I
need your help. I wouldn't ask if there was anyone else
I could turn to. Ginny, please, just listen, that's all I
ask."

"The guys I told you about—they know I'm here. In

fact, they brought me into town. I've got an hour to raise some money to make a loan payment, or they get rough." He began to cough and reached into his pocket for a handkerchief. As he pulled out the handkerchief two poker chips clattered to the table.

Ginny looked at the two colored disks. "That's your problem, Marc. Not mine. I've bailed you out for the last time."

"I swear I wouldn't have gambled again, except they gave me a stake and told me to turn it into a substantial payment on my loan."

"And instead you lost it. Oh, God, Marc, won't you ever learn?"

"That's the way these guys operate. They suckered me into owing even more. I guess I'm still sick, or I'd have realized it."

"What about your promise to go to a Gamblers Anonymous meeting?"

He looked at her slyly. "If you'll just loan me enough to get these guys off my back, I'll go to a meeting. In fact, you can drive me to one and see for yourself."

She regarded him silently for a minute, fighting the old familiar battle in her mind. She no longer loved him, but he'd been a part of her life for so long that she knew only too well the guilt she'd feel if he really were beaten up by loan sharks. "How much do you need?"

"Five hundred," he said tentatively, then seeing her shocked expression quickly amended, "but I think they'd leave me alone for two-fifty."

"Do you know of a G.A. meeting being held somewhere this evening?"

"Why, sure. There's always a meeting someplace."

"You'll get the money at the end of the meeting. I'll drive you there. Then we say good-bye, Marc. Forever."

*   *   *

"Hi," the portly man with the pallid face and cunning eyes said. "My name's Harry, and I'm a compulsive gambler."

"Hi, Harry," chorused the men seated on folding chairs in the community room of the savings and loan branch office.

Ginny was the only woman present, and she sat in the back row. Marc was seated in front. The group had divided themselves into subgroups and sat with their own particular type of gambler. They also seemed to dress differently, according to their gambling preference. Marc had pointed out the horseplayers, the crapshooters, the Vegas gamblers, and poker players. Ginny had never seen so many white or two-tone shoes.

The twelve steps of the Gamblers Anonymous program—based on the same twelve steps of the Alcoholics Anonymous program, substituting "gambling" for "drinking"—had been recited, and the business part of the meeting concluded.

There had been several "pitches" by the men present. They spoke of their abstinence from gambling or their fall from grace. The others nodded and murmured agreement or encouragement. Now it was time for their main speaker.

Harry smiled ingratiatingly. "This is my three-hundred-and-sixtieth day of abstinence." There was a burst of applause, and he continued. "I always wanted to be a professional gambler, even when I was a kid. My old man left me money, and I went through my inheritance in eleven days . . . I always figured I could beat the system. I did for a while—I won on a baseball system I worked out. But then it went sour. I lost jobs; lost three wives; lived on the beach with a girlfriend for a while and spent every dime she had."

Ginny looked at the faces around her. They were

smiling broadly, nodding. She supposed they were
empathizing with Harry, but she felt revulsion. Marc
had warned her that she didn't belong at the meeting,
that she wouldn't understand their sickness. He'd also
told her he would not "pitch" in her presence. He'd
wanted her to wait across the street at a coffee shop,
but she wanted to see him in the group. It would have
been too easy for him to duck out and return for her
later.

Listening to Harry's chronicle of betrayal and exploi-
tation, she understood why Marc didn't want her there.
If it hadn't been for the fact that she had to drive him
home, she would have left. Harry's life story became
increasingly more lurid and degraded as he told how he
allowed his compulsion to destroy his life. She was
sickened by his methods of obtaining gambling stakes,
realizing that Marc's perfidies, bad as they'd been, were
not as vile as Harry's.

Ginny tried to feel pity for him, but it was difficult to
feel sympathy for someone who had used his family and
friends so callously. Harry even told of taking money
set aside for his youngest child's tonsillectomy, of
deserting his first wife when she was in the maternity
ward having their second child. He had tricked gullible
old people out of their savings, sold unnecessary health
insurance policies to retirees already covered. The list
went on and on.

She noticed that even now, when he spoke of gambling, Harry's tiny cunning eyes lit up with an inner fire.
But eventually he spoke of being dragged to a G.A.
meeting by a reformed gambler friend and finding
salvation there. He had turned his life over to a higher
power, he said, and was at last able to control his
obsessive urge to gamble.

The meeting ended with the group joining hands to
recite a prayer, then much backslapping and hug-

ging, and everyone urging everyone to "keep coming back."

Driving back down the highway, Ginny felt Marc's eyes on her, but she concentrated on the road. At length he said, "I told you you wouldn't be comfortable."

"It doesn't matter how I feel: the main thing is that you keep going back. That you use one of those telephone numbers that were passed out if you feel the urge to gamble—call one of those men and let him talk you out of it."

"I promised, didn't I? I'll do it. Did you . . . bring the money?"

"There's an envelope in my purse—" Marc had reached for it before she finished, "I don't want to see you or hear from you again after tonight."

But he was too busy stuffing the fifty-dollar bills into his inside pocket to reply.

Tony hadn't called. Two weeks had gone by without a word, but Ginny was both too proud and too busy to call him. She had found an apartment in a better neighborhood than her first one, and Julius had been given permission to move into the building he wanted to convert to a factory before the escrow closed.

The building had formerly been a large hardware store, and he lost no time in installing sewing machines, cutting tables, and all of the paraphernalia necessary to the trade. Seamstresses and cutters were hired.

Ginny watched the outlay of capital and wondered again where he was getting the money. Besides working on new designs, she supervised the work on the fall line in a partitioned area with good southern exposure via a window overlooking the rear parking lot. It was one of the vagaries of the business that with spring bursting at the seams she had to think in terms of winter clothes.

One late afternoon she sat staring at a blank page
and became aware that the hum of sewing machines in
the adjacent area had stopped. Glancing at her watch,
she realized that everyone must have gone home. She
stood up, lifting her hair from the back of her neck with
her hands and stretching cramped muscles. Julius, she
knew, was meeting with the department store head
buyer today. Tomorrow she would go on a buying trip
herself, to find the fabrics she needed.

She resolutely shoved thoughts of Tony out of her
mind as she contemplated how she would spend the
evening—the first she hadn't worked for two weeks.
She had rushed back to her apartment each evening to
work on the wedding dress she'd been commissioned to
design and make for the singing star of one of the
largest hotels.

As she walked through the cutting room she saw that
the door to Julius's office was ajar. She paused, looking
around the deserted building and listening, but there
was no sound other than the muffled traffic noises from
the street.

Julius usually kept his office locked when he wasn't in
it. He'd hired an assistant, a man named Lou Mando to
whom Ginny had spoken on the phone a few times but
never met, since he spent most of his time shopping for
equipment. It had become a standing joke between
Julius and her that Lou Mando didn't actually exist. He
was just a voice on a telephone wire. Now she wondered if he was in Julius's office.

She called "Lou? Is that you?" But there was no
response. She crossed the room slowly, all at once
noticing the long shadows cast by furniture and machines. There was no light on in the office. There was
no one there. Would there be something in his desk
that would indicate where he was getting his capital?
She might not get another opportunity to find out—

especially when Lou Mando finished acquiring equipment and moved in to the adjacent office to Julius's.

Pushing open the door, she looked inside. The familiar red-enameled desk had been delivered, along with his black leather chairs, but as yet the black carpeting he'd ordered had not been installed. Walls and ceiling had been painted black, however, and already Julius's imprint was all over the room.

She shivered, remembering the night he'd waited for her with champagne and strawberries, both spiked. But she was too valuable to him now for him to risk driving her off . . . or was she? There were plenty of hungry young designers whose talent was equal to hers—she'd just been lucky in getting the break. If he was to return and somehow get his heavy-footed bulk across the bare tile floor without her hearing him, couldn't she simply say she was looking for the last batch of sketches she'd given him? That she wanted to make some changes?

Crossing the room to the desk, she glanced quickly at the files and papers lying on the red surface. Mostly invoices and purchase orders, some correspondence. She opened the top drawer of his desk—nothing of importance in there either. The bottom drawer on the right contained a handgun. She stared down at its sinister shape for a moment, then quickly closed the drawer.

She couldn't find any information that indicated where his capital was coming from or whether he was involved with a ring of casino thieves. The worst evidence she could find against him was a copy of a memo he'd written, urging the Castle's manager to pay "tokes" to taxi drivers who delivered patrons to the shows there. But this had been a common practice in Vegas: Taxi drivers who steered their fares to certain restaurants or motels or hotels were given a couple of dollars for doing so. It was a practice many businesses had begun to fight, since the "tokes" were continually being raised. She looked at the desk, making sure it appeared undisturbed, and wondered about her motives in searching it.

Whatever else Julius was guilty of, the Julius line of sportswear was legitimate. Why was she trying to prove he was a crook—in effect, digging her own grave? Was it to impress Tony . . . to bring him back into her life? Did she really want to call him and say, "I've discovered evidence against Julius . . ." and thereby dash her hopes of continuing her career? Yes. That was exactly what she had in mind. A way to get in touch with Tony without coming right out and saying, "Please come back. I miss you—need you, love you, so much."

There was a filing cabinet on the wall behind the door. She went to it and slid open the top drawer. It contained half a dozen folders holding job applications and various other employee forms. She was about to go to the second drawer when an insistent, pungent scent assaulted her nostrils. She hadn't heard a sound, but she froze, her hands still on the drawer pull. *Someone was standing on the other side of the open door.* And that someone was wearing cologne that shrieked . . . the same cologne worn by the man who had broken into her apartment demanding information about Al Vernon's whereabouts just before he was found murdered.

Chapter 14

HOSHI CAME RUNNING FROM THE OTHER END OF THE penthouse suite as Brad's gargantuan housekeeper opened the door to admit Tony. He heard Hoshi's excited cry, "Brad? Honey, is that you?" When she skidded into the entry hall, Tony said, "Sorry, just me. I was hoping to catch him in. Is he still at the school?"

"I expect so." Hoshi's smile faded and was replaced by a worried frown. "Come on in, Tony. We might as well eat before dinner is completely ruined."

"Oh, listen, I didn't come for dinner."

She slipped her hand through his arm. "Please? I finally got you-know-who—" she glanced over her shoulder to be sure the housekeeper had disappeared back into her room "—to let me fix dinner, and wouldn't you know, Brad's working late."

145

He allowed her to lead him into the dining room, since he didn't have the heart to refuse, despite the fact that he'd already eaten. "What did you make?"

"*Chiles Rellenos*—and they won't keep another minute. The tortillas are shriveling into cardboard."

"Mexican? You're kidding! Don't you ever cook Japanese food?"

She shrugged, "Guess I never felt I could compete with my grandmother's cooking. Besides, I love Mexican food. Would you like a glass of wine?"

The *chiles rellenos* weren't the best Tony had eaten, but maybe the steak he'd had earlier had blunted his appetite. He watched Hoshi covertly, noting the lines of tension on her lovely face, the way her delicate fingers clenched her fork, her frequent glances toward the clock on the wall beside her.

Damn Brad for being so inconsiderate. Perhaps he'd been a bachelor too long; perhaps it was simply that Brad had always been one of those golden souls so favored by the gods that they never considered they might have to work for the approval of other mortals. Tony remembered something Lonnie had said about Brad, back in their Vietnam days. "When that ole boy fixes to have you do something for him, man, he gives that lazy smile of his and you're a goner."

Tony put his fork down and said, "Hoshi, I think it's about time both of us came clean. I didn't drop in to see Brad; I came to see you. I wanted to find out what you knew about Ginny and Marc Noland. And I think maybe you've got something on your mind too."

Her lips formed a silent *Oh, no*. She sighed. "I told her she ought to tell you about Marc. Tony, please don't ask me to betray her confidence. I can't tell you anything except that she isn't in love with him anymore. Please believe that."

"But she *is* seeing him. I saw them together."

"She couldn't help it. Honestly; he was sick and—" She broke off. "No, I'm not going to say another word. If you want to know, call Ginny and ask her. It isn't fair to poke around behind her back."

"You're right," Tony said, feeling more of a snoop than she could have imagined. "I've deliberately kept away from her; tried to get her off my mind. I suppose I thought that it was somehow less prying to ask you what she was doing. But it isn't, is it?"

"She's been busy, Tony," Hoshi said, apparently feeling sorry for him. "For the past couple of weeks she's either been working for Julius or working on a wedding dress at home for some big-name singer. She hasn't seen Marc, or anybody else. I'll tell you that much."

He glanced at the wall clock. "You think she's home now?"

"Either at home or at the office. I've got both numbers. Why don't you call her? Would you mind going down to a pay phone? I want to keep our line clear in case Brad calls."

"Why, sure. But Hoshi, I did suggest we *both* come clean. Why don't you tell me what's bothering you?"

She bit her lip, obviously fighting an inner battle with herself. Tony said softly, "It's Brad, isn't it? He forgets to let you know he won't be home on time . . . don't worry about it, it just takes some guys time to get used to having somebody worry about them. And he always was the kind of guy who needed time to himself. I think maybe it comes from being always "on" when other people are around. But you should get after him. Don't sit quietly back and keep it to yourself. He won't change if he doesn't know how he's worrying you."

Hoshi's face crumpled slowly. She clasped her napkin to her mouth and began to cry. Tony was on his feet and had circled the table before he realized he'd moved. He slipped his arm across her shoulders. "Hoshi, don't . . . what is it? What happened?"

"Brad . . . he's seeing another woman . . ."

Ginny drew a deep breath and said, "I know you're there. Behind the door. You might as well come in and show yourself."

The pungent cologne wafted ahead of the man who stepped into the room. Her heart thudded against her ribs as she looked up at a burly man dressed in a crumpled linen suit. Small unblinking eyes almost lost in their sockets, a hawk's nose descending to a mouth that even the kindest critic would have to describe as morose. In the instant's appraisal she gave him, the thought flashed through her mind that it was essential that he not realize she knew he was the intruder who had ransacked her apartment that night.

Trying to control the shaking of her voice, she said briskly, "If you're looking for Julius, he's out at present. May I help you? I'm Ginny Hooper."

It seemed to Ginny that the man stared at her for an eternally long moment. She maintained the blankest expression she could manage, the kind of look given to a total stranger. His eyes went from her to the filing cabinet, then back to her face. She thought of the handgun in Julius's desk drawer, but it was too far away. Whatever he had in mind, she would try to talk him out of it. She added, "I was just going home, soon as I find some sketches I want to work on. But if Julius is expecting you . . ."

Slowly an ingratiating smile spread across his face, without quite reaching his eyes. "We've talked on the phone, Ginny. I'm Lou Mando."

Julius's assistant. *Of course!* Momentary relief was replaced by even more dread. Lou Mando was the man who had broken into her apartment, roughed her up, demanded to know where Al Vernon was shortly before Al was found murdered. She was sure of it, not only from the cologne, but from his build, the way he moved, his voice, which sounded different in person than over the phone.

"You're working late. I didn't expect anyone to be here," he said. "I wanted to get my office ready. I'll be moving in tomorrow."

He kept looking at her in that peculiarly unnerving way and didn't move out of the doorway. Was he trying to decide whether she could possibly have seen his face in the darkness that night? Was that the reason he'd spoken to her on the phone several times before meeting her face-to-face—to see if she recognized his voice? She hadn't: it sounded much deeper over the phone. Was it just possible she was wrong? Maybe she was putting too much faith in her sense of smell; besides, other men no doubt used that awful cologne. She forced a smile to her lips and extended her hand, "Nice to meet you in person at last, Lou."

His hand was dry and cold and squeezed her fingers painfully. She kept her smile intact but was afraid the overpowering scent would make her sneeze. "Yeah, you too." His voice had risen another couple of octaves, and she realized he consciously attempted to pitch it lower. Somehow the falsetto tones were even more sinister in a man of his size and obvious strength. Those eyes had seen plenty of violence, she was sure of that.

She forced her hand to go limp in his as he continued to hold it. A numbing panic spread upward from his touch. Then the phone rang in the outer office, and he jumped, spinning around in the direction of the sound. Ginny said "I'll get it" and ducked around him to run for the phone.

A familiar voice said, "Ginny? Hope I'm not interrupting anything. Hoshi gave me this number."

Ginny could have wept with relief. She exclaimed,

"Tony! Darling! Where are you? I thought you were picking me up here? You do know how to get to the new building, don't you?" She gave him the address and careful directions, then said, "What? Oh, Tony, why didn't you say you were just around the corner? At the coffee shop? I'll be right over."

Ginny dropped the receiver and looked at Lou Mando, who had followed and was watching her. She said, "Well, got to run; a friend's waiting for me across the street. I'll see you tomorrow. Good night."

It seemed to her that those tiny pitiless eyes bored into her back as she ran for the door, grabbing her purse from her desk en route. She darted across the street, heedless of traffic, and earned a few blasts from the horns of irate motorists.

The coffee shop was packed, but she was too nervous to do anything but pace. She saw Tony's XK come flashing into the parking lot in what seemed like record time and flew outside to greet him.

Although it was completely dark now, the parking area was well lit. Heedless of passersby, she flung herself into his arms as he jumped from the driver's seat. He held her closely. "Ginny, it's okay, I'm here. What happened? You're shaking like a leaf."

"Could we go somewhere, away from here?"

"Sure. Come on, we'll get your car later."

He drove to the same old-fashioned restaurant where they'd talked for hours that memorable night. They sat at a corner table, and Tony ordered wine and appetizers. Ginny said, "Thank you for coming so fast."

He gave her a half-smile. "I was lucky I didn't get a ticket. You know, when you called me 'darling' on the phone . . . I probably could have flown over here. But I was scared as hell for you. I knew something was wrong, from your voice. What happened?"

She told him about Lou Mando, his cologne, and her

fears. When she had finished, Tony said, "That does it. You're not going back there."

"I have to. I can't give up everything now. Besides, during the day there are plenty of people around. I just won't ever work late alone again. I mean, I can't be absolutely sure Lou Mando is the same man just because he uses terrible cologne. And even if he is the same man, how do we know that Julius has any other connection with him besides the fact that he hired him to run the factory?"

Tony strummed the tabletop with his fingers. "I'll run a check on Mando, see what I can turn up. Meantime, you've got to be careful." He paused. "You said you were searching Julius's office when Mando walked in."

"Yes. A lot of good it did. I didn't find anything incriminating."

"But you searched . . . you were taking a chance, Ginny. Please don't do that again."

She felt a need to be completely honest with him. "I think I wanted an excuse to call you—to tell you that I'd got something on Julius. I missed you, Tony, the past couple of weeks."

His eyes found hers and held. She felt as if she could swim in the endless blue depths. He answered, "Not half as much as I missed you. I stayed away because I knew you were seeing Marc Noland again. Since you didn't call me, that seemed an indication it was all over between us."

Ginny felt the last vestiges of color drain from her face. So that was it! "But how—"

"I saw you with him."

It was such a relief to talk about it, to tell someone all her feelings, her frustrations, and fears about Marc. She concluded, "I don't know why I didn't tell you he was back. I suppose because I didn't want you to get the wrong idea. Just goes to show—you did anyway."

Tony listened quietly as she told him about the loan sharks and of driving Marc to the Gamblers Anonymous meeting.

When she had finished, Tony said, "Ginny, *he* has to do it. Not you."

Ginny looked into Tony's eyes, seeing clear through to his soul, it seemed. She said simply, "Take me home, Tony, please. I need to be in your arms."

He drove her to her apartment, and they went inside, his arm around her, fingers entwined. She switched on a light and said, "I haven't eaten; I could scramble some eggs—then broke off as Tony started to chuckle. "What's so funny?"

"Nothing. I was just wondering what steak and potatoes, followed by *chiles rellenos*, followed by scrambled eggs, would do to my waistline."

She put her arms around him and murmured, "Your waistline is just fine . . . and on second thought I'm not that hungry, after all." She raised her mouth to his, and they kissed with a passion that was partly the relief of being together again, but mostly the electric tension they generated when they were together.

Tony's arms went around her and he lifted her from her feet, murmuring against her mouth, "Where's the bedroom?"

"You don't want to go in there . . . it's a mess. I wasn't expecting company."

His tongue touched her lower lip and their breath mingled. She dropped her head to his shoulder, then nuzzled his neck. The scent of his skin reminded her of the wild chaparral in the hidden canyon, elusive, yet compelling. "Ginny, love, I do so want to go in there. . . . How much of a mess can one woman make?"

He picked her up and carried her to the nearest door, discovered it was the kitchen, and backed off, accompanied by Ginny's giggles. The second door he tried was the guest closet. "Dammit, woman, I may have to have my way with you standing up in here among the coats. I'm not sure I can wait much longer."

"The bedroom's over there . . ." Ginny said, still laughing, "But you really don't want—"

She had swatches of material all over the bed, all over the floor. The dresser was covered with different colored spools of thread. Her sewing machine stood in the center of the room, also draped with fabric. Tony ignored all the trappings of her trade as he flung off his own clothes and, despite the fact that she was still convulsed with giggles, removed hers.

Ginny found herself lying atop several different textures of cloth. Cool cotton under her feet; a rough bouclé tickled the backs of her knees. There was a lovely, sensuously soft piece of velvet beneath her hips that, combined with the hard pressure of Tony's manhood insinuating between her thighs, drove her wild. She gasped her pleasure and arched her back to invite his entry.

He bent to kiss her breasts and touch her erect nipples with his tongue, and the swatch of satin under her upper back gently massaged her skin so that she felt surrounded and engulfed by so many wonderful sensations it was like floating in a sea of sensuality.

Twisting her head, a drift of dark blue chiffon slid from her hair to lie softly across her throat. Tony's lips touched her flesh through the delicate material, warm and pulsing with a vitality that was strangely enhanced by the veiling.

He moved within her now, strong and sure and filling every need she had ever known. She heard her breathing quicken, felt the scalding rush of desire take them both climbing up to that plateau they had made uniquely their own. There was no longer any fear or doubt. There was only the two of them in perfect unison. Two halves making one wonderful whole.

Chapter 15

JULIUS PACED AROUND GINNY'S DESK, HIS VOLUMINOUS caftan rustling as he angrily waved a newspaper. He looked, Ginny decided, like a dusty black hippo on the rampage. Lou Mando stood watching from the doorway. Mando always seemed to stand in doorways, blocking entry, or perhaps exit. Julius said, "Those designs belong to *me*—you work for *me*. I own you, Ginny Hooper, and everything you do. You had no right to moonlight on your own—peddling your best work under your own name."

Ignoring the file folder that got in the way of the swinging caftan and went sliding to the floor, Ginny returned Julius's stare without blinking. "That wedding gown wasn't designed on your time. I did it at home, and I sewed it on my own machine."

She wondered how much angrier he'd get if he knew her phone had rung off the hook since the wire services picked up the newspaper article about the singing star's wedding dress. Ginny had calls from as far away as Florida and Texas, asking about her "line" of bridal gowns.

"Look at the agreement I signed again, Julius. I'm your employee; I agreed to run the boutique and design sportswear for the Julius label without taking credit for my work. There's nothing that says I can't free-lance, so long as it's not in competition, and bridal gowns hardly compete with sportswear."

Julius stopped pacing and glared at her, then glanced in Mando's direction. For a split second Ginny thought he was going to order the man to punish her in some way. She stifled a grin, thinking how much easier it was to be brave in the bright light of morning with the hum of machines and conversation in the background.

Still, Ginny was more than a little nervous when Lou Mando was around. Mando was some sort of body-guard and general flunky, rather than the manager he pretended to be, although Tony's check on him hadn't turned up any criminal record. All Mando seemed to do was hang around his office and look menacing.

Ginny said softly, "Of course, you can always fire me."

Julius flung the newspaper on her desk, turned and marched past Mando, shoving him aside. Mando gave Ginny one of his fish-eyed stares and followed his boss.

Still smiling, Ginny looked down at the article. AT LAST, the heading read, A FRESH APPROACH TO TIME-HONORED TRADITION. The article described the wedding of a "well-known Las Vegas singer" and the sheer romantic beauty of her gown, "designed by that exciting young designer, Ginny Hooper, whose dramatic flair and innovative use of fabric has rocked the fashion world and finally brought bridal gowns out of the doldrums and into the spotlight, where they belong."

If she had written it herself, she couldn't have hoped for better exposure. One call last evening had been an offer of financial backing and Ginny might have been more receptive if it hadn't been for the fact that she and Tony were making love at the time the call came in.

For the past few days they had been content to simply be together, to laugh and play and talk and make love, without questions or analysis or discussion about anything more serious than which restaurant to go to, which show might be fun, whether they could get a Bogart movie on the late show, or if what they really wanted was to spend the evening making love. They swam in Tony's pool, had midnight snacks under the moon, and Ginny sometimes drifted off to sleep to the sweet sad strains of his clarinet.

It was a breathing space, allowing them to become close again, after their brief but devastating estrangement. There would be time enough to confront the deeper problems of their relationship when they'd bridged the chasm that Marc's return had opened between them.

When she wasn't working, Ginny wanted no more from life than to be with Tony. Yet they were both wary, treading carefully around each other, she knew. There had been angry words tossed between them, not easily forgotten. It was almost as if they had an unspoken agreement that for now they'd take time out just to be, to feel—not to think, or reason, or question motives.

They were so wrapped up with each other that one evening as they swam lazily in Tony's pool under a midnight sky sprinkled with a million stars, she was somewhat dismayed when he said, "Ginny, much as I want to keep you all to myself, I wish you'd have lunch with Hoshi and try to talk some sense into her. She's driving me crazy, wanting me to check up on Brad."

He told her of Hoshi's suspicions about Brad seeing another woman. There had been phone calls, Hoshi told him, a woman's voice who refused to identify herself, and Brad often stayed out all night or went on business trips without his wife.

They swam to the side of the pool and Tony hauled himself up onto the deck, then pulled Ginny up beside him. "Brad's been used to just picking up and going whenever he pleases. He supplies various agencies in Southern California with operatives, and often goes there, and now he's opening a new security personnel agency in Reno too. He sold his Cessna recently, I suppose he needed capital for the new school. Anyway, that means he has to fly on commercial airlines. He's a busy guy, and his school and business both bring him into contact with a lot of women . . . but I'm sure he isn't cheating on Hoshi."

"Have you told Hoshi this?" Ginny asked, squeezing the water from her hair.

"Her only comment was that the caged bird always wants to fly away . . . old Japanese proverb. Then she said a wife always knows when her husband is seeing another woman. I couldn't fight female intuition. Maybe you can."

"I'll give her a call," Ginny said. "I just hope you're right about it, and she's wrong."

She was silent, thinking about Hoshi and Brad, about her own parents, other married couples she'd known. Was the exclusivity of marriage the reason it wasn't working too well for so many people? Could one person possibly fulfill all the needs of another? Strangely, the more she thought about it, the clearer it became that Tony certainly seemed able to fulfill all her own needs. But what of his? That was the unknown quantity in their relationship.

At her side Tony said softly, "I didn't mean to cast a pall over a very pleasant evening. Come on, let's swim another couple of lengths, then I'm going to dry you off, inch by inch, using only my hands and lips, and then . . ."

Ginny slid into the warm water and splashed him, then set off for the other end of the pool with a graceful sidestroke that wasn't fast enough to evade Tony's powerful crawl. He caught up with her a third of the way across and his arms went around her as his mouth found hers.

Treading water, Ginny felt their bodies slide together, fitting into each other so perfectly as they hung suspended in the sensually warm water. She relaxed against Tony, allowing his body to support her.

They hadn't bothered with swimsuits, and her breasts settled against his chest, her thighs aligned with his as he rolled over onto his back, taking her with him. The movement of his feet, kicking slowly to keep them afloat, teased her to a state of almost unbearable erotic longing.

He submerged the lower part of his face and blew bubbles at her. Laughing, she said, "We're in deep water, Tony."

"You bet we are. We've been in it since the minute we met."

"So what are we going to do about it?"

For answer, he kept his arms around her and began to kick more strongly, propelling them to the shallows. When she felt the bottom of the pool under her feet, Ginny wrapped her arms around his neck and kissed him with an urgency that his mouth communicated equally to her.

Moments later they lay entwined in each other's arms on the soft bank of grass that swept down to the edge of the pool. A warm breeze whispered over them, drying her, even as Tony fulfilled his promise to dry her skin with kisses and caresses.

She felt the grass under her, saw the stars overhead, but distantly, because her whole being was totally involved with this man and her need for him. His touch was featherlight, drifting down over the swelling of her breasts, finding the silken skin of her inner thighs.

"Tony . . ." she whispered weakly, "Tony, don't hold back."

He raised his head and looked down at her, his breath still ragged, and it was obviously an effort for him to speak. "I never want either of us to hold back, Ginny. I want all of you."

His mouth claimed hers again with a hungry ardor that was both commanding and tender. She lost herself in the fever heat of passion, straining toward him until he plunged into her, and together they fell into the inferno.

Much later, she remembered what he'd said about wanting all of her and allowed herself to wonder what he had meant. Surely she had given him all of her, mind, body, and soul. Then she realized that Tony had recognized something that she had blocked from her consciousness. That her giving of herself was with reservations, not with the abandon that had once come so easily. Perhaps it never would again, and would Tony ever accept that?

Tony felt his hackles rise as Marc Noland strolled into his office, hands shoved in the pockets of his cream linen pants, a dark silk shirt open at the neck revealing the inevitable gold chain. Tony rested his hands on the surface of his desk and tried not to clench his fists. He said, "Have a seat. What can I do for you?"

Noland's dark eyes flickered over his face, took in the faded Western shirt Tony wore, noted the office furni-

ture and the computer whirring softly in its corner of
the room, the screen displaying the main menu. Tony
felt as though he and every item in the room had been
appraised, catalogued, and filed neatly away. The hard
crafty stare of the compulsive gambler, always disguised by the affable smile, was very much in evidence
on Marc Noland's handsome features.

Noland said, "Glad to meet you at last, Tony.
Ginny's told me a lot about you—hey, listen, I'm not
dragging you away from a stakeout or a . . . roundup
or anything, am I?" He chuckled at his own wit.

Tony had never considered it necessary to wear
business suits and was more comfortable in well-worn
cotton shirts and jeans. His choice of clothes, he felt,
was one of the privileges of rank. He was the boss here
and could wear what he pleased. Besides, he spent
more time out of the office than in it. Brad used to call
him "cowboy" occasionally in an effort to get him to
dress differently but had given up years ago. Funny how
Noland's crack about dragging him away from a roundup could make Tony all at once aware of the expression
"Clothes make the man." Was it, he wondered, that
the man across the desk in the immaculate slacks and
shirt, nails manicured within an inch of their lives, was,
after all, a rival for Ginny's affections?

"What can I do for you?" he asked shortly.

Noland's restless gaze had found the clarinet case,
lying on top of a file cabinet. "You play the clarinet?"

"Yes. I also run a business. What is it you want?"

"Ginny and I had a little spat, but we were together
for two years. You don't wipe out that kind of relationship overnight. She must have told you about me?"

Tony glanced at his watch. "You've got exactly two
minutes to tell me why you're here."

"Okay, okay. I know you've got the hots for my girl,
and she's using you to make me jealous. Well, maybe I
could be persuaded to get out of town, leave you a clear

field with her. For a slight financial remuneration . . . a loan, of course."

Tony was on his feet, advancing around the desk. Brad had once told him that when he was angry sparks flew out of his eyes and scared the hell out of the object of his anger. Noland was no exception: he ran for the door, but Tony beat him to it. He grabbed a handful of silk shirt and slammed him up against the wall.

"You stay away from Ginny, understand? She wants you out of her life, and I'm here to see you keep out of it. Now it would give me great pleasure to pound you to a pulp, but I'm going to let you go with just a warning, this time."

He yanked open the door and sent Noland sprawling out into the reception area. Frances glanced up from her computer keyboard and inquired, "Is Mr. Noland leaving?"

Noland scrambled to his feet and strode toward the outer office door. Over his shoulder he gave Tony a venomous glance. "I promise you, you're going to be sorry for this."

Tony turned to Frances. "Get Brad on the line for me, will you?"

"Get him yourself; I'm busy," Frances growled. Tony sighed and went back into his own office to make the call.

For a change Brad was in. "Hi, Tony, what's up?"

"Anything from the people you put into the Castle yet?"

"Nope. If there's anything going on, they haven't found any evidence. Maybe now Julius is out of the picture . . . ?"

"Why kill Al Vernon to keep him quiet and then stop skimming?"

"Maybe Julius is laying low until the heat's off?"

"I'm not a hundred percent sure Julius is the top man."

"Wait a minute . . . you don't suspect your own brother, do you? Vince is kind of weak, and he's a big spender, but I don't think he'd steal from his own father."

"I hope not . . . but the old man is inclined to be a tightwad—he still lives in the days when steak was fifty cents a pound. He pays Vince a salary he thinks is generous, but you know what this town is like."

"I'll tell my people to watch *everybody* at the Castle. Tony, while I've got you on the line . . . do you think you could loan me about five K—just for a couple of weeks. I've a cash flow problem at present, what with the new business and Hoshi redoing the apartment and all."

Tony chuckled. Brad asked, "What's so funny?"

"I'll be glad to loan you the cash, Brad. I was just thinking, today's my day to be hit up for loans." He told him about Marc Noland.

There was a moment's silence. "You want me to get one of my hotshots to escort the piece of slime out of town?"

"No, thanks. I've already taken care of him."

Ginny tightened the knot in the dark-green sash that cinched the waist of her ecru dress, a free-flowing float of natural gauze, decorated by green and turquoise beads around a drawstring neckline. She put on a dark-green straw hat with a wide brim that brought out the emerald flecks in her hazel eyes, then slipped her feet into high-heeled tan leather sandals. She picked up her overnight bag and went outside into the fierce heat of the late afternoon.

It was Friday, and in an hour she would be taking off in Tony's private plane with him. He'd been mysterious about their destination when he suggested they go away for the weekend, and Ginny hadn't been sure how to dress.

She decided they were probably headed for Tahoe to visit his father again. Last time they had driven, partly because Tony wanted her to enjoy the scenery from the ground, and partly because the plane was being serviced. The dress and high heels, she felt, would be appropriate for a visit to Tony's father. Older men always preferred dresses and, come to think of it, younger men were beginning to grow weary of unisex clothes.

Although Tony worried constantly about the reliability of Ginny's old VW, she had insisted on driving to his house rather than having him come into town to pick her up. She wanted to retain a certain measure of autonomy. It was all too easy, she knew from past experience, to allow a man to take over completely, dictating that she not do this or that because he was "worried about her." She supposed that the intensity of her feelings for Tony was partly responsible for this clinging to independence. She was falling more deeply in love with him with every passing hour, and she was more than a little apprehensive about how vulnerable that made her.

A barge of a car, ridiculously elongated and blinding with chrome, was parked next to her VW, obscuring it from view. She went around the front of the other car and stopped abruptly as the Volkswagen came into sight. Marc was behind the wheel.

"Hi, kid. You look great. How've you been?"

"What are you doing here?"

"Now, is that any way to greet an old friend? I'm waiting for you—what else? I didn't think you got off work this early . . . see how long I intended to wait out here for you? Man, it must be a hundred and twenty degrees today."

He wore new clothes, she noted, and he'd had a haircut. The old familiar gloss was back. The savoire faire, the easy charm, the devastating good looks. His black hair gleamed in the sunlight and his skin, although still pale, was smooth and taut over classic cheekbones.

"Get out of my car, Marc; I'm in a hurry. If you'll recall, I told you I was through—finished—I don't want to see you again."

"I thought we could celebrate," he went on as though she hadn't spoken. "I've got a job."

"I'm glad to hear it. Are you still going to G.A. meetings too?" Damn, she hadn't meant to pry. She knew she shouldn't push Marc that way; it merely let him know there was a way he could manipulate her.

A slow smile curved Marc's sensuously full lips. "Why, sure, I go two, maybe three times a week. How about it, Ginny, will you have dinner with me?"

"No. Please get out of my car." She really had to start locking her car when she parked it.

"You're asking for trouble with Tony DeLeon."

She blew out her breath slowly, counting silently to ten. "I'm not going to ask how you found out I was seeing Tony; I'm not going to discuss him with you. Either you get out of my car right now, or I go back inside and call the police."

"A lot of people in this town don't like DeLeon. He thinks he's some kind of policeman, got to keep everybody in line. But his old man made his money the same way everybody else did. You know, I'm surprised you'd hook up with another gambler."

"I'm not, as you put it, hooked up with anybody. But for your information, he isn't a gambler." She was letting him draw her into an argument, she knew, but she was too angry to walk away.

"Hell, Ginny, everybody here is a gambler. Some of 'em just do it in secret, that's all. I could take you to dozens of all-night poker games behind closed doors where the town's leading citizens—"

Ginny turned to walk away. She heard the car door

open behind her and Marc's voice conceding, "Okay, okay, I'm leaving."

He held the door as she got into the driver's seat. "I even kept the seat cool for you." He leaned closer, trying to peck her cheek, but she pulled away. He kept his hand on the door. "You'd do better to stay with a reformed gambler, you know. Sooner or later, the active ones are going to get into trouble." He closed the door, grinned, and turned to the oversize car parked beside hers.

She watched, her own car key still poised in front of the ignition, as Marc climbed into that very expensive barge. He rolled down the window and leaned out. "I got a *very* good job, Ginny—paid off my debts—I'm in the clear. You sure you don't want to have dinner with me?"

The engine of the VW roared to life, and she backed out of the parking space. All the way out to Tony's house she wondered how Marc's fortunes could have improved so radically in such a short time. It wasn't likely that he could have won enough at the gaming tables or slots to finance that car and those clothes, not without a considerable stake to begin with, which she knew he didn't have.

As much as she told herself Marc was no longer her concern, the nagging worry persisted that he was a threat to her happiness with Tony. She wasn't sure in what way, but he was up to something. She recognized that smug, barely concealed excitement he always displayed when he thought he'd come up with a fool-proof system for beating the odds.

Chapter 16

TONY SEEMED TO EXHIBIT BOTH ANTICIPATORY EXCITEMENT and slight apprehension when Ginny arrived. Glancing at her overnight bag, he asked, "You look great, Ginny, but I hope you have some comfortable clothes and shoes in there."

"Oh, yes. I came prepared for almost anything. But I thought we were going to Tahoe again?"

"Not this time."

"You going to tell me where?"

"Nope. I want your mind a complete blank on the subject, so I can watch your reaction."

He piloted the Cessna himself, and sitting next to him in the cockpit, Ginny felt a small thrill of pride in the understated efficiency of everything he did.

She put his silence down to the fact that he was concentrating on the controls, and beyond asking where and when he learned to fly, and being told he had started off as a chopper pilot in Vietnam then moved on to fixed-wing aircraft when he came home, there was little conversation.

She hadn't told him about her encounter with Marc, afraid of what his reaction might be. Perhaps when the weekend was over she'd bring it up, but she didn't want to spoil their time together.

They landed at an isolated airfield in a wide valley of open range land. From the air Ginny could see several herds of cattle and clusters of trees around ranch houses. Small private planes were parked around the airstrip.

As the wheels of the Cessna bumped gently on the runway, she gave Tony a short round of applause and said, "What a beautiful valley."

From the way Tony's face lit up she knew that she'd said the right thing and that wherever they were going, it was important to him that she like the place. He said, "I used to come here with my father when I was a kid."

Ginny unbuckled her seat belt as the plane taxied to a halt. "I bet he was really the dashing romantic when he was young. You know, the riverboat sort of gambler —always rescuing a damsel in distress or donating his winnings to the poor widow about to be evicted."

Tony shook his head in disbelief. "Incredible. A couple of hours with my father and you weave a romantic background for him that you know is far from the truth. Yet when you met me you were ready to hate me on sight simply because my name was DeLeon. What is it about gambling men that makes even sensible women turn into such complete fools around them?"

"I don't know," Ginny said, thinking of Marc. "A

certain recklessness, disguised as zest for living, perhaps. I've never met a gambler who wasn't an utter charmer when he wanted to be. Have you?"

He didn't reply, but Ginny saw the line of his jaw tighten slightly. She reached behind her seat to retrieve her overnight bag and hat.

Walking across the tarmac, which still radiated heat from the sun now blazing its final glory across the western sky, she asked, "Where do we go from here?"

As if in answer, a lanky man wearing muddied boots and a trail-dusted Stetson, lounging against the side of a dusty pickup truck, hailed them. "Over here, Tony."

Tony said, "This is Josh Englefield. Josh, say hello to Ginny Hooper." The Stetson was swept from a head of grizzled curls above a face as tan and lined as old leather. Ginny smiled and said, "Hello, Mr. Englefield."

"Call me Josh, please, ma'am. My father's name was Mr. Englefield." Grinning, he took their bags.

"Gladly, Josh, if you'll call me Ginny instead of ma'am."

Tony helped Ginny up into the cab of the pickup and climbed in beside her. As Josh went to put the bags into the back, Tony said, "First time I saw Josh, he was busting broncos, and I thought he was the toughest hombre I'd ever seen." He broke off as Josh returned and swung his sinewy frame up into the driver's seat.

They drove into the setting sun, soon leaving the paved road behind for a narrow dirt track that wound upward into the lower slopes of the foothills, the only sign they passed a CATTLE CROSSING warning.

Wedged between Josh and Tony, Ginny watched the shadowed countryside fly past the windows. She was conscious of Tony's lean frame settling back, relaxing, as if all the cares and tension were leaving body and mind. There had been a similar change in him the day they had hiked into Lost Canyon. When he was ready, he'd tell her the purpose of this trip, but for now it was enough to know that they were going to spend the weekend at a remote ranch house.

During the entire half-hour drive Josh regaled them with the glories of the ranch house. Spring roundup, it appeared, had been a colossal success, and the beef market was booming.

"What's the name of your ranch, Josh?" Ginny asked.

He chortled. "My ranch! Don't I wish! I'm the foreman, ma'am. Run the place for an old dude who wants to retire—sell up and move to the city someplace."

Ginny glanced at Tony, but he didn't comment. She had been wondering if this trip had anything to do with his one-time goal of owning a ranch, mentioned to her by his father.

It was almost completely dark when they reached a wrought-iron archway that informed visitors they had arrived at the Lazy Q Ranch. Josh drove past a bunkhouse, and Ginny caught a quick glimpse of a lit television screen inside. She said, "I thought cowboys strummed guitars for entertainment—when they weren't talking to their horses."

Josh laughed and said, "Main house up ahead. Mr. Quinlan—the old dude who owns the place—is in Carson City this weekend. He took the missus along, so you'll have to put up with my cooking."

"And if you'll settle for a clarinet instead of a guitar . . ." Tony said, slipping his arm across her shoulders.

The ranch house was a rambling redwood structure nestled against the side of a rocky butte, and although everything about it was on a massive scale, it reminded Ginny a little of Tony's house on the outskirts of Las

Vegas. Watching him as he stood on the old adobe-tiled floor and looked lovingly around the man-size living room, she felt he had the air of a man who has come home, that his own house on the edge of town was just a temporary replica of what he really wanted.

Two hound dogs with impossibly soulful faces who had been sleeping beside the fireplace stirred, recognized the visitor and hurled themselves at Tony, licking his hands and nuzzling his face ecstatically as he bent to greet them. A sleek marmalade cat purred loudly and rubbed against Ginny's legs.

"You two relax while I throw on the steaks," Josh said, and went through a wide archway into a kitchen as big as Ginny's apartment. Tony said, "I'll put the bags in the bedroom. The bathroom is down the hall to the left."

Ginny followed Josh into the kitchen, where the light played on a collection of copper pots hanging from the ceiling. An indoor barbecue flamed to life as Josh turned on the gas. The heavenly smell of baking beans came from a large crock on the stove. A moment later two fat steaks were sizzling over the fire.

"So how do you like the Lazy Q?" Josh asked, prodding the steaks with a long-handled fork.

"It's magnificent. I can't wait to see it in the daylight. What can I do to help?"

"How about sticking those biscuits back in the oven to warm? Tony's been coming here since he was a boy—anytime the town started closing in on him. His father and Mr. Quinlan were friends from way back when. Both started out in Nevada about the same time but took real different directions, I reckon. Sometimes I think young Tony wished the Gypsies would've stole him and left him on Mr. Quinlan's doorstep. The Quinlans never did have any children."

"Now, Josh," Tony said coming into the kitchen,

"don't be giving Ginny the wrong idea. I was always proud of my old man."

Tony slipped his arm around Ginny's shoulder in a casual gesture of affection that, unaccountably, made her want to cry. Somehow the moment, the man, and the place were just too perfect. She wondered why human beings always became so apprehensive when they felt happy, why they never expected it to last.

As soon as they were seated at a dining table of heroic proportions and the food was steaming on their plates, Josh bade them good night.

"Aren't you going to eat with us?" Ginny asked.

"Why, thank you, ma'am, but I ate hours ago."

Tony told her about the beef cattle and buffalo the Quinlans raised, about the sheer size of the ranch and how, like his father, Mr. Quinlan was simply getting too old for the demanding task of supervising such a spread.

"You really love it here, don't you?" Ginny asked when she again saw his eyes taking in every detail of the room then finally returning to her as though seeking her confirmation that it was as beautiful as he felt it was.

"I suppose I come here to renew myself. I feel like I turn into a human being again when I'm here. Maybe it's the nature of my work, I don't know . . . but there are times when my own thoughts are my worst enemies. You know, I actually found myself getting suspicious of my own brother the other day . . . that was when I knew I had to come back here."

"I'm glad you brought me. Come on, let's clear the table and go sit by the fire, and you can play for me. I want to hear 'Ginny's Song' again, in this setting."

Tony played the clarinet, and Ginny curled up in front of the fire with the dogs and cat and listened, feeling relaxed, content, and at peace. When he put down the clarinet and came to lie beside her amid the warm bodies of the dogs, she nestled closer to him and put her head on his chest, suddenly feeling very sleepy. He asked, "Have you ever ridden a horse?"

"No," she murmured against the comforting roughness of his shirt. "I think I'm afraid of them."

"You're not afraid of anything." He stroked her hair, and she fought to stay awake but was too relaxed. She fell asleep in his arms, lulled by the sound of his voice as he told her the story of how the Quinlans had started out raising beef to sell to his father's restaurants.

She awoke in the center of the biggest bed she'd ever seen, with no memory of being taken there or of having her clothes removed. Sunlight crept in through the slats of the blinds, and she turned over, stretching and feeling almost sinfully rested. She didn't remember the last time she had slept so soundly.

The impression of Tony's head was on the pillow next to her, but he was gone. She rolled over and pressed her face to the pillow, inhaling the faint scent of wild chaparral left behind by his hair.

A glass of orange juice stood on a tray on the bedside table, along with a small bunch of wild lupines in a little vase. Smiling, she drank the juice and jumped out of bed. She found her overnight bag, pulled out her jeans and a cotton shirt, and went into the bathroom.

Fifteen minutes later she went into the kitchen and found Josh waiting with a pot of coffee and bacon and eggs at the ready. "Tony went for a ride; he said to feed you good and he'd be back . . . reckon any time now, he's been gone an hour."

A veranda ran all around the main wing of the ranch house, and after she'd eaten Ginny went outside to await Tony's return. She saw him come over a rise about half a mile from the house. He was astride a beautiful mare. Josh, coming out to join her, said,

"Ain't she something? She's an Arabian. She belongs to Tony. The Quinlans let him stable her here."

Ginny caught her breath at the sheer beauty of the animal. Muscles rippled in the sunlight, and a silken mane flew in the breeze as she came galloping toward them. Knowing nothing about horses, Ginny could only think that the Arabian looked like some splendid mythical beast come to life, and Tony, her rider, was more a part of her than any other rider could have been.

As she watched him dismount and tenderly stroke the mare, Ginny felt another pang of regret without name. She wasn't sure what it was she feared, but the feeling persisted. A nagging sense of things coming to an end. She recalled the last few days before Marc had walked out on her when the same premonition had tried to warn her.

Tony came bounding up the veranda steps, swung her into his arms, and kissed her. "Good morning, love. No need to ask how you slept! Come on, I'm going to give you the grand tour."

"Not aboard a horse, you're not," Ginny said, still trying to shake her premonition.

Josh grinned and swung himself over the veranda rail. He loped off toward the cluster of outbuildings next to the house. Tony laughed and hugged her. "Look at that view—no neon signs, no traffic . . . is this God's country, or what?"

A few minutes later Josh came back sitting atop what had to be an antique buggy, pulled by a pair of docile horses. "Come on," Tony said, "You'll need a hat."

She saw only a small portion of the ranch, met a few of the ranch hands, and when Tony reined the horses near a copse of cottonwoods and lifted her down to the ground, she saw that his rather watchful expression had returned.

They sat on a grassy slope in the shade of a cotton-wood that whispered overhead. Tony said, "You're very quiet this morning."

"I—think I'm waiting for the ax to fall. I'm not sure why."

He picked up her hand, squeezed her fingers slightly. "The last week or so it's been great, Ginny. A carefree time for us both. But nothing is ever static—life keeps moving forward. I'm thinking of buying this ranch."

"Yes. I had a hunch you were."

"I'd be giving up my house and my business. Working here full-time. It's isolated, and I suppose some people would think it lonely."

"You belong here, Tony. I'm happy for you." A leaden lump had formed somewhere in the region where her heart used to be.

"Ginny . . . I know you were angry with me when you said it . . . but I have to ask you: When you said that your career came first and you'd take off for New York or Paris with never a backward glance if the opportunity arose . . ."

Her breath had stopped somewhere in her throat. She thought in sudden panic, He's going to ask me to live out here in the wilds with him. I'd be doing what I did with Marc—giving up all my own dreams to simply be a part of a man's dream . . . and how can any modern man respect a woman who does that? Oh, God, he's going to ask me to choose between him and a career. There's no way I can run a business way out here. Yet she didn't want to lose Tony; she loved him. Frantically her thoughts tossed her this way and that, and the only immediate solution seemed to be to play for time, to forestall the question.

"You're right, I was angry at the time," she said quickly. "My career certainly isn't all I want out of life. But right now I don't really have a career, and I do need to concentrate on giving it my best shot. I was going to tell you this weekend that I've asked Julius to replace me. I'm going to design and make wedding dresses. I probably won't be able to see you as often, which makes me sad. But you know what the early days of a new business are like."

He still held her hand, and over their heads the leaves of the cottonwood still rustled bewitchingly. Against the endless blue of the sky a pair of golden hawks circled slowly, then swooped in a majestic but deadly dive earthward. Ginny watched with glazed eyes, seeing but not comprehending.

The unspoken words lay between them. Had she made sure, with that little speech, that he would never say them? She fervently hoped not. But with a man like Tony, strong-willed enough to give up breathing if he so decided, she was sure that had she let him make a declaration and then turned him down, she would never have seen him again.

She could hardly say, "I want it all, Tony. I want you and a home and children and everything there is, including expressing myself through my work. Your Shangri-la is lovely, but it's just too remote. Please ask me what you were going to ask me after I'm established as a designer. Not now."

Even to her most uncritical self, that seemed too coldly practical for words. Yet the memory of her struggle to support herself after Marc Noland walked out on her was a specter that not even Tony's warm caring could obliterate from her nightmares.

Tony stared across the rolling valley, his eyes fixed on the soaring hawks. At length he said, "Where do we go from here, Ginny? Along separate paths?"

"Oh, God, Tony, I hope not."

She wasn't sure who moved, but they were in each other's arms, holding each other in a fierce embrace that conveyed without words that the pain of parting would be unbearable.

Ginny sank back into the soft grass as his body closed over hers, and if wishing could have made it happen, at that moment the earth would have stopped spinning on its axis and they would have spent eternity locked in each other's arms.

Chapter 17

SUNDAY MORNING AND THE SUN WAS A SCIMITAR RISING into a sky of dazzling blue. Ginny donned a pair of shorts and a halter, turned up the air-conditioning in her apartment, and regretfully decided not to serve Tony lunch on the balcony. They'd fry to a crisp out there.

She gathered up the swatches of cloth that littered her small living room, thinking of the time Tony had joyously made love to her amid a riot of velvet and chiffon spread over her bed.

Tony had made the Quinlans an offer for their ranch, which they had accepted. He was in the process of closing down the agency and wrapping up the pending cases, not least of which was cracking the skimming ring. Frances had decided to get her own investigator's license and had enrolled in Brad's school.

Ginny and Tony's relationship had been somewhat strained since their return, even though they tried to recapture the carefree time they'd enjoyed before. Had their love affair reached a point of no return? Ginny wondered. As Tony had pointed out, no matter how wonderful things were, life could never be static. Commitments needed to be made, or their romance would wither and die.

Still, it was fruitless to whip herself with "if onlys." If only she hadn't wasted two years of her life with Marc Noland; if only he hadn't destroyed her trust; if only she'd met Tony later when her wounds were healed and she had a successful career and was less insecure about the future.

When he arrived, his smile was warm but his eyes were heavy with fatigue—shattered eyes, eyes that expressed their weariness at forever being forced to witness the pain humans inflicted upon one another. It was little wonder he wanted to spend the rest of his life on a remote ranch.

Taking her into his arms, he kissed her mouth lightly. The kiss was without passion, and she felt he was holding back his hunger. He said, "What would you like to do? It's a barn-scorcher out there, but if you'd like to go somewhere . . ."

"Later perhaps, when it cools off. I've got salad fixings and sun tea."

Ginny tore lettuce into a bowl as he sliced tomatoes. She told him about the wedding gowns she'd been commissioned to design, and he told her about his frustration at being unable to crack the ring that was stealing from his father. She knew that his deep personal involvement in the investigation was because Tony secretly worried that his brother, Vince, might be part of the ring.

Preparing lunch together and talking, Ginny wondered for the thousandth time how she would get along when he left for the ranch. They shared their triumphs and problems, hopes and dreams, both large and small, and troubles were halved, joys doubled. There was such an effortless blending of thoughts and feelings that the prospect of losing Tony was like facing the amputation of a part of herself.

But once before a man had beckoned, and she'd followed, blinded by love, by that purely feminine and utterly unexplainable need to subvert her own ambitions and pretend she could fill her entire life waiting around for bits and pieces of his. *No, Tony, not even for you . . . because eventually my sacrifice would not only destroy me, it would also kill what you feel for me.* It was so simple. No decisions to make. No agonizing over what could have been. Why, then, did she feel so totally, completely desolate?

They sipped tea, shoved bits of salad around their plates, feeling drained by the heat of the day, artificially tamed with blasts of cold air from a machine. Or drained, perhaps, by their own emotions.

Tony put his fork down and said, "It's no use, is it? We can't go on pretending we don't know we're at the crossroads."

She jumped up and began to gather the dishes, in some blind panic that was designed to ward off the inevitable good-bye. As if in answer to a prayer, the telephone rang. Ginny snatched up the receiver in the manner of a drowning person clutching a straw.

Frances's gravelly tones came over the wire. "Ms. Hooper—sorry to bother you on a Sunday, but is Tony with you?"

"Yes," Ginny answered. "He's here. Just a minute."

"Tell him I just had a call . . . I've got the office answering machine hooked to my home phone. She said she'd call him again this evening—that it was urgent. I figured maybe he'd want to go to the office and wait for the call."

"Who was it?"

"Paula Phillips."

At midnight Tony stretched out on the leather couch in Frances's office, convinced that Paula Phillips wasn't going to call back as promised but reluctant to go home just in case she did.

Questions hammered at his brain. Why was she calling him, rather than Brad? Was it something to do with what she'd uncovered at the Castle? Why had she waited this long? What about the letter she'd sent to Brad, indicating the only reason she'd disappeared was because of a troublesome ex-husband? Was it . . . and this was the most disturbing possibility of all . . . because what she'd stumbled into was a skimming ring headed by a DeLeon . . . Vince?

No, Tony didn't want to believe that of his brother. The old man idolized him; all Vince would have to do if he needed extra cash was to ask. But Vince—all the DeLeons—had a fierce pride they guarded jealously. Perhaps Vince wouldn't have asked.

The prospect of speaking with Paula Phillips had hovered over Tony's day with Ginny like an approaching storm cloud. Although they'd spent the afternoon together and eventually had fallen into each other's arms and made love, simply because when they were together, no matter what their rational minds dictated, their bodies craved each other, they had not, as he planned, discussed their future together.

What future, he asked himself with a bitterness he hadn't felt since Lonnie's death and, hard on the heels of that loss, Tony's broken engagement. Within weeks he had lost two people he cared deeply about. Damn, how could he have been such a fool as to let himself care for somebody that much again? All the warning flags had been up when Ginny appeared in his life. Why hadn't he heeded them? Her abandonment by Noland, her fierce need to prove herself in the highly competitive fashion business. She'd made it pretty clear, when he took her to the ranch, that she had no intention of giving up her newfound independence. At least she'd let him save face by forestalling his proposal.

He considered the irony of all the years he'd waited for old man Quinlan to decide to retire so that he could buy the Lazy Q. Now, when Tony wasn't even sure he wanted to move to the valley, it became available. Everything had conspired to force decisions upon them that neither he nor Ginny were ready to make.

Remembering how he'd reacted to seeing the wedding dress sketch, Tony wondered if that was when he really blew it with Ginny. She'd just begun to reach out to him, coming out of her withdrawal, when he, like a fool, shoved her back into her shell.

One of the unlisted phone lines rang, and he leapt to answer it. Hoshi's voice, startled, said, "Oh, Tony . . . I wasn't expecting anyone to answer. I didn't think anyone would be there in the middle of the night."

He didn't ask why if she thought that she had bothered to call. "Something wrong, Hoshi?"

"I . . . uh . . . I guess I'm calling every number in Brad's personal phone book . . . to see if he's there."

Tony swore under his breath. "He probably lost track of time, Hoshi. Why don't you go to bed? I'm sure he'll be home soon."

"You see Ginny today?"

"Yes. We spent the afternoon together."

"I wish you could talk her into quitting working for Julius right now, or at least give him a week's notice, instead of waiting around for him to get another designer. As long as Ginny is there, he isn't really going to try. I'm worried about her. Have you taken a look at that Lou Mando character? He's a hit man if I ever saw one."

Tony considered letting Hoshi in on the fact that he'd assigned one of his best operatives to maintain surveillance on both Ginny and Lou Mando but decided that Hoshi might let it slip to Ginny, who undoubtedly would be furious if she knew. But Tony, too, had been worried about her. "I'll keep an eye on her, and Mando, so don't worry."

"I didn't know I was calling your office when I called this number, you know. Brad has a page of numbers that are only identified with symbols. There's a star beside this one."

"I suppose it represents a sheriff's badge," Tony said. "It's an unlisted number for a private line to the office."

"I've called every number except one. I always get a busy signal when I call it. I think the phone's off the hook." Hoshi's voice trembled on the verge of tears. "I guess I'm not sure if I want somebody to answer it or not."

Damn Brad to hell. Tony was losing patience with his friend's treatment of Hoshi. Before they were married, it was easier to accept Brad's consummate selfishness. He had it down to a fine art, but so charmingly perpetrated that everyone, Tony included, shrugged and put up with it. He said, "Give me the number, Hoshi; I'll try it for you."

As he scribbled the number on Frances's message pad, he realized from the prefix that it was in the northern part of the state, somewhere near Virginia City. An unlikely place for Brad to be in the middle of the night. Curious, Tony asked, "What symbol did he use beside this number?"

"It looks sort of like . . . a ghost. You know, a cartoon ghost—a sheet with pointy head and eyes."

After he finally talked Hoshi into going to bed, Tony

called a friend working the night shift at the police department. "This is DeLeon. I need a favor and you owe me one." He gave him the telephone number from Brad's book, absently drawing a cartoon ghost beside it on his desk pad as he spoke and wondering what it represented. "Can you get me a name and address to go with that? Call me back at the office, I'll probably be here all night."

Just before dawn Tony fell asleep. Paula Phillips hadn't called again. But Tony's friend at the police department had.

Even though it was still early morning, the heat bounced up from the parking lot and sizzled Ginny's feet through the thin soles of her strappy sandals. She wore a simple yellow linen chemise that skimmed her body, and her only jewelry was a matching pair of outsize earrings, to compensate for her severely up-swept but neck-cooling hairdo.

Sunlight shimmered on windshields, reflected from windows, turned buildings into ovens that threw searing rays back on passersby. Still, despite the rapid approach of a desert summer, there were plenty of sleepy tourists and die-hard gamblers around.

Three steps from her car, the heel of her left sandal snapped. Since it was closer, she limped to the back door of the building and kicked off both shoes, then dropped them into her briefcase. Unlocking the black door with the red-lettered sign JULIUS, she was met by a blast of icy air.

She had come in a couple of hours early in order to avoid the hot journey from her apartment in her un–air-conditioned VW when the sun was higher in the sky and had expected to be the first one in.

Her stockinged feet took her silently through the cutting room into the sewing room, and there she stopped, aware of the high-pitched tones of Lou Mando's voice, obviously speaking to someone on the phone. ". . . you do as you're told or you're out. Understand me? I catch you making any deals on the side, and I'll separate you from your head, got it? No, I don't want you to bring it over here. Take it to the usual drop point. You stay away from here—meet your lady friend away from the business."

There was a pause, then Mando said, "Don't give me that—he saw you, waiting for her in her car. And the boss says to remind you that you'd better come through pretty soon with your end of the deal—she still says she's quitting. It's time you persuaded her to change her mind, right?"

Ginny reeled back, leaning against the wall. *Mando was talking to Marc.* Marc was working for Julius— Marc was driving an expensive car, wearing expensive clothes. Marc was back in the money. And there was little doubt that all three of them were involved in robbing the casinos. On top of everything else Marc had apparently led Julius to believe he could influence her to continue working for him. So that was the reason for Marc's patient wait for her in the parking lot the day she and Tony flew up to the ranch.

She crept silently back to the rear door and slipped outside. The cement burned her feet. She had to put on her shoes and drag the broken heel around to the front door.

Mando, whose office had a window overlooking the front entrance, looked up suspiciously as she walked in. He stepped to the door of his office as she crossed the reception area. "You're early."

"You driven a bug in the heat of the day lately?" Ginny continued walking to her office. She called over her shoulder, "Besides, I want to leave early."

As soon as the rest of the staff came in and the whirr of sewing machines covered the sound of her voice, Ginny placed a call to Tony's office. She had to see him, tell him about Mando's conversation. She was also curious about the call he had been expecting from Paula Phillips. The press of outside events was suddenly so great that there was no time to dwell on the fact that she and Tony were coming to the end of the line with each other. It was almost a relief to have other things to worry about.

Frances's impatient voice softened slightly when Ginny identified herself. "Why, no, honey, he isn't here. I found him asleep on my couch when I got in this morning. From the look of him he was up most of the night. I—excuse me a minute, will you?"

Ginny heard a muffled comment that sounded like Frances covering the receiver and telling someone to "go right in—leave it on his desk." Then she said to Ginny, "He may have gone home. You want to call him there, or shall I just put a message on his desk? I'm leaving in a few minutes; I've got a class this morning. Did Tony tell you I'm going to Brad's school for private investigators? All I've learned so far is that you need some sort of receptacle in your car to relieve yourself in on long stakeouts." She gave a throaty chuckle, then abruptly her voice became sharp. "Hey, hey, what's the matter? Wait a minute!"

Without warning Ginny heard the phone drop to the desk and Frances's voice fading as she evidently ran after someone who was leaving. Ginny heard her call for the person to come back, then a door slammed.

A few minutes later Frances, sounding breathless, came back on the line. "Ginny, you'd better call Hoshi. I don't know what's wrong, but she just lit out of Tony's office in tears."

Chapter 18

GINNY FORCED HER TIRED EYES TO FOCUS ON A DELICATE silk thread as she coaxed it through a needle so fine that if it fell to the floor, it was gone forever. She could have glued the tiny beads to the wedding dress, but her bridal gowns were made to last, to go into attic trunks and someday be worn again by granddaughters.

The radio in her apartment played softly, and she stopped sewing as a clarinet solo began. She leaned back, closed her eyes, and listened, knowing that for the rest of her life she'd never be able to hear a clarinet without thinking of Tony.

After a moment she opened her eyes and began sewing again. The tedious work helped calm her nerves a little. Her head ached; her shoulders were stiff. It had been a very long day, but the finishing touches had to be put to this dress tonight for delivery tomorrow.

She had spent half the day making futile phone calls trying to find Hoshi, who wasn't at home or anywhere else Ginny could think of, and Brad, whom she'd called at his office, hadn't known where she was either. By the end of the day he was calling Ginny, trying to find his wife.

The reason for Hoshi's disappearance became obvious when Ginny finally called Tony, and he quickly put the pieces together. He swore soundly. "Frances shouldn't have let her go into my office."

He told Ginny of Hoshi's after-midnight phone call, and of the telephone number he'd checked on. "The address is a private residence in or near Virginia City. The phone is listed under a woman's name, Sally Smith, but the house, I found out, is owned by my good friend Brad Sutcliffe."

"Oh, Tony, no!" Ginny exclaimed. "Hoshi was right. Brad *is* seeing another woman. You think Hoshi saw something in your office—that she knows?" Ginny's heart ached for her friend.

"She couldn't miss it. I was so punchy last night I scribbled the information all over my desk pad—the phone number, a symbol Brad used to identify it, a cartoon ghost, Sally Smith's name, the street address, and a note that the house was owned by Brad."

"Tony, do you think Hoshi's gone there—to the house?"

"The only information I didn't leave was the name of the town. It's a Virginia City address, but the house is out in the country somewhere. So all she has is the name of the street. No, I don't think she'd go there anyway. I can't see Hoshi confronting the other woman, can you?"

"No . . . what shall we do?"

"You sit tight at your place in case she calls. I'm going to see Brad."

In all of the confusion of Hoshi's disappearance Ginny had not had an opportunity to tell Tony about Lou Mando's conversation that morning. She glanced at her watch. Nearly ten o'clock. Hoshi had been gone all day. But Tony would surely come over or at least call her soon.

As if in response to the thought, her doorbell rang. She hastily draped the wedding dress over the back of a chair and ran to open the door. Marc Noland shoved the door fully open and was inside the apartment before she could stop him.

She turned angrily to face him. "I'm warning you, Marc—"

There was desperation on his face. "Please, Ginny, I'm in big trouble. No, no, this time I'm not exaggerating. This time they'll kill me for sure—"

"Get out!" she said, her voice shaking. "I never want to see you again, do you hear me?"

"Ginny, I've been steering players over to crooked poker games. They're taking place in hotel rooms without the knowledge of the owners. And I've been picking up money at some of the casinos, carrying it out like it was winnings. I deliver it to—well, never mind where. There's a whole network of people involved—including your boss, Julius, and Lou Mando."

"Tell me about how you were also supposed to persuade me to go on working for Julius; might as well make a complete confession," Ginny said, walking across the room to the telephone.

He reached her side before she could lift the phone. His fingers closed around her wrist. "Don't call the police, Ginny. I'm telling you, I'm desperate; don't push me. Listen, it's true I let Julius think you and I were still an item. That I'd talk you into going on working for him."

With his other hand he reached out and touched her cheek. He smiled ingratiatingly. "Ginny, baby, you're so pretty. And so clever. You don't know how clever, do you? Julius says you're going to be the greatest woman designer since Chanel. Talk to him—tell him you'll stay with him if he keeps Mando off me. . . . I just need a little time to repay—"

Ginny groaned, jerking her head away from his hand. "You didn't! Oh, Marc, you didn't steal from *them?* The money you picked up from the crooked games, the money they skimmed from the slots, you carried it out like it was your own winnings and you got to thinking it was, so you decided you'd use it as a stake, is that it? But you lost, didn't you? When will you ever learn?"

"Just give me a little time. I can win it all back, I know I can. I've got a new system—"

"I can't help you, Marc. And there's no way I'll go on working for Julius. Especially now I know he's involved with a gang of thieves."

"Please, please, Ginny. I'm begging. Just a couple of thousand, and I'll go away, I'll never bother you again."

"Your promises are worthless. You swore you'd go to G.A. meetings."

"Honestly, I will, I swear. I'll go to a meeting every night if you'll just help me out this one time."

"No, Marc. I can't and I won't. Just go. Get out."

Behind him the outer door opened silently, and two seconds later Tony had an armlock around Marc's neck. "I warned you; now I'm going to show you what happens when you don't listen."

The expression on Tony's face chilled Ginny. She saw his unbridled anger and feared where it might lead him. She screamed, "Tony, no—no, please don't!" She ran to him, tried to pluck him away from Marc. "Tony, listen to me. He's a witness. He just implicated Julius and Mando."

Tony slammed Marc against the wall, keeping one hand on his throat. "Okay, Ginny, calm down. I'm going to take him out of here. You lock your door after us, and let me take care of things."

Ginny was still shaking when, minutes after they left, her phone rang. Brad's usually buoyant voice had been replaced by a husky monotone that she barely recognized. "Ginny, would you do me a favor?"

"Brad? Is that you?"

"Yeah, it's me. Hoshi's in L.A. She's gone to her grandmother's house. Will you talk to her—get her to come home?"

"What if she doesn't want to come home?"

"She won't talk to me. You've got to explain to her that she's got it all wrong. There isn't another woman."

"She knows about Sally Smith, Brad."

"She thinks she knows: Sally Smith is just a woman I helped out. She's nothing to me—nothing. I swear to God."

"Oh? Then, why is she living in a house you own?"

"Damn Tony DeLeon to hell! And to think I taught him all he knows. . . . Okay, it's true I own the house —you ever hear of a tenant?"

"Not one who lives in a house that the landlord's wife doesn't know about."

"Ginny, please, at least call her and tell her I love her and I want her to come home. Tell her that I know we can work things out, and I won't leave her alone so much in future, I promise. If she'll just come back, I'll explain everything about Sally Smith. No more secrets, I swear."

"Give me the telephone number. I'll see what I can do."

"Thanks, Ginny. Thanks."

She dialed the 213 area code and the Los Angeles

number Brad had given her, and when a man's voice
answered the phone, Ginny asked if Hoshi was there.

There was a pause. "Who may I say is calling?"

"I'm sorry, I should have explained. This is Ginny
Hooper; I'm a friend of Hoshi's."

She heard a long sigh. "I'm Hoshi's father. Her
grandmother is with her . . . I'm afraid—wait, I'll see if
Hoshi will come to the phone."

As she waited Ginny's fingers traced the pattern of
beads around the hem of the wedding dress, now
covering the kitchen table. After an interminable five
minutes Hoshi's father came back on the line. "Miss
Hooper, I'm sorry. My daughter isn't able to speak
with you personally. She asks me to tell you that she
isn't coming back to Las Vegas."

Ginny felt her apprehension about Hoshi suddenly
become acute. She said, "Please—it's very important
that I speak to her."

"I regret I cannot force her to come to the telephone.
I'm very sorry."

Perhaps if I call again tomorrow, Ginny thought as
she carefully hung the wedding dress on a padded
hanger, wrapping it with tissue and plastic, ready for
delivery. Happy endings, she thought, looking at the
dress. Oh, for simpler times, when wearing a bridal
gown meant living happily ever after. The image of the
radiant Hoshi on her wedding day refused to fade from
Ginny's mind.

Restlessly, despite her exhaustion, Ginny began to
tidy up the apartment. Tony would return after he'd
taken Marc to the police, she was sure.

It was well after midnight when he arrived, his face
set in tight lines of anger. "They're questioning him,"
he said in answer to her unspoken question, "but I
doubt they'll be able to hold him."

"But if I were to tell the police what he told me—"
Ginny began.

Tony pulled her roughly into his arms. "Locking up Noland, or even Julius and Mando, doesn't get us the top man."

"You don't think Julius is the top man?"

"No, I don't." He switched to a Bogart growl: "Look, kid, leave the detective work to me, okay?"

Ginny slipped her arms around his neck. "Sometimes I have this wonderful fantasy that you and I are the last two people left on earth. Do you realize how much other people manage to intrude into our lives?"

He looked down at her, his eyes softening. "Do you really mean that?"

Over his shoulder she could see the wedding dress, hanging over the back of the closet door. She sighed. "Come and sit down. I have to tell you about your friends Brad and Hoshi."

The trouble with Los Angeles, Ginny decided the following day, was its sheer sprawling size. By the time she'd taken a taxi from the airport to Westwood it was already really too late in the evening to make unannounced calls. But her nagging worries about Hoshi persisted, and she decided for once good manners had to be thrown to the wind.

Tony had suggested that Ginny go to see Hoshi at her grandmother's house. Ginny suspected he wanted her out of the way in case Marc's confession to the police led to a break in the case.

Hoshi's grandmother received her courteously, showed her in to a comfortable living room, furnished in Early American style, and offered her a choice of tea or soft drinks. Ginny declined politely.

It was easy to see from whom Hoshi had inherited her beauty. The old lady was a slightly faded and fragile version of her granddaughter. She said, "It is very kind of you to travel so far because you are concerned for your friend."

"Is she here? May I see her?"

There was a long pause. The old lady's lips compressed slightly and her eyes squeezed shut, as though she were holding back tears. Ginny felt apprehension swimming through her mind, rushing about searching for possibilities. Something, she knew, was terribly wrong. "Please," she said again, "for just a minute?"

A frail hand was raised, beckoning, and the old lady wordlessly turned to lead the way. They went up a narrow staircase, and Hoshi's grandmother indicated a door, then turned and went downstairs. Ginny caught a glimpse of the tears running down her face as she went by.

Ginny knocked on the door and called softly, "Hoshi . . . it's me, Ginny. Please, may I come in?"

There was a muffled response that Ginny decided to interpret as an invitation. She opened the door and stepped inside. The room was in darkness. She could make out a denser shadow that was the bed, with a vague shape reclining on it. She said, "Hoshi? Could I turn on a light?"

"No, please don't. Put out your hand; there's a chair to your right."

Ginny's groping hand found the back of a chair, and she slid into it, straining into the darkness to try to see her friend. "Brad called me. He wants to talk to you, to explain everything. Hoshi, running away isn't going to solve anything. Give him a chance."

"Did Tony tell you about Sally Smith?"

"Brad says she's just a tenant in a house he owns."

"If that's so, why didn't he tell me about her? Why did she call at all hours of the day and night and hang up if I answered the phone? Why did I try to write checks on our personal account and find there wasn't any money in it, because it had been wired to a bank in Virginia City? I thought it was needed for Brad's new business up north, but when Tony found out about

Sally Smith, I called the bank, pretended I wanted to be sure the money Brad had wired had been picked up. It was—by Sally Smith."

"Circumstantial evidence, Hoshi. Give Brad a chance to explain."

"Will he be able to explain why he left me alone so much? I never told you; I was so ashamed. He was gone more nights than I care to remember."

"Oh, Hoshi . . . I'm so sorry. What can I do to help?"

She stood up, stubbing her toe in the darkness but wanting to hug Hoshi, to convey by her touch that everything would work out for her.

Ginny's foot connected with a table, and she practically fell across the bed, feeling Hoshi's delicately boned shoulders under her hands. But there was something different about those shoulders . . . Ginny gasped and pushed herself up from the bed. She swung her hand in a frantic arc, seeking a lamp.

The light flooded the bed. Hoshi raised her tear-streaked face. Wisps of black hair stood up in forlorn and ragged spikes all over her head. *"Oh, no!* Oh, Hoshi . . ."* She had cut off her long beautiful hair, leaving less than an inch of length.

Chapter 19

TONY PICKED GINNY UP AT THE AIRPORT AND DROVE HER directly to his house. En route he told her that Marc had been released for lack of evidence. He'd refused to repeat his accusations against Julius and Mando to the detectives, claiming that he only agreed to go to the police because he was afraid if he didn't, Tony would beat him up.

Noting that Ginny was tense and withdrawn, Tony didn't question her about what had happened in Los Angeles, other than to ask if Hoshi was all right. When they reached the house and went inside, Ginny turned to Tony and whispered, "Hold me, please. Hold me very close."

His arms went around her, and she buried her face in his neck, drawing comfort from his nearness, from the dearly familiar scent of wild chaparral that seemed to cling to his skin. He asked softly, "Do you want to talk about it?"

"No, not yet. I just want to be with you and not think about anything else."

His fingers drifted down her spine. "You're tighter than a bowstring. Come on, I've got an old-fashioned remedy someplace for what ails you."

Taking her hand, he led her along the inner hall to the guest bathroom, which had a wall-size window overlooking a tiny private atrium filled with flowering bamboo. There was a huge sunken tub, and he flipped on the water and then began to rummage through the contents of the cupboards under the washbowl. "Aha! Here it is." Straightening up, he displayed a slightly dusty bottle of bubble bath.

Ginny raised a questioning eyebrow.

"When my mother was alive, she never went anyplace without her bubble bath. She claimed it was the only way she could get relaxed enough to sleep in a strange bed."

"I wish I'd known her," Ginny said, kicking off her shoes.

Tony poured a generous amount into the tub, which immediately turned into a snowy mass of froth, delicately fragrant. "She was quite a lady. I miss her. I remember once she told me, back in the days when I still thought I was immortal and could have anything I wanted in life, that it was a good idea at moments of great happiness to take a second to shut my eyes and ask myself what I most wanted to remember about that particular moment in time. Then I could be sure I fully experienced what would become a treasured memory."

"She was very wise."

Tony's eyes held hers, and neither spoke for a moment. Then he said, "Relax in your bubbles. I'll have cold drinks ready when you're through."

He started for the door, and Ginny said softly, "Bring the drinks back here. Something about a bubble bath in the middle of the day makes me long for the luxury of having my back washed too."

She had just settled into the warm scented water, leaned back and closed her eyes, when she heard the door open again and Tony's footsteps on the tiled floor. Her hand was fished out of the bubbles and a frosty glass placed in it. She took several sips of the wine cooler, murmured her appreciation, and laid her head back, feeling most of her tension drain away.

Tony removed the glass from her hand and picked up a sponge. He ran it gently over her shoulders, down the length of her arms. She watched him through half-closed eyes. He'd removed his shirt but kept on his jeans.

When he plunged his hand into the water and raised her leg, she said, "You know, I think I could hire you out to do this . . ."

The sponge traveled from toes to thigh and back again, and he said, "Yeah, it's a rotten job but somebody's got to—"

She splashed him, and he blew bubbles at her. Soon the bathroom was awash with bubbles, and his jeans were drenched. He peeled them off and rolled over the edge of the tub and into the water with her.

There was another flurry of bubbles, and he captured her in his arms, pushed her wet hair out of the way, and nuzzled her neck vigorously.

"You know," Ginny said, laughing, "When I was a little girl, I thought if you let a boy kiss you on the neck you'd have a baby."

Raising his head, he looked at her. "I see that little girl in there sometimes, Ginny. You should let her out more often. She's a helluva lot of fun."

"Oh, Tony—" Ginny wasn't sure why, but suddenly she wanted to cry. Instead she offered him her mouth, and he claimed it in the way only he knew how. The kiss went on and on while their hands stroked slippery wet bodies and the cooling water in the tub took on a new dimension. It had become a volcanic pool, pulsing with energy and bursting with need. Ginny abandoned herself to her desires, offered herself to Tony's. They were two creatures of the deep, meeting in some strange and wonderful new ocean. When her fingernails suddenly bit into his shoulders and she moaned softly, he said, "We'd better get out of here before we drown."

Her passion was almost at its zenith, and she was scarcely aware of him wrapping her in a towel and carrying her to the massive bed in his room. The sheet was cool under her damp back, and Tony's body was warm and full of promise. They came together, limbs entwined, mouths hungrily seeking. The first thrust of his entry brought a cry of pleasure to her lips, and then they were back on some wildly beautiful shore and the surf pounded out the rhythms of the sea as their bodies undulated toward fulfillment.

When the moment of release came, it was a shattering of the universe, a breathless rush to earth, and then they were clinging to each other, savoring an aftermath of total contentment and joy.

Tony's hand touched her cheek. "You've got your eyes closed . . . are you asking yourself what you want to remember about this moment?"

She nestled closer but didn't open her eyes. "No matter what happens in the future, Tony, knowing you, being a part of your life, is the best thing that ever happened to me."

"Look at me, Ginny," he commanded. When her eyelids fluttered open, he said, "Why are you speaking in the past tense? As if we're never going to see each other again."

Because, she thought in sudden weariness, *nothing*

has changed. You're still going to live on a remote ranch, and I'm going to be the best woman designer since Chanel. . . . It's only in moments of high passion that we're really together. They were two strong individuals who could never be happy giving up their own dreams to be a part of someone else's. Yet their dreams were light-years apart.

"I'm sorry," Ginny mumbled. "I didn't mean to sound so fatalistic. I suppose I'm coming out of my rosy glow and remembering Hoshi . . ."

"Tell me what happened in L.A.," he urged.

After she had described how Hoshi had hacked off her long beautiful hair, she added, "It's a funny thing about women: When they get into emotional deep water, they often seem to take it out on their hair. I had a friend who was a hairdresser once—"

Tony interrupted, "I think it was a gesture of defiance aimed at Brad. He loved her long hair. What's she going to do? Stay in L.A.?"

"I talked her into coming back here. She agreed so long as she could stay with me. She'll be here in a couple of days. Tony—we shouldn't push her. When she's ready to talk to Brad . . ."

"Don't worry. I don't care for the way he's treated her either."

When Tony stopped by her apartment the following weekend and saw Hoshi, Ginny sensed his shock— despite being prepared—at the sight of Hoshi's ultra-short hair. Still, Tony masterfully kept from showing his feelings. "Well, there she is, the pearl of the Orient. What did you do to yourself, Hoshi? Let's see, you either lost weight or shaved off your mustache, I can't decide which—but you do look slightly different."

Hoshi giggled. "I missed you, too, Tony. You caught any bad guys or punched any cows lately?"

Tony fished in his pocket and solemnly presented

each of them with a Hershey's bar, warning, "Don't spoil your dinner. I'm taking the pair of you out to my favorite restaurant."

"Gee, the last of the big spenders," Hoshi said, unwrapping her chocolate and taking a bite. "Thanks for the dinner invitation, but, well . . ." She glanced sideways at Ginny.

Ginny said, "Hoshi's going to talk to Brad."

Hoshi shrugged. "Yeah, well . . . I phoned and Godzilla said it was her night off tonight, so . . ."

"We'll drive you over there," Tony said. Ginny was glad he didn't question Hoshi or comment on her separation from her husband.

Later, after they'd dined in the quiet restaurant well away from the hubbub of the Strip, they lingered over an excellent bottle of house wine.

The candlelight played softly over Ginny's hair, gilding the bronze with fire. The summer sun had brought sun-bleached highlights to her hair and tawny color to her cheeks. Her shoulders were tanned and bare tonight, exposed by the strapless white cotton dress with full swinging skirt she wore. She looked, Tony decided, unbelievably, breathtakingly lovely.

His hand slid across the table and found hers. "Sometimes when I look at you, I wish I were a poet, so I could tell you how beautiful you are. I think right now I'm composing another piece of music to you, in my head."

She smiled. "I've missed you so, these past few days. What have you been up to?"

"Still trying to find the mastermind behind the skimming operation. If it hadn't been for what Marc Noland said about Julius and Mando, I'd probably have given up. Nobody in this town wants to talk to me. Including my father and brother. They all think I'm paranoid about it. Did I tell you my father's back in his office, just an hour or so a day, but enough to keep

Vince on his toes. What about you? Hoshi been a problem?"

"Not really. I've been so busy. I have three new weddings to design for, and I have to do everything myself: design the dress, make the patterns, do the fittings, to say nothing of picking up the pins, selecting fabrics and sewing, and all the paperwork. Hoshi's going to give Brad a chance to explain about Sally Smith, I think."

Tony cradled her hand in his, rubbing his finger lightly over her smooth flesh. He wondered whether to share with her the information that Brad had spirited Sally Smith away from the house he owned—where, Tony hadn't been able to determine. He decided against it, afraid it would spoil the mood. Nor did he want Ginny to know that Marc Noland had vanished into thin air. Oh, God, Tony thought, don't let him turn up dead like Al Vernon did. She can't take that right now; she'd be torn apart with guilt.

Aloud, he said, "I signed the final papers on the ranch today. It's all mine."

The merest suggestion of a shadow flickered across Ginny's eyes. He wanted to squeeze her fingers and say urgently, "Tell me you'll go there with me, Ginny . . . tell me you can't live without me, any more than I can live without you." But he didn't. Nor did he add that he hadn't made any immediate plans to move to the ranch. He pretended, even to himself, that he had to stay in town and crack the skimming ring. But he knew better.

"Congratulations. I'm happy for you," Ginny said, not meeting his eyes.

He said carefully, "You know, Ginny, sometimes when two people are at an impasse, a compromise is possible."

She replied, "You mean Hoshi and Brad? I don't think so. She wants a full commitment from him, and he hasn't given it."

Was she deliberately misunderstanding him? he wondered. "I talked with him yesterday. He's really broken up about her leaving him. I believe he'll try to turn over a new leaf. I've never seen him so serious about anything. When I was leaving, he suddenly said, 'I know what I have to do to get her back,' and I can't describe the look on his face—relief, and something else . . . a realization that the answer had been there all along, but he hadn't seen it."

"It wasn't that hard to see. All she wanted was to share his life. He excluded her from big chunks of it." Ginny still didn't meet his gaze, and he thought, Are we talking about them or about us?

He said, "Good marriages don't happen overnight. Brad had been a bachelor for a long time."

Now her eyes were raised to his, and he saw the questions there but couldn't define them, but they were overlaid with—not pain exactly, but perhaps the anticipation of being hurt. And why not? First Marc Noland destroyed her trust, then she watched Hoshi's fairy-tale marriage disintegrate. "Ginny. Don't project negatives back at yourself or at us. When I mentioned compromise, I wasn't talking about Brad and Hoshi—"

She interrupted swiftly, "Compromise means someone has to defer to someone else. Neither of us wants that, do we?"

"I wouldn't ask you to give up your career, Ginny."

"And I wouldn't ask you to give up your ranch."

He drew a deep breath and said, "Supposing—"

"Excuse me, sir." The waiter's voice floated down over his shoulder. "There's a telephone call for you."

"Not now," Tony snapped. But the telephone was placed on the table in front of him. The waiter said apologetically, "The lady said it was extremely urgent, Mr. DeLeon."

He picked up the receiver, and Frances's gravelly

tones came over the wire. "Boss? I'm on my break at the school for P.I.'s. Can you get over here right away?"

"What won't keep till morning?"

"Look, boss. I'm not doing well in this class, my desk at the office is piled with work, the bank's refused to give me a loan to open my own agency, and my scale tells me I gained six pounds this week. I don't need any more hassles, understand? Now get over here—what I've got for you won't keep."

Ginny was smiling when he replaced the receiver. "I heard every word. It's all right, Tony, really. You can drop me off en route. I really should get back to my apartment in case Hoshi doesn't get back together with Brad and goes back there."

"Okay. But you and me, babe," he said in his best Bogart growl, "have some heavy decisions to make—and soon."

When Ginny arrived back at her apartment, Hoshi was already there, sitting in the dark watching television. Her heart sinking, Ginny flipped on a lamp and asked, "How did it go?"

"Well, he was appalled at what I'd done to my hair."

"I can imagine."

"He swore that Sally Smith was just a woman who'd gone to his school for P.I.'s. That she got into a jam working on a case. He felt he owed her, so when she wanted to disappear, he bought the house and let her move in and kept everything secret. It was all very plausible when Brad was telling it, but . . ."

"You don't believe him?"

"Ginny, I love Brad, and I think I know him almost as well as I know myself. He wasn't telling me the truth. Maybe a partial truth, but that woman isn't just an ex-employee—she means a great deal more than that to Brad. There was . . . I don't know, a feeling of despair, obsession . . . something, when he talked about her. I almost felt like I was inside his skin, experiencing his emotions. I honestly felt that he wanted her to be out of his life but didn't know how to say good-bye to her, that he couldn't, in fact. I watched him going through an inner battle with himself and . . ." Hoshi's hand went to her shoulder, patting absently as though searching for the curtain of hair that used to hang there. "And . . . losing."

"What about you?" Ginny asked. "Are you going to be able to simply stop loving him? It isn't that easy, Hoshi."

Hoshi gave her a wan smile. "Can't live with 'em, or without 'em, right? Tell me, Ginny, have you realized yet just how much you love Tony?"

"Oh, yes," Ginny answered. "I love him to distraction. I've stopped kidding myself that I don't."

"And he loves you. So have you told each other?"

"It's not quite as simple as that."

"Ginny, listen to me. I don't want you soured on marriage because of what happened to me. I guess I should have seen that there was always a part of Brad that he didn't want to share with me. I sensed it but wouldn't admit it. Maybe his Sally Smith could share that part of his life, and I couldn't. But it's not like that with you and Tony. Be honest now: even when you're not with him you're thinking about him, talking about him. Just as he is about you. Except for your work, neither of you wants to go off by yourselves and do things alone . . . like Brad did."

Except for our work, Ginny thought. Isn't that a rather major factor? But aloud she said, "You're right, Hoshi. But I still don't know how it would be possible for us to make a life together. But enough about me. What are you going to do about Brad?"

"He begged me to move back. He said he was going

to do something that would give us a fresh start. He didn't want to tell me what it was, but he said it was the only hope he had. I told him if he couldn't confide in me, completely, then I couldn't live with him."

"And?"

"He asked me to call him in the morning. He thought maybe he'd be able to talk to me then. Listen, all of a sudden I'm beat. Let's call it a night, shall we?"

"Good idea. I don't know about you, but my early-morning decisions are usually better than my nighttime ones."

Ginny awakened to Hoshi's frantic whisper close to her ear. "Somebody's trying to get in." Ginny sat up, hearing the faint scratching sound that came from the apartment door. The air-conditioning system had failed, and it was stiflingly hot, pitch-dark, and silent except for that ominous rattling of the lock.

"The phone!" Ginny swung her feet from the bed.

"No! It's in the living room. If he gets the door open—"

"You stay here. Open the window and get ready to yell if you hear the door give."

"We're too high up. Nobody will hear."

"Look for a weapon of some sort, then." Ginny was already crossing the bedroom. She stubbed her toe in the dark and bit back a cry. Now that she was in the living room, she realized the intruder was using a key or a wire or something on the lock. Her hands touched the back of the couch and she fumbled with cushions, trying to find the end table that held the phone.

The receiver was in her hand when the door opened. Silhouetted in the light from the outside hall was the shape of a brawny male. Ginny stabbed frantically at the operator button on the phone. It was still ringing as the intruder hurtled across the room and grabbed her. The receiver slid from her hand as she fought off the grasping hands. She wasn't aware she was screaming until Hoshi's piercing shriek joined in. In the darkness the two women were flailing at the man, Hoshi with an umbrella. He cursed and swung his arms, trying to grab first one and then the other.

Ginny heard a crash and Hoshi's winded gasp. He'd evidently knocked her to the floor. The next instant Ginny felt a hand close around her throat, and her nostrils were assailed by a powerful, unpleasant scent of cologne.

Mando's voice hissed in her ear. "Where's he hiding? Where's your boyfriend? I want Marc Noland, and don't tell me you don't know where he is."

Tony parked his car behind a gas station on the highway and surveyed the meager lights marking the tiny town to which Frances had sent him.

An hour's drive from Las Vegas, it was one of those gas, food, and lodging towns that you'd miss if you blinked—a combination motel and coffee shop, a small casino, grocery store, a few mobile homes, and the wood-frame church he could see nestled against a bleak rise of foothills. As he walked quickly in the direction of the church, he saw there were a number of cars parked around it—not as many as were parked in front of the casino, but enough for it to be a surprise on a weekday evening.

Surely Frances had been wrong? But no, she wouldn't have sent him clear out here on a wild-goose chase. Tony had long known that Frances was probably the best investigator he had, and if she'd been younger, he'd have sent her out into the field.

In front of the small church a few spindly shrubs fought to survive the harsh climate of the desert. Tony moved silently past a sign reading: TONIGHT AT EIGHT G.A. MEETING.

The meeting was already in progress in an anteroom.

Tony stepped into the entry hall and stood pressed to the wall outside the open door. The room was crowded, almost all of the chairs taken. Smoke clouded the air, not quite obliterating a faint scent of incense and musty old prayerbooks. Someone was pitching, his despairing voice telling of his misdeeds, of his constant battle with himself to quit gambling, to go away from this mecca of his obsession. The man on the floor finished speaking and sat down.

Almost at once someone else took his place. Tall, good-looking, blond, oozing charm. . . . He said, "Hi, my name's Brad, and I'm a compulsive gambler."

Chapter 20

GINNY STRUGGLED IN THE DARKNESS WITH MANDO, FEELING consciousness ebb away. Somewhere beyond the threatening bulk of the man, she could hear Hoshi sobbing.

Suddenly the overhead light went on and a strange female voice yelled "Back off!"

Blinking, Ginny looked first at her attacker. Lou Mando had turned in the direction of the voice, his hand relaxing on her throat. A calm-eyed young woman stood with one hand on the light switch and the other held a pistol. "Okay," the latest arrival said slowly, gesturing with her gun to Mando. "You—no sudden moves. Get over there, on the floor. Face-down."

"You'd better do it, Lou," Ginny croaked, as the pressure on her throat eased.

"You know him?" the woman asked as he lowered himself to the floor.

"Yes. He works for Julius—as I used to. But who the heck are you?"

"I'm one of Mr. DeLeon's operatives. I'll show you my ID as soon as I get cuffs on your visitor."

Ginny helped the shaken Hoshi to her feet. Fortunately she seemed to be more scared than hurt. "We'll take your word. But how—where did you come from?"

"Mr. DeLeon assigned me to watch this apartment. He was afraid this might happen. Say, would one of you call the police now?"

"I can explain this," Mando said, from the floor.

"Breaking and entering, assault; tell it to the police," Tony's operative said.

"Will you make the call, Hoshi?" Ginny asked.

Mando said, "I wasn't after you. I was looking for your boyfriend, Noland. He has something that belongs to Julius."

"When Julius visits you in jail," Ginny said, "you can tell him I was through with Marc a long time ago. I don't expect to see him, or Julius, or you, ever again."

Half an hour later, after two policemen took away the handcuffed Mando, the woman with the gun said, "Do you mind if I use your phone to report to my boss what happened?"

"Tony . . ." Ginny said, collapsing into a chair. How she needed him. "Yes . . . and I'd like to speak to him too."

She awoke the next morning in the comforting circle of Tony's arms, aware of the enormous size of the bed in which they lay. The masculine lines of the furniture came into focus, along with bright bands of sunshine squeezing between the slats of shuttered windows.

Floating serenely toward consciousness, Ginny felt wonderfully protected and safe in Tony's bed, in his house. She remembered that he'd brought Hoshi and herself here late last night. The episode of Mando breaking into her apartment now seemed more like a nightmare than reality. The sun was already high in the sky and Tony was awake, watching her.

"Hi," Ginny whispered sleepily, wondering how she'd ever be able to sleep alone again. "I can't believe how soundly I slept."

"You were pretty tired last night." He pushed her hair back from her brow, allowing his finger to trail down her cheek.

"And you were awfully quiet about why Frances wanted to see you so urgently."

"I didn't want to talk in front of Hoshi. Brad will be here to pick her up soon. I'll tell you everything after they leave."

Ginny sat up. "You told him you were bringing her here?"

"Yes. But let's not exchange another word until after breakfast."

Despite Ginny's protests, he slid out of bed, pulled on a robe, and headed for the kitchen. Ginny followed a few minutes later and found him studying a note on the refrigerator door.

"It's from Hoshi," Tony said. "She decided to call a cab and go home on her own, rather than wait for Brad to come for her."

Tony opened the refrigerator and took out a pitcher of orange juice. When he turned to bring it to the table, she saw that he was frowning slightly.

"What is it? Aren't you glad she's gone back to him? I am," Ginny said.

Tony sat down and stared moodily at the orange juice. "Funny how you can know somebody for years and not know a damn thing about them."

Ginny opened a cabinet and found glasses. She poured juice while Tony continued to stare into space. When he still hadn't spoken after several minutes passed, she said, "You never did tell me what Frances had discovered that sent you rushing off last night."

"I went to a G.A. meeting."

"G.A.?" Ginny drew in her breath sharply. "Marc—"

"No, not Marc. Brad."

"Brad? At a Gamblers Anonymous meeting? But—"

"Frances overheard him calling a G.A. number to find out if there was a meeting last night, somewhere out of town. I stood outside and heard him pitching about the misery he'd caused himself and his wife by his gambling, the terrible debts he's always juggling, how he'd sneak off to a poker game and then lose track of time."

"The times he left Hoshi alone . . ." Ginny said slowly, everything falling into place, "he was gambling." All at once she realized why she had been both drawn to Hoshi and afraid for her. That particular lethal charm of the compulsive gambler, both she and Hoshi had been caught in its deadly spell.

Tony said, "When she walked out, I guess that was the catalyst he needed to admit his compulsion and go to G.A. I'd wondered about Brad. I saw him in a few poker games when we were in the army. I remember when he and Lonnie and I were in 'Nam, Lonnie was afraid Brad was selling army equipment to the black marketeers—he told me then that Brad had been on a losing streak. But lots of guys in the army play cards. I didn't think much about it, especially when Brad swore he'd stay away from any high-stakes games. And I never did see him in another game, either there or after we came home. Yet there were always those times when he was incommunicado . . ."

"Hoshi didn't suspect either. It seems incredible that

Brad would let her think he was seeing another woman rather than tell her he was going to a poker game, but then, I remember how Marc was. When they're in the grip of the obsession, there's no rhyme nor reason to their actions, and they'll go to any length to hide the fact that they're gambling again. I think maybe that's the one characteristic of all compulsive people—they try so desperately to cater to their addiction in secret. Even after I'd found out about Marc's gambling, he'd never let me stay with him while he was at the table."

"Well, at least Brad has taken the first step. It took a lot of soul-searching and real determination for him to go to a G.A. meeting and admit he has a problem."

"Does he know that you know about him?"

"No. I got out of there before the meeting broke up. It bothers me that Hoshi doesn't know, yet it's Brad's place to tell her. I think he will. It's her influence that sent him to G.A. I'm sure he doesn't want to lose her."

"You're right. We should stay out of it. But I hope he won't waste any time in telling Hoshi that the other woman in his life is Lady Luck."

Ginny glanced at the wall clock and jumped to her feet. "Gad, look at the time! I've got to get back to my apartment and go to work."

Tony intercepted her before she reached the door. He caught her in his arms and said sharply, "Ginny, don't run off. We need to talk." The look on his face drove all thoughts of dress patterns from her mind. He said, "Last night we were interrupted. Now I'm telling you—to hell with your work, and my investigation, and Brad and Hoshi and everybody else. If one of us doesn't do something fast, we're going to take off in separate directions. Do you want that? I don't."

"But, your ranch . . . Tony it's lovely, but I couldn't live there with you. I need to be where my business is, where my clients are, and the fabric centers and—" His mouth covered hers, tongue seeking to rekindle all the fire that their physical closeness had always generated. For an instant she responded, then fought him off. "Tony, you said you wanted to *talk*."

"I'm just shutting you up so you'll listen." He put his hands on her cheeks, pressing lightly as he held her face close to his. "I love you, Ginny."

She felt her heart skid, then pound. She was looking into the depths of his eyes and seeing a blazing honesty and caring there that was boundless. That look in his eyes said he was about to sacrifice his own dream for hers.

Several emotions swept over her simultaneously. Happiness that was beyond anything she'd ever known, a desire to give that happiness back to him, and at the same time a distant warning voice hammered at her conscience. *If you let him give up his dream for you, it will be just as bad as your giving up yours for him.*

"Oh, Tony . . . I love you, too, so much."

"Ginny, about the ranch—"

"No! No. Don't you dare say you're not going there. It's what you've longed for and worked for all your life."

"It doesn't matter anymore. Don't you see— sometimes the anticipation is more alluring than the realization. I just want to be with you, Ginny."

"But, Tony, I can't live with that kind of self-sacrifice. You—me—our relationship to each other, would all be diminished."

His mouth twisted into a small lopsided grin. "What do you suggest, then? A weekend romance? I'm not sure I'd be satisfied with that. Ginny, don't you understand, I'm trying to tell you that you are more important to me than anything else on earth. The ranch is a piece of property. I can leave Josh in charge and still own it. I don't have to live there."

"But you *want* to, don't you?"

"If you wanted to live there too—yes. But not without you."

She clung to him fiercely. "You'll never know how much I want to be with you. You'll never know how much I love you—but that's the problem. I love you too much to let you give up your dream of living on the ranch. Don't you see, I couldn't handle the guilt. I'd be afraid that in time you'd resent my selfishness."

"Ginny, Ginny . . . it would be *my* choice."

"No," she said stubbornly. "I remember when I was with Marc, how much I resented being dependent on him for all the stimulation in my life. I'd never want to put another person in that position."

"I'm not Noland," Tony said with unexpected savageness. "Besides, I'm not going to hang around doing nothing while you design your clothes."

"No? What will you do—go back to being a P.I.? You told me yourself you just slipped into investigations as an alternative to working in your father's casino. That you've dreamed since you were a little boy of owning a ranch. Or maybe you'd go to work for your father? And you know how I feel about gambling tycoons. Don't you see, you wouldn't be the man I love if you weren't being yourself—the you that's worked all these years to move to your great outdoors."

"Okay, I give up. I *do* want the ranch, and I want to work it. I don't want to be an absentee owner. What now? We say 'Good-bye; it's been nice knowing you'?"

"No! I—I just want to see you when I can. Surely we can get together sometimes—"

"Ginny," he interrupted. "I'm not a part-time sort of guy. Don't try to put me into a compartment and expect me to pop out when you have time for me. I want more of a commitment from you than that. I couldn't stand just being handed fragments of your time."

"Please don't force a decision on me now, Tony." She ran her hands distractedly up and down his arms, touched his hair where it fell in a tousled sweep across his brow, as though she were afraid he might demateralize before her eyes. How easy it would have been if she loved him less than she did. But what could she do when she loved him so much that she had to consider every aspect of his life and whether he would be happy with the changes he was so ready to make for her? Yes, it would have been so simple if she could have just selfishly accepted what he wanted to give.

Releasing her, he kissed her lightly on the tip of her nose. "Okay, kid. I know when I'm licked." There was a finality in the gesture that frightened her. The casual words and gesture masked a deep sense of resignation, she was sure. He'd offered all he had to offer, and she'd refused the gift of his unconditional love. For a man like Tony that meant he'd have to construct a hard shell over his emotions to hide his hurt.

Don't misunderstand my motives, Ginny thought in sudden desperation. I'm trying to be as unselfish as you. But now she realized that twice he'd wanted to make a commitment and she'd run scared. How can I be such a fool, she asked herself, when I want him so much? I've lost him this time for sure.

She cast about in her mind for something to say that would express the depth of what she felt for him, to explain that she was thinking about him and his needs rather than her own. But it wasn't a moment for explanations, it was a moment for decisions. For a long minute they looked at each other, eyes locked, the palpable force of their feelings lying between them, uniting and dividing them. The image of a demon that shoved them together only to drag them apart danced in the back of her mind.

At last Tony turned from her and said, "You want breakfast before you go?"

"No, thanks," Ginny answered, her voice a whisper. "When will you be going out to the ranch?"

"I don't know. Soon as I wrap up this case, I guess. I think maybe now that Mando's in custody, there'll be a break."

She walked to the door, hesitated, and asked, "Will you . . . call me?"

Over his shoulder, he gave her a raised-eyebrow glance that made her feel foolish, and she instantly saw the incongruity of telling a man that she wasn't prepared to spend her life with him but didn't want him to leave her either. She added quickly, "I mean, about the case. I do have something of a vested interest in it, you know."

"Sure, Ginny. I'll let you know how it turns out. Now, I'd better throw on some clothes and drive you back to town."

Ginny was both aware of the passage of time and oblivious of it. She decided the only way she was going to survive the loss of Tony's love was to work eighteen hours a day and not give herself time to think about anything but wonderful wedding gowns. Damn . . . why had she become a designer of wedding dresses? Tony hadn't actually asked her to marry him, but oh, how she wished she were designing a dress for her own wedding.

Had two days gone by since their last meeting? Or was it three? She fell into bed, exhausted, after midnight, tossed restlessly all night, and got up again at dawn. There had been no word from Hoshi other than a brief call to say that she and Brad were trying to work out their problems. Hoshi didn't mention whether or not she knew Brad was a compulsive gambler.

Tony didn't call, and at last Ginny couldn't stand it any longer and, thrashing in bed trying to sleep, decided that if she didn't hear his voice, she would die. She picked up the phone and dialed his number.

His voice, alert, businesslike, snapped "DeLeon" in response to the second ring.

"Tony, it's Ginny."

"Ginny? Hey, I'm glad you called. How's it going?"

Her heart fell. The question was friendly but hardly that of a pining lover.

"Oh, okay. I just wondered if you were any closer to finding-out who the top man in the skimming ring is."

"Believe it or not, I finally connected with the mysterious Paula Phillips tonight; she called me."

"What did she want?"

"To sell me information—and proof—about who is behind one of the most elaborate skimming operations in this town's history. She wants a large sum of money so she can get herself and her son out of the country. I have a feeling maybe she's been blackmailing somebody and is either afraid they're going to quit paying or maybe get ideas about shutting her up, permanently."

"Are you buying?"

"I'm going to see her. I was going to call you and tell you, because I'm uneasy about leaving you alone here. Julius is still on the loose, and God knows how many others. Your friend Marc is up to his ears in it, but he's gone underground, and we haven't been able to locate him. I don't like not knowing where he is or what he's likely to do."

"Where are you going to meet Paula Phillips?"

"She wants me to meet her at an old ghost town in the California desert called Gingham Junction. There's no airstrip anywhere nearby, so I figured I'd drive the Jeep down there. . . . I'll probably leave early in the morning to beat the heat."

"Tony, have you thought what you'll do if this Paula Phillips implicates someone close to you?" She didn't have to add, "Like your brother, Vince," because Tony knew whom she meant.

"Yes. It won't make any difference. I can't condone murder, even if I could overlook the rest of it. Look, Ginny, I don't want to scare you, but I'm worried for you. Mando and Julius think you know more than you do about Marc Noland's whereabouts. I wish you'd go away for a few days, until after I've seen Paula Phillips and found out who's running the ring. Could you do that?"

Ginny thought quickly. She'd been working such long hours she was more than caught up with current orders. Fortunately most brides planned their weddings months in advance, so she wasn't under the gun for deadlines.

A light blazed suddenly at the end of the dark tunnel she'd been in. A momentary vision of the first time she and Tony had made love, amid the spring wildflowers in the lost canyon, dazzled her with the brilliance of its perfection. It was a memory she had taken out and polished many times in her mind, and it never failed to move her deeply. Perhaps if they could get away from everything again, out in the desert somewhere where all the clutter of civilization was swept away . . .

Drawing a deep breath, she plunged headlong into her plan of action. "Tony, yes, I could get away for a couple of days. And you know, I've always wanted to see Gingham Junction. It's one of the last unspoiled ghost towns left, isn't it? It never became a mecca for tourists because it's so difficult to reach. Didn't it spring up in the high desert, around a bunch of mines?"

"You've done your homework. The only way to reach it is aboard a horse or mule, or in a four-wheel-drive vehicle. Ginny, are you telling me you want to go with me?"

"Yes," she breathed, "I am."

"I don't know . . . what if someone other than Paula Phillips is waiting for us there?"

"You said she wants to sell you information; even if she has an accomplice, why should they kill the proverbial goose with the golden egg?"

There was a long silence while he considered. At last he said, "Okay. I doubt a woman with a child in tow is going to plan an ambush. She sounded pretty desperate to put a lot of distance between them and the skimming gang. But before we go I have just one question."

"Yes?"

"Does this call mean that you've been missing me and you're ready to reconsider my proposal?"

"Proposal?"

"In my roundabout way the last time I saw you I was trying to ask you to marry me." After a moment he asked in a worried voice, "Ginny, are you crying?"

"No," she said, choking back her tears. "But—"

He went on quickly, "I've been doing a lot of thinking since the other day. I know that maybe we'd be apart more than most married couples, but maybe we could still make a life together. Who knows, perhaps the quality of our time together would make up for the quantity. I thought about what you said about loving me as I am, and that's how I love you too. We're two people who need each other but need space to grow too . . . I believe we love each other enough to give it. I figured we could spend some time together on the ranch, and when you had to travel on business, I'd take off and go with you. I suppose I'm saying the main thing is that we try to work it out so we don't part company, now or ever."

Not trusting herself to speak, she could only murmur his name.

"Who knows," Tony went on, "maybe the reality of becoming a rancher wouldn't be as much fun as I think, and before you tell me I shouldn't continue working as an investigator, let me remind you that I also happen to be a talented musician and composer. I could probably make a living with my clarinet."

She found her voice at last. "Oh, Tony, I love you. Let's get married the minute we get back from Gingham Junction."

Chapter 21

THEY LEFT FOR THE CALIFORNIA DESERT THE FOLLOWING morning, allowing themselves one long kiss and the affirmation of all they'd promised before tossing backpacks and water flasks into the Jeep and roaring off in the predawn darkness.

Ginny hadn't been able to resist calling Hoshi right after she talked with Tony, to share the news of their engagement and at the same time to tell Hoshi they were going away for a couple of days. She explained about Paula Phillips and asked Hoshi to keep quiet about it until their return. Hoshi had sounded somewhat preoccupied, but that could have been due to the lateness of the hour. Ginny promised herself that as soon as possible she'd spend some time with Hoshi. If she now knew about Brad's gambling, then she was going to need plenty of support.

This morning Ginny was both exhausted and exhilarated. The vision of life with Tony stretched before her in all its infinite wonder but nights without sleep were taking a physical toll. She leaned back and dozed, waking when the dawn split the horizon with brilliant silver light.

Tony took advantage of the straight highway and scant early morning traffic to make good time, knowing that desert roads and, eventually, no roads, would slow them down.

Even before the sun began to climb in the sky the summer heat of the desert caused them to reach for their flasks. "We can fill them again when we stop for breakfast," Tony said.

He reached for the car radio and flipped it on, twisting the dial to try to bring in a local station. "I'd like to get a weather forecast," he explained. "I don't like the look of those thunderheads to the east."

Turning, Ginny saw the cumulonimbus clouds piled up over the distant hills. She asked, "Do you think Paula Phillips knows enough to keep her child and herself out of the dry washes?"

"Maybe we'll reach them before the weather does," Tony answered. The radio crackled with static, and he turned it off.

Ginny watched the sun-hazed desert fly by. Gravelly sand stretched to infinity, dotted with creosote and mesquite or an odd cluster of yucca standing like a huddle of old men in conversation. Except for an occasional truck or speeding car on the highway, they might have been on some alien uninhabited planet.

Paula Phillips had chosen her hideout well, Ginny thought. Most travelers headed for the better-known western ghost towns boasting adjacent motels and restaurants. Gingham Junction had neither, and any

trails into town had long since been obliterated by
sandstorms or flash floods. She wondered how a woman
and child had managed to find their way to such an
inaccessible spot.

Tony pulled into a straggle of roadside businesses
where the highway intersected a narrow road snaking
off across the desert. "Last chance for breakfast. We'll
eat and fill the canteens, then gas up before we leave.
Gingham Junction is nothing but a rotting collection of
old buildings almost swallowed in sand."

Ginny stepped from the car into intense desert heat
and steadily increasing humidity, immediately losing
any appetite she'd had.

There seemed to be a film of grease over everything
in the tiny diner next to the gas station. An overweight
waitress yawned and poured coffee for them, set two
glasses of ice water in front of them, and handed them a
stained menu.

Sipping the coffee, Ginny asked, "What time are we
supposed to be there?"

"I told her I'd try to arrive about noon. I figure we've
got at least another couple of hours drive into the
desert from here. Better eat something."

"Paula Phillips must really be afraid of somebody, to
want to meet you at such a godforsaken spot."

"Remember what happened to Al Vernon? I think
Paula's afraid of ending up in a shallow grave too."
Tony stood up, "Order ham and eggs for me, will you?
I'm going to call my office to be sure she didn't phone
again and change the plans."

He returned just after the food arrived, and the look
on his face brought Ginny out of her heat-induced
lethargy. "What's wrong? Did Paula call again?"

"No . . . but there was a message on the answering
machine from Hoshi."

"What did she say?"

"It was a frantic whisper, like she was afraid someone might overhear. She just said, 'Tony—for God's sake be careful—Brad knows.'"

The food stuck in Ginny's throat. "Brad knows what?"

"I haven't a clue. Unless she meant he knows I found out about him going to Gamblers Anonymous. But what difference would that make to anything?" Tony looked as baffled as Ginny felt.

"Do you think we should call Hoshi and find out?"

"I tried. Nobody answered. We'll try again before we leave."

Tony asked the waitress to fill their canteens with water, bought a six-pack of soft drinks, and ordered some sandwiches to go. Then they went outside to call Hoshi again.

"Let me try," Ginny said, "She might be a bit more communicative with me."

The telephone was located next to the gas station on the highway, and an occasional truck roared by as Ginny dialed the number, listened to the electronic voice tell her how many coins to insert, then waited as the phone rang in Brad and Hoshi's apartment.

Hoshi answered the phone on the first ring. "Ginny? Oh, God, I didn't know. I didn't realize what I was doing—"

"Calm down. Take a deep breath. Now, what are you talking about?"

"I told Brad where you and Tony were going."

"So? There's no reason Brad shouldn't know."

"Ginny, Brad and I talked all night long. All about his gambling and his debts and the things he's done to cover them up and get money and . . . and he said he wanted to stop, to live a decent life with me, but he couldn't let all the mistakes he'd made in the past stop him . . . that it all had to be buried."

"Well, that sounds—"

"*Buried!* Ginny, I'm terrified that he's gone to kill

her, to keep her quiet. He was so angry. He said he'd done everything she asked: got her out of town, bought a house for her and got her child to her, paid her so she could live there and not have to work. He said he did it for me, for us, that there'd been a time when he'd have shut a miserable blackmailer up for good, but that he was really trying to be the man I thought he was."

"Blackmail? . . . bought a house—*kill* her?" Ginny repeated, puzzled and frightened. "You're talking about Sally Smith?"

"Sally Smith—*alias Paula Phillips*. Sally Smith was the name she used when she went into hiding. I told Brad you and Tony were going to meet her at Gingham Junction to buy information from her about who was the brains behind the skimming ring and who ordered the Al Vernon killing. That's when Brad told me Paula Phillips had evidence that could hang him. He just stormed out of the house. Ginny, you've got to get to her, quickly—get her away from there."

Tony, who had listened with his ear pressed to the other side of the phone, removed the receiver from Ginny's shaking fingers. "When did he leave? Okay, take it easy, Hoshi. We're on our way."

Ginny knew from the look on Tony's face that they'd better move. They ran to the Jeep, and the tires squealed as he jammed down the accelerator. They turned off the highway onto the dirt road, sending dust flying.

"Tony, you don't really think Brad would—"

"He left before we did. But he knows he can't make it in his car, so he'll have to stop and rent a four-wheel drive. That could have bought us a little time. But, Ginny, I've been a blind fool."

"How could you know it was Brad who got Paula Phillips out of town? How could you guess that she and Sally Smith were one and the same person?"

"I kept looking for somebody who had access to the

hotels and casinos, someone who knew all the routines for handling cash and who wouldn't be suspected. I even considered my own brother—but Vince didn't fit as the headman, either, because he only knew The Sand Castle setup, not the other hotels. Who better than the guy in charge of security personnel? Free to come and go, and with knowledge of all the safeguards and routines!"

"Brad organized the ring that was stealing from the casinos? *He's* the headman?" Ginny said, shocked beyond belief.

"And no doubt used some of his own security officers to stash the loot, ready for pickup. Paula Phillips must have stumbled onto what was happening and thought it was just one crooked employee; tried to call Brad to report him, couldn't get hold of Brad, probably because he was in a secret poker game, so she called me. Before I reached her Brad got her message off his answering machine and got to her first. In the meantime she discovered Brad was the brains behind the ring, and foolishly let him know that she knew. Any other crook might have made sure she didn't tell anyone else, but he took pity on her, got her out of town, and paid her off. And I don't believe he intended for Al Vernon to be killed; I think that was Mando's idea. Because Brad had met and married Hoshi, and he was changing—I really think he was. So he paid Paula Phillips to leave town that night; promised he'd get her kid to her later."

"Then threw you off the scent with a faked letter from her."

"Brad's been having financial problems; probably dropped a bundle at the tables. He borrowed money from me recently. Maybe Paula thought the well was going to run dry; maybe she heard about Al Vernon's killing and got scared."

"But Paula kept some sort of proof, linking Brad to

the ring. And Brad knows she wants to sell it to you. Oh, can't you go any faster?"

"We're doing sixty on a dirt road—I can't make this thing fly. Remember when I found out about the house Brad had bought in the northern part of the state? Hoshi said Brad had used symbols on the phone numbers in his personal directory, and the one for Sally Smith, alias Paula Phillips, was a little cartoon ghost. Well, the house Brad bought for her was near a Nevada ghost town not far from Virginia City. Paula told me on the phone that she'd come across a list of western ghost towns and got the idea of coming here because the list said this one was seldom visited because of its inaccessibility."

Five minutes later they skidded in a cloud of stinging sand onto the open desert. "Well, we just ran out of road," Tony said, slowing down.

Ginny looked with dismay at the vistas of rolling badlands. Sand dunes stretched for miles, almost devoid of plant life. Swirling sandstorms had long ago obliterated what was left of the road while howling winds had come through the canyon and swept this part of the vast desert plain.

Against the glare of sand-reflected sun they could see a few bleached buildings scattered in a canyon between rocky hills about five miles away. Gingham Junction looked as ghostly and deserted as a mirage.

The black-bottomed clouds piled along the top of the hills were now closer, more threatening, and the air so humid it seemed to hang over them like a damp veil.

"We're going to get caught in a cloudburst," Tony said, braking beside a cluster of boulders. "That could make things tricky. Still, I'm going to leave the Jeep and you here, out of sight, and go in on foot."

"Tony!" Ginny protested.

His hand closed around her arm. "There were two sets of tire tracks back there. It could be that Paula came here first, then had to drive back to the highway to call me, but I want to play it safe. Please don't argue with me, Ginny. Do I try to design wedding dresses for you? This is my job, not yours."

Sighing, Ginny tipped her hat low over her forehead and settled back into her seat as Tony climbed out of the Jeep and headed toward the ghost town.

After the sound of his boots crunching the gravelly sand had faded into the distance, Ginny felt the hush of the desert and the oppressiveness of the approaching storm close about her. A dust devil danced down a dry wash, and a slow-moving honeybee buzzed over a dried-out clump of sagebrush, making faint sounds in the vast stillness. Feeling slightly faint with the humid heat, Ginny got out of the Jeep to seek the shade of the boulders.

She was about to lean back against the shady side of a rock when she heard an ominous rattle somewhere over her head. She leapt backward, falling down and rolling over the baked-hard sand in her haste to put distance between herself and the unseen snake.

Picking herself up, she began to run after Tony. He heard her coming and stopped to wait, his expression stern until she caught up with him and breathlessly said, "A rattlesnake—back there in the rocks. I'm going with you. I'd rather face Brad than a sidewinder any day."

Tony shook his head slightly but said, "Okay, come on. I guess we don't have anything to fear from Brad if he's here. We're his friends."

Neither gave voice to the thought that Brad was a very desperate man driven to the breaking point by Paula Phillips's blackmail, and there was no telling what he might do. The only way to be sure a blackmailer didn't talk was . . . but Ginny didn't want to think about what Brad might already have done to Paula.

As the ghost town came closer into view they saw it consisted of only a single street of dilapidated buildings. A pickup truck covered with a heavy layer of dust was parked beside the remains of a horse trough. There was no sign of another vehicle or of any life.

Tony stopped and offered her the canteen. "It looks like we're in luck—that must be Paula's wheels, and I don't see anything Brad could have driven."

Ginny swallowed the water gratefully, then watched as Tony took a drink. Despite the suffocating heat and the unseen menace of Brad, she wanted to put her arms around Tony and tell him again that she loved him, that no danger or misfortune would be beyond bearing if he was at her side. At the same time the full realization that nothing she might ever do in the future would be fulfilling unless he were a part of her life, overwhelmed her.

Realizing she was watching him, he smiled at her and replaced the cap of the canteen. "We seem to find the darnedest things to do together, don't we?" Then, studying her expression for a moment, he seemed to read her mind, and there was an instant answering flash of recognition in his eyes. His arm went around her shoulders, and he pulled her close to him for a quick kiss. "Come on. Let's get Paula and get the hell out of here. You and me have better things to do."

They quickened their pace, closing the distance rapidly to where Paula's truck was parked beside the horse trough. When they reached it, Tony called out, "Paula? It's Tony DeLeon. Where are you?"

Only the sound of a broken shutter, flapping against a wooden wall, broke the silence. A faint breeze, hotter than a dragon's breath, moved down the street. "Paula?" Tony called again. He started toward the nearest building, and Ginny followed.

They entered what had probably once been a store of some sort, but the inside was gutted. Only a collection of rotting, broken boards and unidentifiable debris was scattered about the floor, all covered with a thick layer of sand. But it was cooler inside, and Ginny let out her breath. "Phew! What a relief to get out of the sun. But she isn't in here. Where can she be?"

"You wait here. I'll check out the other buildings."

"No way. I'm going with you."

"Ginny, I wish you wouldn't. God knows what we may find."

She shivered, despite the heat. Paula's body? Please, no! "I want to go, too, Tony. There may be more rattlers around."

"Okay. But stay behind me, will you?"

"Aren't you going to get your gun out?" Ginny asked as she cautiously stepped over the debris to the door.

"What gun?"

"You don't carry one?" She was shocked. "What kind of a private eye are you?"

"The kind that searches for missing persons. I hate guns. Who do you want me to shoot, anyway?"

"It's just that it's so eerie. The pickup truck is there but no sign of Paula, and the . . . silence." She lowered her voice as they went back out onto the street.

It didn't take long to check all the buildings on one side of the street. They had probably been stores, a couple of saloons, and a livery stable. All were deserted. They crossed to the other side and found a larger, fancier saloon with a staircase leading to an upper story.

"Probably the local bawdy house," Tony said, approaching the staircase. "Wait here. I don't like the look of those stairs." He went up them carefully, disappearing for a moment.

Ginny felt very alone and nearly jumped out of her skin when something scurried across the floor and vanished into the shadows. She called "Tony!"

He came scrambling back down the stairs. "What is it?"

"I think I saw a rat."

"Terrific. Did you ask if it had seen Paula?"

"Let's get out of here. She would have come to us by now if she were still here. Brad must have got to her first, and they've driven off in his vehicle. That would explain why her pickup is still here."

"I'm going to check all the other buildings first, to be sure. Come on."

As they emerged from the saloon Ginny glanced over her shoulder at the walls of the canyon stretching behind the ghost town, enclosing a sandy wash that disappeared into the barren hills. She clutched Tony's arm. "Look—in the wash—way up toward the hills. There's a cloud of dust."

"A dust devil?" Tony asked, turning and shading his eyes from the sun. "No! It's a motorcycle—a dirt bike. It must be Brad."

"Is there a passenger? Does he have Paula? Why is he going that way?"

"I can't tell how many people are on it, but he must have seen us coming and be trying to get out through the canyon. He should have checked the maps. There's no other way out than the way we came in. It's a box canyon."

"What are we going to do? . . ." Ginny began, and in that second the clouds began to move, blotting out the sun, and the air was rent with a violent clap of thunder. Like a mighty avenging djinn, the desert storm was upon them.

Chapter 22

A GREAT GUST OF WIND WHIPPED DOWN FROM THE HILLS, bearing a dense cloud of sand. Suddenly, at midday, darkness descended as the sun and sky were blotted out by masses of clouds and the accompanying sandstorm.

Tony grabbed Ginny and pulled her toward the shelter of the nearest building as the first rain fell, audibly spattering on the dusty street. Lightning ripped through the whirlwind of sand, and thunder exploded, so close that Ginny clung to Tony in fright.

He drew her back, away from the doorway, kicking debris out of the way, then groped in the darkness until he found a fairly well-preserved packing case. "Sit down, Ginny. We're not going anywhere in that."

Ginny perched on the edge of the box, amazed and

strangely exhilarated by the violence of the storm. "What about Brad and Paula?" she asked in the brief interval between claps of thunder.

"They'll have to come back this way. There's no other way out. Besides, even a desperate man knows he can't ride a motorbike in zero visibility. They may have found shelter somewhere up there in the canyon."

"Tony . . . the walls of that canyon looked awfully sheer."

"Brad will have enough sense to anticipate a sudden rush of water with rain this heavy. Stay here. I'm going over by the door to watch for them. No, Ginny, you sit here. No sense in both of us getting drenched to the skin."

But as the rain drummed in increasing intensity on the roof, jets of water streamed down on her, finding a way through the upper floor of the building. Her cotton shirt was soon soaked, as was her hair. The storm seemed to be centered directly over the ghost town. She was somewhat protected from vicious gusts of wind, which at times had Tony hanging on to the rickety doorway. Minutes passed as he strained through the wind-whipped sand and torrential rain to watch the street.

Ginny called to him, "Can you see anything?"

He waited until a long rumbling roar of thunder passed overhead. "Not a thing. I don't even know if I'd hear the bike coming."

Feeling isolated as the midday darkness deepened and Tony became an obscure shadow, Ginny wanted him to keep talking. "How do you feel about Brad? I was wondering if it was any easier for you to take than if it had been your brother in charge of the ring."

"Matter of fact," Tony answered slowly, "I keep flashing back to Vietnam. To Brad and Lonnie and me . . . and Lonnie's suspicions about Brad . . .

shortly before Lonnie was killed. Brad saved my life when I went to root out that rats' nest of black marketeers who knifed Lonnie in the back, but it never occurred to me to wonder *what Brad was doing there with them.*"

"Oh, God, Tony! You don't think that Brad killed Lonnie?"

"No. But I do think that Brad was dealing with the gang, so was as indirectly responsible for Lonnie's death as he now is for Al Vernon's. What do they say about not being able to lie down with swine and come up smelling of roses?"

The pain in his voice made her want to cry. Bad enough that his best friend had been killed, but to have to face the possibility that another friend had been responsible would be unbearable. She found herself praying that when they caught up with Brad, he'd have a story about Lonnie's death that Tony would believe.

She rose to her feet and went to his side, putting her arms around him. "I know how you must feel. But don't jump to any conclusions yet. Even a compulsive gambler is innocent until proven guilty, right?"

"Ginny, I'm not going to go on wearing blinders when it comes to Brad. When he comes back here, I want you to stay out of sight and let me handle him."

All at once a different sound made itself heard. Above the staccato crack of thunder and howl of wind, over the pounding rain, came a steadily increasing roar, like the rumble of an approaching train.

Instantly Tony grabbed her and dragged her away from the open doorway, back to the rear of the building where rotting stairs went up to a second story.

"What?" Ginny began.

"Upstairs! Quick!" Tony yelled, holding her hand as he practically lifted her from the floor.

They were halfway up the staircase when the rush of

water hit the side of the building, shaking it to its foundations. The flash flood had roared down the hillside, collecting dead chaparral and rocks, small drowned rodents and uprooted yucca. Now it rampaged through the derelict town, slamming into buildings, swirling in muddy eddies three or four feet deep.

As they gained the upper floor they heard the wrenching sound of one of the age-rotted buildings collapsing, somewhere across the street. Rainwater was seeping through the gaping boards of the side of the building. It was the former bawdy house, Ginny now realized, and it seemed certain that either wind or rain or flash flood must tear their precarious shelter to shreds.

Tony kept one arm around her and braced himself against the wall. He yelled, "Hang on to me. Let's get under that doorway over there. If the roof goes, it will be the safest place."

Nodding, Ginny moved sodden boots over the uneven landing, feeling her toes squish water, sure that at any second the whole house would explode under the impact of the flood.

They reached the doorway, which had a sturdy beam overhead, and Tony wrapped both arms around her and held her close. Unseen objects thudded against the side of the building as the flash flood raged on. She could feel the floor shake under her feet and didn't dare contemplate what would happen to them if it gave way.

The roar of rushing water eased, but it was obvious that the street was flooded, as was the ground floor of the bawdy house. They could hear water sloshing around in the darkness below.

Tony let out his breath. "At least the house didn't wash away."

"What about the Jeep? You think it's still drivable? Can we get back to it?"

"As soon as the rain eases up, I'll check and see how deep the floodwater is. If it's too deep to wade through, we'll find something to float out on. The Jeep should be okay; it's parked out of town on fairly high ground."

"What about Brad and Paula?"

"After I get you to a safe place I'll come back and look for them."

The rain gradually diminished, and the wind dropped slightly. As the sky lightened Tony peeled Ginny away from him and went to the top of the stairs. He called over his shoulder, "Stay where you are. I'm going down to take a look."

Ginny shivered in the damp heat. She didn't dare think what might have happened to Brad and Paula—was her small child with them?

A moment later Tony came back. "I estimate there's at least three or four feet of water down there. Not to mention a few unpleasant things floating in it."

"Snakes?"

"They're probably just as interested in finding a dry place as we are. There's a door still attached to one of the rooms downstairs. I'll try to get it off and see if we can rig up a raft. Look around and see if you can find anything to use as paddles."

As she searched the debris and found a couple of boards that might serve the purpose, she heard wrenching, splashing sounds from down below as Tony tore the door from its hinges. She also stifled a scream as she came face-to-face with several pairs of beady eyes clustered in a row along the balustrade. The rats had evidently followed their example in seeking the safer upper floor.

Tony called to her, "Come on down—carefully."

Inching her way down the staircase, Ginny felt a pang of fear as she saw the brackish water filmed with floating dust and littered with broken boards and dead mice. Something went curling by, flashing in the direction of the open door, and she realized it was a swimming snake.

Tony was on the last step above the water, holding on to a fairly substantial-looking door. The wood seemed sound enough, but it was disconcerting to see that the door floated slightly below the surface of the water. With their weight on it, wouldn't it sink even lower?

Sensing her fear, Tony said briskly. "Come on, hop on. We've got to get out of here before another cloudburst hits us. I doubt this place could withstand another flash flood."

He took her hand, and she stepped onto the door, then sat down. When Tony joined her, the door sank lower, but he grabbed one of the boards from her and pushed off from the wall. She paddled furiously with the other one, anxious to at least be out in the open.

As soon as the makeshift raft cleared the door and they floated out onto the street, the current of the floodwater flowing swiftly downhill picked them up. They sailed along at a terrifyingly fast pace, only using the paddles to steer away from the walls of the buildings still standing. Several of the derelict buildings had collapsed.

At the bottom of the street Paula Phillips's pickup truck had overturned. Ginny said a silent prayer that their Jeep was still serviceable.

Once clear of the ghost town, their raft slowed down as it struck the tops of submerged yucca and mesquite bushes. The water had cut a deep wash into the desert sand, with sheer sides several feet deep. Tony used his paddle to guide them toward a partially uprooted Joshua tree protruding into the wash. He shouted, "When we hit that Joshua, grab something and hang on."

The raft slammed into the Joshua, tilting alarmingly,

and Ginny grabbed the rough trunk, wincing as it cut into her hands. Tony held on to her with one hand as he pulled himself up onto the sandy bank. A moment later she was standing beside him, watching their raft hurtle off to the desert floor.

After they caught their breath Tony said, "Well, at least we won't have to cross that again to get to the Jeep. Come on, it's behind that boulder over there."

Too winded to reply, Ginny plodded along in her wet boots beside him. "Over there" was several hundred yards away, and although the rain had stopped, the clouds were again piling up along the ridge of hills behind the town.

Ginny could have wept with relief when they went around the boulder and saw that the Jeep was high and dry. She climbed into the passenger seat and began to unlace her boots.

Tony reached into the back of the Jeep and produced a length of rope, which he wound around his shoulder. "Drive back to the highway, Ginny, and call for help. Tell them we need a chopper and probably paramedics."

That jolted her out of her sense of deliverance. "Tony, don't go back. Let's go and call for help together."

"If they're hurt, they may need immediate first aid. Go on. Get out of here, and be careful how you handle curves in this thing: take 'em too fast and you'll overturn."

"But how can you possibly get into that canyon? It's flooded."

"I'm going to have to climb in. There'll be a ridge somewhere along the side of that mountain. Hurry, Ginny, please."

She nodded, peeled off her wet socks, and hit clutch and accelerator with her bare feet. She also made the mistake of glancing over her shoulder to watch Tony begin the arduous climb up the rocky mountain. In that split second before he disappeared from view, she was filled with an overpowering fear that she would never see him again, and with it came an agonizing regret that she'd ever believed anything in her life was more important to her than he was.

Chapter 23

TONY'S HANDS GRIPPED THE WET FACE OF THE ROCK AS HE inched around the side of the mountain, his feet searching for precarious footholds. There was a narrow ledge over his head, but it would have been foolhardy to place his hands anywhere he could not first check with his eyes. Rattlesnakes could very well be lurking up there. Below, his worst fears were confirmed. The narrow canyon was now a raging river of water. There was no sign of Brad or Paula.

Tony hadn't answered the questions in his mind as to what he'd do when he met up with Brad. That same Brad who had once saved his life . . . with whom Tony had shared so many good times. All his energy had to be concentrated on finding him and perhaps staying alive.

He tried not to worry about Ginny but found it impossible and had to keep reassuring himself that she was brave and resourceful and wouldn't have any trouble finding her way back to the gas station on the highway.

The sun appeared briefly, sending a beam of light through the clouds and flashing on something wedged in the mud and debris at the base of the mountain where the floodwaters had been dammed by a rockfall. Tony sucked in his breath sharply as he realized he was looking down at the upturned wheel of a motorcycle.

Okay. Keep going, he reassured himself. *They could have abandoned the bike to try to climb to high ground.* But as he pressed on around the ridge, he saw only sheer rock walls above the water, and, at least from this altitude, no sign of chaparral, or accessible ledges they could have hung on to.

The sky was again darkening ominously, and several drops of rain hit his face. He slid one foot in front of the other, scrambling upward toward the highest ridge. From that point he would be able to see the entire box canyon.

Gasping for breath, he reached the ledge where the mountain met the sky. Looking down, he yelled, "Brad—Brad, are you down there? It's me—Tony." His voice echoed eerily back at him.

At first he thought he was too late, then something fluttered on the periphery of his vision. He looked down to see a woman clinging to the sheer side of the cliff, waving frantically. The water seemed to be trying to pluck her away from the tiny ledge where she huddled. She screamed something that was muffled by the low rumble of distant thunder.

Tony didn't take the time to consider that Paula Phillips was on the opposite side of the canyon. Even if he was able to negotiate the difficult descent, there was still the rushing water, filled with obstacles, to cross.

Nor did he want to ask the question *Where was Brad?* Was he waiting in ambush? Was he that desperate?

No time to worry about it. He had to get to Paula before more torrential rains hit. If the water rose, she'd be swept from her perch. Large drops of rain were now falling, making the rock even more difficult to negotiate.

Halfway down, he heard Paula calling to him in a terrified voice. "Please—please hurry. I can't hold on much longer."

Turning, he called back, "You're going to be okay, Paula. I'll be with you in a minute. Where is your little boy?"

"Safe. I took him to a friend before I called you."

"What about Brad?"

Tony cursed as his feet suddenly slid out from under him and he went crashing down the side of the rock. Paula's scream of fright didn't help much. A jolting blow to his back stopped his fall and knocked the breath out of him. He had hit a jagged rock and was draped over it, arms and legs in midair. Drawing a deep breath, he cautiously reached out with one hand to try to find something to hold on to. Paula continued to scream until he shouted to her. "Shut up. I'm okay. Tell me what happened."

Anything to keep her mind off their predicament, he decided, when instead of telling him where Brad was at this moment, she began a somewhat hysterical recital of the events preceding her flight to the ghost town.

The facts were quickly arranged in Tony's mind. Brad had been juggling gambling losses and several large loans, and as was always the case when someone robs Peter to pay Paul, he had kept very accurate financial records. The night Paula had observed one of Brad's security men taking skimmed profits to a drop point, she had called Brad, but he was probably in a secret poker game. She then called Tony, but before he arrived she became afraid the security man had realized she'd seen him, so she went to Brad's office.

Fearing the security man would return while she was there, she hid in a closet. Only it was Brad, along with Julius and Mando, who showed up. It was quickly clear from their conversation that Brad was the mastermind behind the skimming ring and crooked poker games.

After Julius and Mando had left, she heard Brad on the phone promising to pay off a gambling debt. Then Brad played the messages on his answering machine, heard the one Paula left, and took off for the Castle. But in his haste to catch up with Paula, he left his financial records on his desk. That book not only listed all the loans he'd juggled but also the monies he was stealing from the casinos his security people patrolled and how the loot was divided up.

As a new deluge of rain hit the box canyon, Tony managed to get back on his feet. He began to scramble down the slippery wall of rock. He called to Paula, "You have that book stashed somewhere?"

"Yes. But it doesn't make any difference now, does it?" She began to sob uncontrollably.

Tony had reached the last footholds just above the floodwaters. He unhooked the rope from his shoulder and looked around for a substantial rock to which to tie it. "Paula . . ." He was almost afraid to ask the question. *"Where is Brad now?"*

"I thought he was going to kill me. He came roaring into the ghost town on that motorcycle. He was so angry because I'd called you and offered to sell you the book; honestly, I wouldn't have told on Brad. He'd been paying me to keep quiet. But Lou Mando found out where I was living, and I thought Brad had sent him to get me, but Brad said that Julius and Mando were getting greedy and they wanted to shut me up, permanently. I had to run again and hide, and I was so scared. That's why I called you and told you I wanted the whole bunch of them locked up."

"What did Brad say when he got here?"

"He just ordered me to get onto the back of the bike. Then we saw a Jeep coming across the open desert—"

"Paula, I'm going to throw the rope across to you. Do you think you can catch it and tie it around your waist?"

"No! I can't move. I'm afraid!"

"Okay, calm down. I'm coming across. Keep talking —what happened when you started up the canyon?"

"We'd stopped when the storm hit. Brad parked the bike and found this ledge and lifted me up onto it. Only there wasn't enough room for him too. Then the water came rushing down the canyon, and he—oh, God—he was just swept away . . ."

Tony felt a piercing shaft of grief slice into him, but he had to shut out the image her words had conjured. The rain was heavier now, and if he didn't act quickly, there would be two more bodies in the floodwaters.

He tied the rope around his waist and lowered himself into the rushing water. Whatever Brad had planned to do to Paula Phillips had been forgotten in that final moment of truth. He'd saved her at the cost of his own life. Tony would be able to believe now that Brad had not been responsible for Lonnie's death either. Halfway across the muddy water, Tony heard the welcome sound of whirring helicopter blades.

Ginny pushed open the unlocked door and paused on the threshold of the house, listening. Purple shadows were claiming the remnants of a scarlet-slashed sky and, released from the punishing rays of the sun, the desert seemed to sigh and relax.

A clarinet played softly in the dimly lit room beyond the entry hall, a sweet melody evocative of poignant

moments between a man and a woman. The music told
of yearnings that grew stronger with the passage of
time, of a love that couldn't be relegated to second
place.

If something had to be sacrificed so that their love
could live, then Ginny knew that no matter how much
she wanted success and acclaim, she would give up
everything else just to be with this man, to love him and
let him love her. But perhaps there was, after all, a way
to have it all. She felt an anticipatory lilt in her step as
she went toward the music, her thoughts on what she
was about to tell Tony.

The music faltered and died. Tony said, "I thought
you'd never get here, Ginny. You see Hoshi off okay?"

Ginny went into the living room, and he rose and
folded her into his arms, holding the clarinet behind
her. All the plains and hollows and curves of their
bodies fitted together in dearly familiar ways. His lips
closed with hers tenderly; kept her mouth locked to his
for a long, entrancing moment. As they drew apart
Ginny said, "Hoshi's on her way to L.A. She said to tell
you good-bye and remind you to be careful when you
ride your steers."

He gave a ghost of a grin. "She's a gallant little lady.
I wish it could have turned out differently for her and
Brad."

"At least she has the comfort of knowing that Brad
lost his life saving Paula. It's tragic, but it could have
been worse for Hoshi. If Brad had been charged with
murder . . . if he'd lived he would have been, wouldn't
he?"

"Brad was the brains behind the operation and an
accomplice to Al's killing even though he didn't order
it, since Mando worked for him," Tony said. "Funny, I
think I always knew Brad would find a way to die a
hero's death. I hope it helped wipe the slate clean for
him."

"In time," Ginny said, "Hoshi will find someone els
to love. Did I tell you that her housekeeper took
rather significant phone call after the news storie
about Brad were released? The call was from a Japa
nese doctor who helped Marc—his name is Shiger
Ayusawa. Hoshi found him for me and, well, it wa
obvious he was bowled over by her. He—Shigero—
very attractive. Anyway, he was here on tour but ha
apparently accepted a research position at a hospital i
L.A. for a year. He's going to pay a sympathy call t
Hoshi."

"From all this information, I take it you think mayb
this doctor friend might someday fill the void in Hoshi
life?" Tony asked.

Ginny shrugged. "It's possible. I think maybe Hosl
will find that in future she's less lonely than she wa
while she was married to Brad. That was certainly th
case with me after Marc left. Women who sit hom
alone waiting for a compulsive gambler to return reall
know the meaning of loneliness."

Tony took her hand and led her to the sofa. They sa
down together, very close, fingers entwined.

"You know that Julius and Marc and all of the peopl
involved in the skimming operation and crooked game
have been arrested?" Tony asked. "And my fathe
grudgingly admitted that maybe I'd been right al
along."

"Has he given up trying to get you to step into hi
footsteps?" Ginny asked, laying her head on Tony
shoulder. "I suppose your buying the ranch must hav
accomplished that."

Tony grinned. "I think it was always a game m
father played with me—trying to turn me into a gam
bling czar. He enjoyed having someone around wh
refused to give in to him. But as a matter of fact nov
that I'm closing the agency, I do intend to take a mor
active part in DeLeon Enterprises."

When her face fell, Tony added quickly, "Not the asinos—I'm talking about hotel management. Vince an handle the gambling end of things . . . but he tends o neglect the rest."

Ginny looked around the room. "I'd forgotten how uch this house resembled the Lazy Q Ranch—on a maller scale. Tony, if you're going to live on the ranch, ow will you be able to manage the DeLeon hotels oo?"

He gave her an enigmatic smile, seemed on the point f saying something, but changed his mind about it. nstead he responded, "I've got frosty cold drinks eady. Kick off your shoes, make yourself comfortable, nd I'll get them."

Ginny did so, leaning her head against the back of he couch and closing her eyes. There had been so little ime to talk these past few days, and now she wanted to avor the moment when she could tell Tony of her very nuch revised plans for the future.

Her eyes fluttered open as she heard the tinkle of ice ubes against glass. Tony bent over her and kissed her orehead, placing the cold glass into her hand. "It must ave been rough for you, feeling as you do about Hoshi."

Hoshi hadn't wanted to see or talk to anyone but Ginny during the past few days. Ginny said, "I didn't lo much but listen, really. Brad's housekeeper took are of everything. But, you know, when Hoshi and I alked about what she would do back in L.A., she said omething about wishing she had a career . . . and, vell, one thing led to another, and the outcome was hat she's going to work for me. She'll do most of the raveling, paperwork, buying fabrics, and so on. I can each her how to take measurements, estimate yardage, nd so on. That will allow me to concentrate on the lesigns."

Tony dropped down beside her, his hand curving

around her neck to play with her hair. He smile
slowly. "And you can work on your designs at hom
. . . on the ranch with me?"

Ginny took a sip of her drink and then placed he
cold lips against his. She murmured, "You catch o
fast. I kept thinking I had to do everything myself—
don't, though. Hoshi wants to invest in my bridal shop
she doesn't even want a salary until we're in the black.

When his kiss became more demanding, she pulle
back slightly and said, "Before we get too carried away
tell me what made you give me that mysterious smile
little while ago."

He shrugged, keeping his mouth close to hers. "Oh,
was just thinking that tonight you're going to relax an
I'm going to barbecue the biggest swordfish steak
you've ever seen."

"Where do you get fresh fish way out in the desert?

"Have them flown in from the Coast." He presse
several kisses in a tantalizing trail from her eyelid to th
hollow of her shoulder. "That is one of the wonders c
this modern age. Distances aren't so great anymore
are they?" He chuckled. "Funny, but that's exactl
what I was getting ready to tell you before you sai
Hoshi would be doing most of your legwork for you s
you could work at the ranch. That we can get from on
place to another in no time in my Cessna."

He played with a strand of her hair, and one finge
traced a gentle path from her throat around the neck
line of her linen dress. "You're so beautiful, Ginny.
could sit and look at you forever and forget everythin
else."

"What are you trying to tell me, Tony?" Ginn
asked. "Aren't you pleased that I'll be able to spend
lot of time at the ranch with you?"

Tony smiled. "It's ironic. We've both been maneu
vering toward the same end. My plan is to keep Josl
Englefield on as foreman of the Lazy Q—he's bee

running the place for years anyway without old man
Quinlan's help. I'll probably go up there—maybe more
often than I visited in the past—but I'm not going to
live there all the time. I guess we all need a Shangri-la
tucked away somewhere, a place where we can go and
restore our souls. The Lazy Q is mine, but maybe I've
been too active for too many years to really settle down
and be a full-time rancher. Besides, the dream doesn't
mean as much to me anymore. Not since I found a new
one . . . and that dream is you, Ginny."

Her breath caught, somewhere between her heart
and her throat. She felt a rush of love for him that made
her feel as if she were suddenly airborne. "Tony, are
you telling me that while I was trying to work out a way
for me to be with you at the ranch and still be a
designer, you were figuring out a way to be with me in
town?"

He nodded, smiling with a warmth that lit up the
room. "I'm going to keep this house, run the DeLeon
hotels, travel with my wife when necessary, and we'll
both fly up to the ranch when we want to get away."

"Oh, Tony, I love you so much, I can't think of a way
to express it."

He took their glasses and put them down and then
drew her into his arms. "Maybe I can." He kissed her
again and murmured against her lips, "I guess we were
both thinking more about the other than ourselves.
Isn't that the way it's supposed to be?" Slowly he eased
her down on the couch, his mouth seeking hers as his
hands slid her dress from her shoulders.

His fingers pressed into her inflamed flesh, and she
returned his kiss so eagerly that he groaned and tore at
his own clothes impatiently. Moments later they lay
naked, entwined in each other's arms, their desire
surging between them, drawing them together in fren-
zied need.

Tony stroked her breasts and inner thighs, pressed

fluttering kisses in the wake of his fingertips, whispered to her of his delight in the silky smoothness of her body. Although she was fully aroused, he made love to her slowly, and she allowed him to set the pace, following his lead, yet marveling that their rhythms could be so in tune.

She had never known such happiness. There had always been that special magic between them, when they touched, when they were together like this, but now it was enhanced by the promise of the future. Of the anticipation of so many romantic nights and wonderful days that they would share. There was no longer a sense of urgency, nor a lurking fear that everything might slip away.

As they came floating back to earth she clung to him, knowing that the harmony in their physical joining was a reflection of a much more mystical bonding that was theirs forever. All at once it became very clear to her how two people's lives could attain a perfect symmetry.

She whispered again, "I love you, Tony."

His hands went to her face, tilting it upward so he could gaze into her eyes. "And I love you. More than you'll ever know."

A long time later, after a leisurely meal and several breathless interludes of lovemaking interspersed between whispered plans for the future, Ginny said, "Play for me. . . . The last thing I want to hear before I fall asleep is the sound of your music."

He picked up his clarinet and began to play "Ain't Misbehavin'," the sweetly melancholy song he'd played the first night she'd met him. She sang softly in accompaniment to the plaintive notes of the clarinet. *"No one to talk with, all by myself . . ."* Pausing, he said, "I was playing that the night you walked into my life. But it isn't going to be *our* song . . . this is."

Abruptly he switched to the piece he'd composed himself, "Ginny's Song." The shadows obscured Tony's face, but his music seemed to say it all. He'd written a new ending, a soaring, wonderful climax that promised a golden future.

When the last notes of the song faded into the still night air, Ginny stood up and moved toward Tony. Wrapping her arms around him, she breathed, "That was beautiful. Thank you."

"Let's get married tomorrow," Tony said, his voice husky.

He felt a slight stiffening of her body and asked quickly, "What's wrong?"

"Nothing . . . I—"

"Tell me," he commanded.

Ginny gave a rueful smile. "I haven't designed my own bridal gown yet."

Tony's arms dropped away from her, and he turned and headed toward the door.

"Where are you going?" Ginny asked, alarmed.

"To get you a pencil and paper," Tony answered.

Laughing, Ginny ran after him, and they kissed again. The drapes were open across the long sliding glass doors of the living room, and outside, the sweeping dunes of the desert lay still and serene, painted with stardust.

RULES FOR SILHOUETTE
DIAMOND SWEEPSTAKES

OFFICIAL RULES—NO PURCHASE NECESSARY

1. Silhouette Diamond Sweepstakes is open to Canadian (except Quebec) and United States residents 18 years or older at the time of entry. Employees and immediate families of the publishers of Silhouette, their affiliates, retailers, distributors, printers, agencies and RONALD SMILEY INC. are excluded.

2. To enter, print your name and address on the official entry form or on a 3" x 5" slip of paper. You may enter as often as you choose, but each envelope must contain only one entry. Mail entries first class in Canada to Silhouette Diamond Sweepstakes, Suite 191, 238 Davenport Road, Toronto, Ontario M5R 1J6. In the United States, mail to Silhouette Diamond Sweepstakes, P.O. Box 779, Madison Square Station, New York, NY 10159. Entries must be postmarked between February 1 and September 30, 1985. Silhouette is not responsible for lost, late or misdirected mail.

3. First Prize of diamond jewelry, consisting of a necklace, ring, bracelet and earrings will be awarded. Approximate retail value is $50,000 U.S./$62,500 Canadian. Second Prize of 100 Silhouette Home Reader Service Subscriptions will be awarded. Approximate retail value of each is $162.00 U.S./$180.00 Canadian. No substitution, duplication, cash redemption or transfer of prizes will be permitted. Odds of winning depend upon the number of valid entries received. One prize to a family or household. Income taxes, other taxes and insurance on First Prize are the sole responsibility of the winners.

4. Winners will be selected under the supervision of RONALD SMILEY INC., an independent judging organization whose decisions are final, by random drawings from valid entries postmarked by September 30, 1985, and received no later than October 7, 1985. Entry in this sweepstakes indicates your awareness of the Official Rules. Winners who are residents of Canada must answer correctly a time-related arithmetical skill-testing question to qualify. First Prize winner will be notified by certified mail and must submit an Affidavit of Compliance within 10 days of notification. Returned Affidavits or prizes that are refused or undeliverable will result in alternative names being randomly drawn. Winners may be asked for use of their name and photo at no additional compensation.

5. For a First Prize winner list, send a stamped self-addressed envelope postmarked by September 30, 1985. In Canada, mail to Silhouette Diamond Contest Winner, Suite 309, 238 Davenport Road, Toronto, Ontario M5R 1J6. In the United States, mail to Silhouette Diamond Contest Winner, P.O. Box 182 Bowling Green Station, New York, NY 10274. This offer will appear in Silhouette publications and at participating retailers. Offer void in Quebec and subject to all Federal, Provincial, State and Municipal laws and regulations and wherever prohibited or restricted by law.

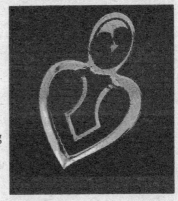

Silhouette Intimate Moments

COMING
NEXT MONTH

VALLEY OF THE SUN
Elizabeth Lowell
Hope Gardener dreamed of finding the water that would
bring her ranch to life. Rio was the one man who could
save her ravaged land, but would he leave her with a
ravaged heart?

THE MALE CHAUVINIST
Alexandra Sellers
Kate Fenton was an ardent feminist. Andreas
Constantinou seemed to epitomize the attitudes Kate had
fought hard to escape, yet his potent sensuality drew her
into his arms again and again.

SOFT TOUCH
Möeth Allison
Chalice York was a Hollywood screenwriter, Joe Dante a
New York playwright. They had nothing in common,
except a fierce competitiveness and an irresistible
passion.

TIGER PRINCE
Erin St. Claire
The island paradise of Jamaica brought vacationers
Caren Blakemore and Derek Allen together in a blissful
fantasy...until Derek's secret life threatened to destroy
their paradise and tear their worlds apart.

AVAILABLE THIS MONTH

DEVIL'S DECEPTION
Doreen Owens Malek

FOOLISH PRIDE
April Thorne

STARDUST AND SAND
Amanda York

COMES A STRANGER
Maura Seger